In *Chameleon* Jillian Kent weaves a fascin... romance. Her research into those who fo... tions within nineteenth-century insane ... pages long past midnight. This is the perfect novel for a rainy evening with a bottomless pot of English tea at one's side.

—SERENA MILLER
AUTHOR OF *LOVE FINDS YOU IN SUGARCREEK, OHIO* AND *THE MEASURE OF KATIE CALLOWAY*

Jillian Kent delights the reader's senses with her second novel in the Ravensmoore Chronicles, *Chameleon*. Lady Victoria Grayson's introduction to London Society becomes a deadly game of cat and mouse as she and the secretive Lord Witt join forces to unmask a brutal assassin. With each suspenseful twist and turn it becomes more certain that Jillian Kent is the bold, new voice of Regency romance.

—MAE NUNN
AUTHOR OF *A TEXAS RANGER'S FAMILY* (LOVE INSPIRED), ACFW CAROL AWARD WINNER

*Chameleon*, Jillian Kent's masterful tale of love and intrigue, weaves through the streets of Regency London and into the reader's heart. Don't miss this can't-put-down story told by a fresh, engaging voice in historical romance.

—DEBBY GIUSTI
AUTHOR OF *THE OFFICER'S SECRET, THE CAPTAIN'S MISSION*, AND *THE COLONEL'S DAUGHTER*

A delicious Regency house of mirrors, Jillian Kent's *Chameleon* is an enthralling mix of Sherlock Holmes meets Jane Austen in a breathless love story that will steal both your heart and your sleep.

—JULIE LESSMAN
AUTHOR OF *DAUGHTERS OF BOSTON* AND *WINDS OF CHANGE* SERIES

Jillian Kent has penned an indomitable heroine, an enigmatic hero, and intriguing circumstances that kept me turning pages with delight.

—LAURIE ALICE EAKES
AUTHOR OF *A NECESSARY DECEPTION*

# Jillian Kent

# CHAMELEON

BOOK II
*the*
RAVENSMOORE
CHRONICLES

REALMS

Most CHARISMA HOUSE BOOK GROUP products are available at special quantity discounts for bulk purchase for sales promotions, premiums, fund-raising, and educational needs. For details, write Charisma House Book Group, 600 Rinehart Road, Lake Mary, Florida 32746, or telephone (407) 333-0600.

CHAMELEON by Jillian Kent
Published by Realms
Charisma Media/Charisma House Book Group
600 Rinehart Road
Lake Mary, Florida 32746
www.charismahouse.com

Scripture quotations are from the King James Version of the Bible.

The characters portrayed in this book are fictitious unless they are historical figures explicitly named. Otherwise, any resemblance to actual people, whether living or dead, is coincidental.

AUTHOR NOTE: Bethlem Royal Hospital has a long and fascinating history. It is the oldest psychiatric hospital in the world. Today it functions as a modern psychiatric facility. It's been infamously known as Bedlam throughout history to denote chaos, confusion, and disorder. Bethlem in its early history was known for the cruel treatment of its patients at a time when little was known about what caused mental illness and how those patients should be treated.

Cover design by Rachel Lopez
Design Director: Bill Johnson

Visit the author's website at www.jilliankent.com.

Library of Congress Cataloging-in-Publication Data:
Kent, Jillian.
  Chameleon / Jillian Kent. -- 1st ed.
      p. cm.
  ISBN 978-1-61638-496-8 (trade paper) -- ISBN 978-1-61638-866-9 (ebook) 1.
Aristocracy (Social class)--England--19th century--Fiction. I. Title.
  PS3611.E6737C47 2012
  813'.6--dc23
                                    2012002338

First edition

12 13 14 15 16 — 987654321
Printed in the United States of America

*For my husband, Randy, who taught me to laugh*

**This book is also dedicated to the broken-hearted, to anyone who has ever felt left out, and to those who hold secrets close to their hearts.**

The Spirit of the Lord GOD is upon me; because the LORD hath anointed me to preach good tidings unto the meek; he hath sent me to bind up the broken-hearted, to proclaim liberty to the captives, and the opening of the prison to them that are bound.

—ISAIAH 61:1

# ACKNOWLEDGMENTS

THIS PAST YEAR has been an incredible year of growth for me as a writer. I experimented a lot with ideas, style, and construction of this novel. My growing pains were eased by the encouragement of my agent, Rachelle Gardner; my editor, Diane Noble; and my acquisitions editor, Debbie Marrie. I appreciate their patience and understanding; in the end it helped me write the best book I was capable of writing at the time. I hope you, the reader, will be pleased.

My deep appreciation is extended to the many behind-the-scenes folks at Realms, including Woodley Auguste, Deborah Moss, Jason McMullen, and Ann Mulchan. My beautiful cover art was designed by Rachel Lopez with William Johnson as the design director. I am in awe of their abilities.

I am so grateful to the authors who took valuable time away from their own busy writing schedules to read this book for the purpose of endorsement; I appreciate each and every one of you.

Each member of my immediate family deserves recognition because writing a book doesn't get done without a lot of support: my husband, Randy, for helping me find the time to write; my mom for reading the manuscript for errors; my daughter Katie for her encouragement and helping me to think out of the box; and my YWAM missionary daughter Meghan, a brave and valiant warrior for Christ who understands and encourages through the words of Scripture, "Be not afraid."

My friends Jenelen and Gerard Dulemba, Laura Spitzig, Mae and Michael Nunn, and Elizabeth Wilkerson, friends extraordinaire, have helped me over many hurdles along the way. Thank you!

Finally, I want to express my appreciation for my church family, LifeSpring Christian Church, my Thursday evening women's Bible study, the Saturday night Truth Project gang, and, of course, for my Creator, Jesus Christ, the Light of the World who planted the gift of storytelling in my heart.

> Then spake Jesus again unto them, saying, I am the light of the world: he that followeth me shall not walk in darkness, but shall have the light of life.
>
> —JOHN 8:12

Society is a masked ball, where everyone hides his
real character and reveals it by hiding.
                        —RALPH WALDO EMERSON

# CHAPTER I

We should come home from adventures, and perils,
and discoveries every day with new experience and
character.
                    —HENRY DAVID THOREAU

*London, 29 March 1818*

ST. JAMES PARK loomed in front of them, shrouded in a
heavy mist that created difficulty for horse and driver as
the coach and four maneuvered its way into the park.

Inside the vehicle Victoria leaned toward the window, straining
to see the outline of trees. "Such a disappointment," she sighed.
"This is not what I expected my very first morning in London.
I'd so hoped to see more on the ride through the park, something
exciting to tell Devlin when we get to his home."

"Don't despair, my lady." Nora, her maid, pulled a heavy shawl
tighter about her shoulders. "'Tis sure to be the same mist that
abounds in Yorkshire. This nuisance will lift eventually. It always
does."

Victoria patted the sleek head of her dog. "Even Lazarus grows
bored." She marveled at her best friend, a behemoth of a mastiff, as
he lowered his bulk to the floor of the coach with a loud groan and
laid his head across her slipper-covered feet, creating a comfortable
warmth. He'd been with her for years, and she couldn't leave him
behind. The poor dear would cry himself to sleep every night.

1

Victoria allowed the clip-clop of the horses' hooves and Nora's penchant for humming songs to lull her into a light sleep. Nora's humming had comforted her all those years she'd been sick at Ravensmoore. While everyone else lived their busy lives out around her, she'd done little but survive, taking comfort in the small things that brought her joy.

A sudden crash caused the coach door to vibrate. Victoria screamed and bolted upright as Lazarus pressed his nose and giant paws against the carriage window. A low growl rumbled in his throat.

She grabbed the dog by the collar. Heart pounding, she turned to Nora. "What was that?"

"Highwaymen!" Nora's hand crept to her neck, and fear filled her eyes.

The coachman drew the horses to a halt and opened the top hatch. "I fear I may have run someone down, my lady, but in this fog I can't tell."

"We must find out at once. Someone may be hurt." Victoria threw open the door, and Lazarus bounded into the mist. "Lazarus! Find!" She called after him, but he was already well on his way. She stepped from the coach, nearly tripping in her haste.

"Wait, my lady," Nora cried. "'Tis not safe. Come back!"

The driver's voice echoed through the mist. "You'll lose your way, my lady. Stop where you are."

But the warning wasn't necessary. Victoria could hear Lazarus snuffling the ground someplace nearby. She bit her lip and told herself to be brave, even as her heart slammed against her chest.

At the same time Lazarus let out a warning bark, the mist shifted. Victoria's hand clamped over her mouth.

A man lay on his side only a few feet in front of her.

She shouted back to the coach. "I've found him! I need help." She dropped to her knees and touched his shoulder. He didn't move.

She touched his arm and gently shook it. "Sir, are you conscious? Are you injured?" But before she could investigate further, strong arms lifted her and turned her away from the sight. She assumed it was Mr. Smythe, the carriage driver.

"This is not something a lady should see," the man said.

But as he turned her from the body, she caught a glimpse of the man's head. She gasped. There was just enough light to see streaks of blood upon one deathly pale cheek.

"We hit him," she cried. "The coach—" She lifted her head expecting to see the kind eyes of Mr. Smythe and met the warm, brilliant, gray eyes of a stranger. "Who...who are you? Who is he? Did we kill him?" She buried her face in her rescuer's shoulder to rid her mind of the sight.

"It does not appear so, my lady," he said, his voice low and comforting.

He deposited her inside the coach. Before she could speak, Lazarus bounded in next to her, rocking the vehicle precariously. She patted his head to calm him, and when she looked up at the man again, she saw only icy gray eyes and a rigid jaw line.

She studied those eyes momentarily and heard Nora say, "You poor dear. What is it that you saw?"

"Not the sight any young woman should witness, miss," the stranger said. "But I believe I prevented her from viewing the worst of the man's injuries." He hesitated, then added, "This was no fault of the driver. Take care of this young woman. I'll get help for the gentleman. Carlton House is nearby."

"Nonsense," Victoria whispered. "Use the coach. Our driver will take you."

He nodded and bowed. "You're very kind."

She wondered if it had been her imagination or if his eyes frequently switched from an icy gray coolness to a warm molten gray in only moments.. She wondered what this meeting might have been like under different circumstances.

"Be still," Nora said. "You've had a shock."

She heard the stranger and Mr. Smythe lifting the injured man to the driver's seat. "God have mercy," the driver said.

"I'll show you to Carlton House through this heavy fog. He can get the help he needs there. Who am I indebted to?"

"I'm taking Lady Victoria Grayson and her maid to the lady's brother."

"And that would be?"

"Lord Ravensmoore, sir."

They approached Carlton House a few minutes later. Victoria clutched the edge of the seat, attempting to recover from what had happened and what she'd witnessed. As if he understood, Lazarus licked her hand. The coach came to a halt.

The fog still lay heavy on the ground. Victoria could barely make out the two figures moving toward the door and into the palace. But even as their images faded, her thoughts returned to the stranger who'd lifted her away from the bleeding man and carried her back to the coach. The stranger with strong arms and fascinating gray eyes.

Victoria found her strength as the fog lifted and patches of sunlight appeared through the trees, dappling the ground with their shadows. London came alive. Though her curiosity remained keen, she turned her thoughts to her brother and kept her mind on the joy it would be to see him again. He'd only been absent from their home at Ravensmoore for two months, but it seemed far longer.

She stared in unabashed awe at the sea of activity that surrounded them as their coach merged with others, making its way through the muddy, rutted streets. The crowded sidewalks teemed with people of all classes. Women in brilliant gowns of color swirled past street urchins and beggars, meshing into an ever-shifting tapestry of humanity.

She'd stepped into a world bigger than York, a world she'd only dreamed about. Victoria leaned back against the banquette and sighed. "Now that I can see it properly, London is magnificent."

"I think it best if you have your brother examine you when we arrive, my lady Victoria. You know how he worries. You know how I worry. 'Tis a blessing to have a brother who is both a lord and physician."

Victoria turned away from the window and assessed her maid. "I am no longer an invalid, Nora, and well you know it." She lifted her chin a notch. "I'm stronger than either you or my brother realize." Nora met her gaze, her brow furrowed with worry. Victoria lifted her hand to dismiss the words of warning she knew were sure to come. But Nora, having been her constant companion the past eleven years and knowing her so well, caught Victoria's hand.

"Child, you're pale and weary from our travels and that horrid incident in the park. 'Tis a good thing we've made this journey, but I think your brother will agree with me that you need to rest."

"I've been resting my entire life. It's time to live and catch up on the adventures that God has in store for me. How many times did you read Jeremiah twenty-nine, eleven to me throughout the years? Did you not believe those words yourself?"

Nora nodded, keeping her lips firmly pressed together in an obvious effort to curb her tongue. A difficult feat, Victoria understood and appreciated.

As if sensing the tension and hoping to break up an ensuing argument, Lazarus nuzzled and nudged Victoria's attention away from her maid and back toward the window to watch a group of young boys chasing each other down the street. He barked and strained against the coach door. Victoria couldn't move him from his place of entertainment if she'd tried.

"Such a window hound you are, Lazarus." Victoria rubbed her hand over his big, sleek head, ruffling his ears. "If you wanted my attention, you would more readily share your window." She smiled and turned her gaze toward the window on the opposite side. Men and women hawked their wares and called to them in hopes of making a profit. "You can do no wrong in my eyes, Lazarus. If you hadn't been with us earlier, that poor man might still be lying in the park." She tried to shake off the sense of dread that seeped through her pores. She refused to allow the upset of the morning to ruin her reunion with her brother.

"I'm sorry, Nora." She studied the dark-haired, blue-eyed woman who was eleven years her senior. Nora had always seemed more of an aunt to her than a maid and companion.

"You're forgiven." A smile quirked the corners of her mouth.

"You really are too pretty to continue caring for me much longer. Why is it you haven't yet married?"

Now Nora chose to gaze out the window to escape further inquiry. "I will when the time and the suitor are right."

Victoria ended that line of questioning, and they rode in companionable silence the rest of the way, each lost in thought.

The busy streets gave way to quieter and more prestigious avenues as they made their way to Grosvenor Square and her brother's London townhome. The quality of the air improved as they moved farther from the central streets and into the areas of the upper crust. The coach slowed and then pulled to a halt in front of number three, Devlin's home.

"I cannot wait another moment." Grabbing the handle of the coach door, Victoria stepped out onto the curb. Lazarus bounded out after her and onto the street.

"Good heavens! It's a bear," an elderly woman said, clinging to her husband.

Victoria smothered a grin. "He's quite harmless."

The couple hurried away from the dog.

Nora bolted from the coach and grabbed Lazarus by the collar, holding him fast as he strained to make chase.

"Thank you, Nora. Just in time."

Victoria gathered her blue velvet traveling skirts and ran up the five steps to the entrance. She reached for the gilded knocker, hesitated, and then, after adjusting her gloves, started to grab the handle instead. But the door opened before her hand reached it.

Devlin's butler appeared. A smile lit his face when he saw Victoria. "Lady Victoria," he said, and then executed a most noble bow. When he straightened, his pleasure at seeing her was still apparent. "Welcome to London."

"Henry!" Victoria said. "It is good to see you. Do you mind taking Lazarus? He adores you almost as much as I do."

"For you I would take Lazarus on a walk to the ends of the earth," he said with cheerful amiability.

"Who is it that you are taking for a walk, Henry?" Devlin appeared in the doorway, tall and handsome with that brotherly smile of his and assessing green-eyed gaze. "Ah, there she is. My favorite imp. What took you so long? I expected you yesterday." He held out his arms. "Are you well?"

"I believe so. We stopped at a nearby inn last evening. The rain made travel a bit difficult." Victoria burrowed deep into her brother's warm, comforting embrace. "I've missed you, Dev," she whispered into his chest and squeezed him tight. "I've missed you so much."

"And I, you." Devlin held her at arm's length. "It's good to see you. Now, come in and tell me all about your journey and how my wife is doing at home without me." He looked up at Nora. "Has she behaved herself on this trip, Nora?"

Her companion grinned. "Nothing out of the ordinary for Lady Victoria, yer lordship."

"That speaks volumes." Devlin gently pinched his sister's cheek. "Henry, I believe Nora would love to hear about town."

"Of course, yer lordship. Welcome to London, Nora. Would you care to accompany me? And allow me to take Lazarus off your hands."

"Bless you for that, Henry. He wears me down too quickly."

"Come along, Lazarus." He accepted the leash from Nora and quickly fastened it to the dog's collar.

Nora nodded. "It will help me find my balance again after a long, bumpy, and perilous ride in the coach. I'll catch you up with all that's happened back at Ravensmoore."

Devlin started to enter the house with Victoria and then turned back to Henry. "And Henry," he called, "don't forget to feed the beast before you return him to Victoria."

"Feed him, sir? And just who should be the sacrifice? Lazarus has a shine to his eyes, and I'm thinking it is for me."

"Get creative, man. Start with Cook."

"Now, there's a right smart answer," Henry said and laughed. "Mrs. Miller will faint dead away."

Devlin grinned, a wicked glint in his green eyes. "If Cook has the nerve to faint, let Lazarus nibble at her."

"Devlin!" Victoria feigned horror. "What an outlandish thing to say." She covered a grin. "That would bring her around faster than smelling salts."

She turned to watch Lazarus leading Henry and Nora down the street. Her thoughts fled to what might be happening at Carlton House. A shudder crept up her spine. She decided to wait to tell Devlin of her experience in the park. Guilt niggled, but she just wasn't ready to divulge that bit of information. After all, her freedom was at stake. One thought of her in danger, and Devlin would ship her back to York before she got settled in. No doubt

Nora would reveal all if she didn't stop her maid when she returned from the walk.

"Are you cold?" Devlin asked, assessing her carefully. "Come in. You must be exhausted."

"Not really. The ride was but a couple of hours."

"No adventures during your journey, Snoop?"

She loved his pet name for her. She was more than a bit curious about everything life had to offer, and Devlin used her nickname more often than her given name. "Adventures? What could possibly happen on a two-hour ride into town?" She swallowed hard, hoping her expression didn't give her away. She would tell him when the time was right.

"Knowing you, just about anything."

"I promise to give you a full report." *Eventually.* And as she stepped into her brother's townhome, she wondered how she could discover more about her gray-eyed stranger and the bloodied man he'd taken to Carlton House.

Jonathon Denning, Lord Witt, nearly collided with the guard on duty while carrying Lord Stone into Carlton House.

"Send for the regent and his physician immediately," he ordered. "There's been an accident. I need a place where Lord Stone can be treated, and privacy is a must. Not a word of this leaves your lips. Do you understand?"

The guard nodded and headed toward one of the pages standing nearby. "You heard Lord Witt. Be off with you, and hurry, Thomas."

Witt watched as the page fled down a long corridor.

"Follow me, Lord Witt. We'll take him upstairs to the guest lodgings. Allow me to carry him."

"I can manage," Witt muttered. "Go, man. Lead the way, and make sure you choose a room that is not easily found."

The guard wasted no time, and after climbing to the second floor, Witt lay Stone on a four-poster bed surrounded by green drapes. Out of breath, Witt collapsed into a chair, mentally taking stock of all that had happened in the period of a mere half hour.

The guard paled when he saw the severity of Lord Stone's wounds.

"Not a word. Remember that, or I'll have your post. Now draw those drapes and leave. Send a decanter of brandy. I need a drink. Better yet, send two."

Witt sat in a chair near the bed and tried to think about what to do next, as the regent was sure to ask his opinion. He'd been a valued spy during the war, and the regent frequently asked his advice. He sat forward and rested his head in his hands. He'd simply gone out for an early morning walk before Parliament, heard the coach approaching, and scrambled to get out of the way before he was run down.

The muffled sounds of an obviously disturbed dog had fired him to action. He ran a short distance through the mist and then had come upon a well-dressed lady, her massive dog, and Lord Stone. One look at the huge dog had almost caused him to retreat, but he couldn't leave a young woman to deal with what he'd seen of Stone's face.

The driver had said the woman was Ravensmoore's sister. Ironic, since he'd been keeping an eye on the "Lord Doctor" at Prinny's request.

Prinny, as the regent was known amongst the ton, didn't know if he liked the idea of one of his lords working as a physician. A nobleman working a trade drew suspicion. What was the point? Although Ravensmoore's reputation had been spotless when he'd come into his title, it was anticipated that he would leave the study of medicine to manage his estate. Instead he'd pursued this obsession that he referred to as *a calling* and allowed his man of affairs to run his estate when he was forced to be absent. Prinny wanted to know if there was more to it or if Ravensmoore was simply eccentric.

He heard the unhappy growling of the regent and his doctor as they neared the suite of rooms. Witt steeled himself.

"What in the name of all that is reasonable has caused this inconvenience?" roared Prinny when he burst through the outer sitting room. He was still steaming as he entered the bedroom with his physician in tow.

Witt stood. "Your Royal Highness." He bowed. "Lord Stone has been attacked. I found him in the park. He needs your physician's immediate attention."

The overstuffed physician huffed. "I'll decide what necessitates immediate attention, Lord Witt."

"Then I suggest you make the determination." Witt nodded toward the bed. The physician hesitated.

The regent said, "Get on with it. I'm busy today. For the love of good food, Parliament reconvenes this afternoon."

The physician huffed again and went to the bed, grabbing the drapes and pulling them back. "Great heavens. What's happened to the man?" He opened the black bag he carried with him. "I'll need a nursemaid."

Prinny then stepped closer to evaluate Stone's condition himself. He sucked in a breath. "The poor devil! Get on with it, doctor. Do everything you can to save him." The regent, visibly shaken, looked at Witt. "Tell me everything. What happened? We must find out who did this to Stone."

"Your Majesty." The physician turned from the bed with a bloody missive in his shaking hand. "I found this pinned to his waistcoat. A warning."

"Who dares?" He snatched the paper away and read it. "Lord Witt, today's session of Parliament must be canceled."

Witt arched a brow.

Prinny handed him the blood-stained parchment.

Witt read the note aloud. "'You have been found guilty of conspiring with sinful men for sinful purposes. I will now handle the situation as I see fit. Stone is only the first. Repent, you lords of parliament.' And it's signed, 'Lord Talon.'"

"Curse this Lord Talon." Prinny looked to Witt for direction. "We must decide the best course of action, and soon. No one has dared attack a member of Parliament since Bellingham assassinated our prime minister, and that was six years ago."

Ravensmoore came to mind, but Witt faltered for just a moment. No doubt the man was the best there was, and his skills badly needed. But his sister had only just arrived in London, and this situation could put her and her brother in danger. An edge of uneasiness rippled down his back.

"Witt," the regent said. "What is your recommendation?"

Witt took charge. "We must proceed with caution. Tell no one about the note. Not yet. And don't say anything to anyone about the signature of this Lord Talon. I suggest we ask Lord Ravensmoore to join us immediately. Having a physician who is a peer can prove most helpful."

The regent paced and mumbled to himself, seemingly in a struggle to make a decision. Finally he said, "Send for him."

# CHAPTER 2

The least initial deviation from the truth is multiplied later a thousandfold.

—ARISTOTLE

*W*ELL, MY DEAR sister, what did you think of your trip?" Devlin cut into a juicy piece of beef but kept his eyes on Victoria. After the long illness that almost took her life, he was constantly on watch for signs that it might return.

"The trip was an adventure, though I doubt that Nora saw it that way. You would not believe how protective she's become. She hovers about like a bee on an English rose."

Devlin imagined that Victoria, with her penchant for landing in the middle of any curiosity that came her way—and delving into any mystery involved, no matter how large or small—had been more than difficult to keep up with every stop along the way. He'd called her *Snoop* since childhood. It was fitting then. And if he guessed correctly, it was even more fitting now.

His thoughts turned toward home. "And how is my beautiful wife? I was disappointed she couldn't come with me, but I'm grateful that she's there to keep our mothers entertained for a while."

"They always hate to see you leave, Dev. But since you discovered Mother, still alive at Aschcroft Asylum last year, well, she's frightened of losing you again."

"I try to reassure her. I don't think she understands that it's difficult for me as well, but since I am the one who left, I can't really blame her."

"We all attended Easter services together last Sunday, and then we had an egg hunt for the children in the village. The weather, for once, cooperated with our plans. The crocuses are everywhere. Beautiful blooms of purple, white, and yellow. Your Madeline is wonderful. I don't know what I'd do without her friendship since Mercy has gone to Scotland."

"I'm glad to hear it. I miss her. I'm hoping that perhaps she can join me in a couple of weeks." He took a swallow of tea and thought about how much he yearned to hold Madeline in his arms, then he forced his attention back to his sister. "You look pale, but I see that usual mischievousness alive in your eyes, which assures me that you are quite well."

"And you, brother, look as though you haven't slept for days. There are dark circles under your eyes, and I gather you have been busy caring for others at the expense of your own health. I think I'll begin tormenting you about your health as you do me. Then perhaps we can call a truce." She hid a smile behind her drinking glass and then took another sip.

"That's why I'm a doctor, Snoop." He never could fool his sister. She'd always had an uncanny sense of knowing how people felt. Probably because she'd fought her own sickness for most of her life. But now she was older and reading the outward signs of his fatigue. She didn't know that some of those dark circles were from the constant battle to improve the lunatic asylums and treatment of those confined within asylum walls, in addition to defending his right to be a physician even if he was titled. Both battles wearied him.

"I do hope you have arranged to take some time off while I'm here so you can show me about and not leave that to someone else." She accepted more rosemary potatoes from the server and ate with a hearty appetite, then sighed her enjoyment. "I'm surprised you're not fat, brother. The food is most enjoyable."

Mrs. Miller entered from the kitchen, carrying a tray of small bowls of bread pudding and clotted cream. The pleasing fragrance of cinnamon and nutmeg filled the air. "He's rarely home to eat his food, Lady Victoria. He's far too busy a man. Perhaps he will be makin' himself more at home now that he's got your company. I hope you'll be enjoying this. 'Tis special for tonight." She set the bowls between them. She added a small bowl of mixed fruits near the pudding dishes.

"Mrs. Miller, you've outdone yourself. Thank you. I can see from the sparkle in my sister's eyes that she is most grateful." He grinned and raised his glass in a toast. "To health."

Victoria did likewise. "To health and to adventure. May this visit prove to be the best of my life."

Devlin grinned. "Best of health or best of adventures?"

Victoria looked at him as if she had more to say on the subject, then just as quickly gave him a reassuring smile. "Both, dear brother. Both."

Before he could comment, voices filtered into the room from the front entrance. Lazarus barked and loped into the dining room to greet Victoria. He tried to pull her with him by clamping his big mouth gently around her wrist.

Devlin sighed. "I think you will have to train Lazarus in the manners to be used here in town, Snoop."

"Where is it you want to take me, dear dog? I'm eating my meal."

Henry entered the room. "You have a visitor, my lordship. Nora and I arrived at the door as he quit his coach."

Devlin stood to greet the man standing behind Henry. "Lord Witt."

"I apologize for this unexpected intrusion, Ravensmoore. But you are needed at Carlton House."

Victoria recognized his voice...and his eyes. But their icy gray had turned to a warm slate blue, or was it green?

His gaze swept over her with such intensity that she shivered. He studied her in the same open manner she'd seen men study women during the country assemblies in Yorkshire. Those gentlemen were besotted by a lady's beauty, but this man's perusal added a hint more of the rogue. Isolated as she had been during her illness, she had learned to depend far more on her powers of observation and deduction than on feminine beauty and ability to flatter.

Before she could recover from his scrutiny, Devlin stepped between them.

"As you can see, my sister is visiting, and this is a most inopportune time. Forgive me. Lord Witt, may I present my sister, Lady Victoria."

Witt bowed, and as he raised his head, she'd have sworn his eyes had flecks of green in them and that he stared at her just a moment overlong.

"Victoria. This is Lord Witt."

Lazarus still held her wrist in his mouth. He pulled her to her feet, and she curtsied. "I'm so sorry if my dog made a nuisance of himself in the entryway. I imagine Nora and Henry intervened on your behalf. He can be quite dangerous around strangers if he thinks you are a threat."

"Obviously you own a very intelligent dog."

Victoria smiled and thought she'd never seen a more handsome man in all her days. Her heart beat much too fast, and she felt a slight blush warm her cheeks.

"So, are you going to tell me why I'm needed at Carlton House, Lord Witt? I've no desire to be away from home this day."

"I'm sorry for that. Ravensmoore. But there's been an attack on Lord Stone. It's rather sensitive, and I wouldn't want to upset your sister by such talk."

"Lord Stone? Allow me to get my medical bag. I'll be right back."

"An attack?" Victoria whispered as soon as her brother was gone. "Surely, you do not mean the man we found this morning…?" She paused, frowning. "Is that why you wouldn't let me get a good look at him? What kind of an attack? Why…?"

Lord Witt held up his hand. "It's obvious your brother is unaware of your morning's adventures." An eyebrow shot up. "When were you planning to tell him?"

Nora entered the room. "I see you have now been officially introduced," she whispered. "Perhaps you should tell your brother the truth." She too shot an eyebrow upward, her gaze on Victoria. "After all, he will eventually learn of it, I'm sure."

"When you tell him is obviously your concern. However, I'm happy to see that you are uninjured, Lady Victoria," Witt said. "Forgive our hasty departure and the need to take your brother from you so soon after your arrival. It is unfortunate."

"Please be discreet. I will tell my brother of this morning's events soon, perhaps as early as tomorrow. I do thank you for helping me this morning. I'm not easily frightened. However, the situation was most unusual."

Devlin entered the room wearing his greatcoat and carrying his medical bag. "I'm not sure how long I will be gone, Victoria. Settle in and get some sleep. Perhaps tomorrow we can have an outing."

"May I come with you?" Victoria pleaded, her eyes wide with interest, especially as she thought about the man beside the road that morning. "Perhaps there is something I could do to help."

Her brother stepped closer, scrutinizing her face. "I can see in your expression that you are concerned, perhaps more than I am. But truly, I don't know why I have been summoned. You must rest from your long journey and settle into your room."

She smiled briefly. "I'd much rather go and be of some help than stay in my room." She hesitated. "Will you be back this evening?"

As she spoke, her brother gave her a curious look. She felt a blush color her cheeks. She was not used to keeping anything from him. She convinced herself it would be acceptable this one time.

He whispered, "I'm sorry, little Snoop. I'm afraid I can't make any promises."

⚜

Witt, with Ravensmoore at his side, walked through the Carlton House main entrance, which was graced with six Corinthian columns. Inside they were greeted by a grand staircase, chandeliers, marble floors, and ceilings painted with scenes of myths and legends. Although he'd seen the place many times, he was again struck by the grandeur, the paintings by Gainsborough and Reynolds, and the portraits by Van Dyck and Rembrandt. Grand indeed.

When he'd last entered only a few hours earlier, it had been through the rear entrance of the palace with Stone dripping blood onto the polished marble. This time his attention was on Ravensmoore and the argument that had ensued in the carriage prior to their arrival.

"Understand this, Ravensmoore," Witt said as they headed across another expanse of marble to the staircase. "I'm not against you wanting to help the sick. I don't understand it, and neither does Prinny. With your title and monies, you could help in other ways. But that discussion is for another time." He halted at the base of the elaborate staircase, locking eyes with Ravensmoore. "Something has happened that may help you if you persist in this direction. But that is not of the utmost importance right now."

Ravensmoore nodded. Witt had the physician's full attention and, from the set of his jaw, a well-controlled bit of the man's ire as well.

"I've been asked to fill you in on events." He turned, expecting Ravensmoore to follow.

"You were asked to fill me in?" To the man's credit, he hadn't budged. "Why didn't you on our ride over?"

Witt laughed, though without mirth. He'd not wanted to allow time for Ravensmoore to ask too many questions regarding the attack, since his sister did not want him informed of what had happened. It'd been difficult to keep him distracted. "You had my ear regarding your sister's visit and your ideas for helping the sick in Southwark."

Ravensmoore raised an inquisitive brow. "I thought that Prinny was unhappy with my methods of practicing medicine."

Witt nodded. "Not so much your methods. More the fact that you do it at all." He began climbing the stairs. "You have a patient who needs tending."

"So, are you going to tell me about these events you mentioned or must I guess?" Witt turned. This time Ravensmoore followed him.

"I'll fill you in as we go."

"Please do."

"As I mentioned at your home, Lord Stone was attacked," Witt said as they continued the long climb to the second floor. "He's been seen by the royal physician and is sedated with laudanum, but his wounds... well, let's just say they're complicated." He stopped at the landing and again turned to Ravensmoore. "Everything you are about to see and hear must be kept in the utmost secrecy. Do you understand?"

"Attack?" Devlin stared at him. "What kind of attack?"

Witt hesitated for a moment, thinking about Ravensmoore's sister. He'd turned her away from Stone before she could fully see the horror of the attack upon the man. At least she'd been spared that nightmare. He only hoped her brother, just by being called to attend to Stone's wounds, would not put her in danger.

"He's been disfigured. But we don't know how or why, though I have my suspicions. He'll not likely survive. You'll be told more once we reach Prinny's chambers."

They continued up the stairs. "Why me?"

"You've been summoned because you're a doctor *and* a peer."

"What can I do?"

"I believe that's what the regent wants to know." A guard opened the door to Prinny's chamber. "I suggested we send for you."

"You suggested?"

Witt had taken him by surprise. Just as well. He really did like the man. He stood back and let Ravensmoore enter the chamber first.

The prince regent, known for his frivolous lifestyle, appeared to Witt as though at any moment he might fall into an apoplectic fit. He rushed to meet Ravensmoore when they entered the room. "Thank you for coming so quickly. We need to treat this situation with the utmost of care."

Prinny's hair and clothing were disheveled, showing how out of sorts the regent was this day. It was well known that he went to great lengths not to fall below the standard that Beau Brummel set for the ton.

Ravensmoore bowed slightly. "Of course, Your Royal Highness. Whatever I can do. But I suggest you sit down before you fall ill."

A few of the other lords nodded. Some paced with their hands behind their backs. Two looked out the windows to the gardens below spreading toward Regent's Park. Others sat in nearby chairs with slumped shoulders and exhausted expressions.

"Yes. Yes, you're right," the regent said. "Please make your own assessment of Lord Stone when we finish here." He slid to a chair and took a deep breath. "Witt has told you what has happened?"

"Only that Stone has been attacked."

"Yes, yes. And terribly disfigured. But there's more. A message."

"What sort of message, sir?" Devlin asked.

The prince regent looked to Witt and nodded.

"The royal physician found a note in Stone's jacket." Witt produced it from his own coat pocket and read, "'You have been found guilty of conspiring with sinful men for sinful purposes. I will now handle the situation as I see fit.'"

"This sounds like Stone did something that his attacker did not approve."

Witt continued. "It continues: 'Stone is only the first. Repent, you lords of parliament.'"

Witt studied Ravensmoore as he absorbed the implications of this information. Shock, surprise, and then anger changed his features.

"Who would do such a thing?" Ravensmoore asked. "Why?"

"That's what we all want to know." Witt handed him the scribbled note stained with Stone's blood. "His penmanship lacks the benefit of practice. Perhaps he's not a learned man, or perhaps he's trying to disguise the fact."

"Using blood as ink. Another form of rage," Ravensmoore added as he studied the missive.

"Whatever the case may be," the prince regent said, "he must be found immediately. God knows what havoc this monster could cause within the House of Lords." He leaned toward the two of them. "I need your help, Ravensmoore."

"Of course, but what can be done? You have the royal physician at your disposal. Surely he can be counted on for his discretion and skills."

"The royal physician has grown soft and is not exposed to injuries like these. We need someone like you."

Witt stepped closer. "You are unique, Ravensmoore. You are both physician and nobleman. You can work with the royal physician, but you also have an ear close to the common man and may hear or see things on the street that others may not. A convenience, indeed."

Prinny mopped the sweat from his brow with a silk handkerchief embroidered with the royal crest. "Witt also possesses talents from his years in my service, and he has agreed to do all in his power to locate this demon and stop him."

"I'd like to see Lord Stone, sir. Where is he?"

"Witt, show Ravensmoore to the suite of rooms assigned to Stone. I'm keeping him well protected in case the madman attacks again. I've dispatched messengers to every member of Parliament to convene early tomorrow morning. They need to be made aware of the danger."

Witt and Ravensmoore stood and bowed. "Your Majesty."

As soon as they'd left the regent's chambers, Ravensmoore let out what sounded like a pent-up, exasperated breath. "So now I'm a convenience."

"Better a convenience than the other words Prinny used to describe you in the past month."

"Yes. You have a point. Better to be seen as a convenience than an embarrassment." He shook his head. "And this attack on a member of the House of Lords, and a threat to the others. What if he can't be found?"

"We'll find him," Witt said. "We must. The difficulty will be stopping him before one of us is killed."

Ravensmoore stared at Witt for a moment without speaking. "We must outsmart him. He rages against some perceived injury or some injustice that if not satisfied could flourish and endanger those we love as well."

# CHAPTER 3

To him who is in fear everything rustles.

—SOPHOCLES

"HE'S NOT REGAINED consciousness," Witt said as they made their way to the bedchamber where Lord Stone lay. "I don't know what attacked him. Maybe it's something you've seen before.

The guard on duty asked, "Do you take responsibility for entering these rooms, Lord Witt?"

"I do. Familiarize yourself with Lord Ravensmoore. He will be coming and going as he pleases and also conferring with the regent's physician if needed."

The guard studied Ravensmoore as requested, nodded, and then opened the door.

They walked through a dimly lit sitting room en route to the sleeping quarters where Stone lay. The bedchamber was dreary as well. A woman sat next to him, rose, and curtsied as they entered.

"He's the same, your lordships. He hasn't awakened, and he hasn't talked in his sleep, but he has been thrashing about and groaning. The regent's physician told me to keep him warm, but he looks too hot to me."

"Thank you. You can go for now," Witt said. The nursemaid scurried away without complaint.

Witt stood aside as Ravensmoore locked the door behind them, leaving the guard and female attendant outside the room. Then he followed the doctor to Lord Stone's bed. The man's breathing was shallow and ragged. The smell of sweat clung to him.

When Ravensmoore spoke again, his voice held a tone of command Witt hadn't noticed before. "There's still not enough light," he said. "Light a candle and bring it here."

Witt did as bidden and returned to the bedside, watching Ravensmoore's face, expecting it to reflect the horror of what he saw. His only thought seemed to be that of his patient, his only emotion that of deep concern.

"Blast it! The man hasn't even been bandaged. Hold the light closer."

Witt did so and watched as Ravensmoore studied the wounds. For a moment he didn't speak, and then he said, "These injuries were inflicted by a raptor, a large hawk or maybe even a buzzard. See these long tears in the skin on the left side of his face and these marks on his forehead?"

"Yes." He could barely utter the word, wanting desperately to turn away.

Ravensmoore then explored Stone's scalp for injury. "Can you see this?"

Witt leaned in closer. Deep gashes had slashed through Stone's scalp, leaving his hair caked with blood.

"A bird of prey does this as he eats flesh. When a kill happens in nature—such as with a hare or a squirrel, it's devoured or decapitated and flown away with the head intact. But when a falconer uses a hawk, the prey is not destroyed because it's caught for dinner."

Witt stood away for a moment to ease the stiffness in his back and mind, a rest from the ugliness of the attack. "Hawks don't attack people."

"Unless they are protecting a nest."

"This kind of damage is excessive even for a raptor with chicks to feed. A hawk would simply chase a predator from the area near its nest. This raptor attack appears to be far more aggressive. I would stake my life on the fact that the bird intended to kill Stone. Why would it do such a thing?"

"A more important question is *who* would do such a thing, wouldn't you agree, Lord Witt?"

Witt frowned. "Is it possible a raptor can be trained to attack a human?"

Ravensmoore frowned. "Anything's possible, I suppose. But right now we have more important tasks at hand than puzzling who, why, and if. Help me strip him out of his clothes. I know one thing for certain about the royal physician. He believes it indelicate to view a naked body." For the first time he gave Witt a half smile. "Let's do this quickly."

Witt's hand brushed against the man's skin as he attempted to free his torso of its torn clothing. "He's fevered."

Ravensmoore nodded as he placed a hand under the man's arm. "Quickly now," he said, almost as if to himself.

They stripped Stone down to the skin within a matter of moments. "Now," said Ravensmoore, "I want you to examine his skin from head to toe on the right side of his body while I do the left. I need your eyes in case I miss anything, then we will do the same but switch sides, and then again when we turn him over. But first let's have a look at both sides of his hands."

"What is it, exactly, that we're looking for?" As Witt fought to keep from turning away, he wondered why Ravensmoore risked his reputation as a nobleman to focus on sick and maimed bodies.

Ravensmoore, already bent low, peered closely at the man's skin. "Any unusual marks, lacerations. Any injuries that might have been missed by the royal physician."

He looked up, shaking his head slightly. "As if it might be possible to examine a man who's fully clothed." Then he added, "It would help if you'll hold the candle where it will do the most good."

Witt took a deep breath to steady himself and moved the candle over Stone's hands. Torn flesh. But not anything like the poor man's face.

"Now raise his arms above his head so his palms face the ceiling."

As Witt did so, Ravensmoore let out a small whistle. "Look at his palms and lower arms. These are defensive wounds against whatever it was that he tried to fight off."

Witt moved the candle to a position where he could better see. "Surely a bird couldn't have inflicted this kind of damage."

"Move the candle down here," Ravensmoore said. "Look at this bruising on his legs. He may have hit something. Hard. He was likely running and fell, perhaps more than once."

"The man was unconscious when I discovered him in the park this morning. There was a coach parked nearby, its occupants worrying they had collided with him. Perhaps they were right, which would account for the bruising." Witt didn't meet Ravensmoore's eyes as he spoke, wondering how the man would feel if he knew one of the vehicle's occupants was his own sister. That, combined with memory of the gruesome discovery, caused him to take a deep breath and focus on Ravensmoore's examination.

"If he hit the coach, I would say he was literally running for his life." Ravensmoore picked up the man's discarded coat from the floor and examined one of the ripped sleeves, then the other. "His attacker tore through his coat sleeves like a blade through cheese. He's going to lose his arms—perhaps his life—if I can't get his worsening infection under control."

"How do you do this kind of work?"

"I don't consider it work." Ravensmoore continued his examination without looking up.

"What is it, then? It's certainly complicated your life."

"It's my calling. Let's turn him on his stomach and look for lacerations on his neck and back." After they turned the man, he continued. "I'm a physician who happens to hold a title. And yes, my life is complicated, but I'm doing what I love and what the good Lord has called me to do. What has He called you to do, Witt?"

"I don't know that I believe in God. I do what interests me. But you're right, Ravensmoore. It must have been some kind of raptor. The tears in the back of his neck show that he was attacked from the air."

"Or something larger than a raptor," Ravensmoore said. "Larger than Stone." He looked up. "Was he on horseback when this happened?"

"There was no way to tell."

"The man is not small. Nearly as tall as you, Witt, and I'd guess you're well over six feet."

Before Witt could answer, Stone shuddered violently and cried out.

"Help me!" he screamed. "Get away! Get away!" He thrashed about, arms flailing. He caught Witt across the face with such violence that it knocked him to the floor. His fear seemed to give him the strength to push past his anguish and continue his fight against whatever he imagined still pursued him.

Witt threw himself across Stone's chest to pin him down while Ravensmoore forced laudanum down his throat. Even as he worked to force the liquid through the man's rigid, snarling lips, he spoke in calming tones. "You are safe now. We're here to help you."

The guard pounded on the door. "What's going on in there? Is Lord Stone all right?"

"Leave us!" Witt called out, struggling to keep Stone pinned until the laudanum took effect.

"Stop! Get away from me," Stone screamed. He pushed Witt away and then rose from the blood-soaked pillow, staring wildly around the chamber and swatting at the air as if trying to escape an invisible winged tormentor.

"Together," Witt yelled. He and Ravensmoore pressed on Stone's shoulders to force him to lie down.

"Help me." Stone, breathless from his fevered exertion, stared at Witt and then at Ravensmoore, but his eyes seemed empty. "Help me, God." His eyes closed, and his shallow breathing softened.

"Let's pray that he's not taken those demons with him as he sleeps." Ravensmoore eased his hold on Stone and stood next to the bed, looking down at his patient. "The caked-on blood from the wounds in his scalp have opened afresh. He needs attention."

Witt breathed deep, released his hold on Stone, wiped his sleeve across his brow, and fell into a chair. "What happened? I've never seen such a reaction. Even on the battlefield."

"His fear empowered him," Ravensmoore said. "Whatever attacked Stone frightened him beyond anything I've seen before. Now I must make sure he doesn't die from his wounds."

"I'll tell Prinny what's happened if you no longer need me here."

"Go on."

"You'll join us when you finish?"

Ravensmoore nodded, already engrossed in further assessing his patient.

❧

"I beg pardon, Your Royal Highness," Witt said as he entered the suite of private rooms lush with hunting tapestries and an ornately decorated Axminster carpet of crème and burgundy.

"Enough with protocol, Witt. Where's Ravensmoore, and what did the two of you think of Lord Stone's injuries?" He speared a piece of venison from his plate and stuffed it into his mouth. Then he pointed to a chair with his fork. "Sit down," he mumbled.

It was no wonder Prinny increased in size every year. The man never failed to eat, no matter how gruesome the occasion. Witt sat in a chair to the left of the regent. "Ravensmoore may prove quite useful." Witt filled him in on the events that had taken place in Lord Stone's bedchamber. Witt felt a twinge of guilt regarding the constant spying that Prinny had ordered. So far, Witt found Ravensmoore genuinely passionate about medicine, though, in truth, he didn't understand, any more than Prinny did, why the man insisted on practicing a trade.

"He's skilled, and he's one of us. I propose that you allow me to further investigate his motives for becoming a physician and find out if those motives go further than simply 'a calling,' as he puts it."

"I don't care what he thinks he's *called* to do, Witt. He's an embarrassment to the rest of us. You agreed last month." He peered into Witt's eyes. "Have you changed your mind?"

Perhaps he had, but he certainly wasn't ready to tell Prinny. "I reserve my judgment. I don't think how I feel is relevant right now. The greater importance is working together to find the person or persons who carried out this vicious act." He paused, thinking how much worse it could get if they failed.

"How could such a thing happen?" Prinny hit the table with his fist so hard that his wine spilled. A footman rushed to clean the blood-red mess. "What kind of monster would carry out such a deed and then threaten the rest of Parliament?"

"Ravensmoore believes it's someone that holds Parliament, or members of Parliament, responsible for a perceived injustice. Who knows what this madman is thinking? But we must find out. The faster he's brought down, the better for all of London." He leaned closer. "And we must consider your welfare, sir, and that of the prime minister."

"Preposterous! You don't think he would be foolish enough to threaten me and Lord Liverpool?" Prinny reddened, grabbed his cup, and drank. Then he slammed his empty cup on the table. "Do what must be done, Witt. Use whatever means you must."

A knock at the door interrupted their conversation.

"Enter!" Prinny stuffed another piece of meat into his mouth.

The aroma of the regent's meal caused Witt's stomach to lurch uncomfortably. He didn't understand how Prinny could stuff himself after seeing Lord Stone's injuries.

A page announced, "Lord Ravensmoore," and then bowed out of the room. Devlin entered, his expression grim.

"Lord Doctor!" Prinny said, his voice laced with sarcasm. "Come in and join us." He pointed to a chair on the opposite side of the table, once again using his fork. "Come. Eat. Drink. Tell me more about how Lord Stone fares." The regent then snapped his fingers at the footman. "Serve these two deserving men, as well."

The footman immediately uncovered venison along with steaming carrots and potatoes from the side board and set the plates in front of them, along with two cups of ale. The aroma sickened Witt. He waved off the footman. "The ale will do nicely."

"Ravensmoore, have you worked up an appetite?"

Ravensmoore slid into his seat. "I'll have cider only, sir. It's been difficult work, and I prefer to wait and eat later."

"In that case, give me your personal assessment of Lord Stone's wounds and needs for recuperation."

"He's near death, sir. His fever is climbing, and infection is setting in. It will be a miracle if he doesn't succumb from his injuries. Your personal physician—"

The regent lowered his fork to the table. "Not my personal physician. If Lord Stone needs a miracle, then it is you who will make certain he gets it and attend his needs. You are the one who is going to stay until he receives that miracle, Lord Ravensmoore."

Ravensmoore frowned and set down his mug of cider. "Your

Royal Highness, my sister is visiting, and this is her first night in London. I'd like to be with her—"

"I'm afraid that won't be possible, Ravensmoore. You must remain here." He fixed his stare on the man. "Is that clear?"

Witt wondered what this combat was really about. Did Prinny just want to make Ravensmoore suffer for what he considered behavior unbecoming to a lord for pursuing his passion for medicine? Was this Prinny's way of punishing Ravensmoore? Or had this crisis made Prinny aware of Ravensmoore's value and he now intended to utilize him as he saw fit? Knowing Prinny, Witt thought it was probably both.

"I understand your concern, sir. I'll do my best to assist Lord Stone."

The regent clenched and unclenched his hands on either side of his plate. "I wouldn't ask it of you if I didn't think it necessary."

"Of course you wouldn't." Ravensmoore finished off the mug of cider, which was immediately refilled by a nearby footman.

"Witt!" Prinny bellowed. "What are you so deep in thought about? A woman, I'd wager."

Witt steepled his fingers. "My reputation does me an injustice, sir. I was thinking of the predicament we all find ourselves in at the moment and how best to manage. And, by the by, my reputation has been greatly tainted by the gossips who can't foist their daughters upon me each season."

"Be that as it may, I don't want this matter to spread beyond the palace any sooner than it's likely to, which is bound to be too soon. Panic and speculation will run through the streets like the plague, and then more problems will abound. I'd like to know if Stone can be saved before hysteria breaks out. No matter what we do, when his family finds out about the attack and how disfigured he is from his injuries, the first thing they'll do is spread word."

"You might buy some time, sir," Ravensmoore said. "Allow his wife to come sit with him. She doesn't need to know the full extent of his injuries. The bandages will cover the worst of it. I'll tell her as much of the truth as possible without alarming her further, but you can make certain she doesn't leave until the time is right. That way both the family and society will temporarily be mollified."

The regent speared a carrot. "Brilliant!" He popped the carrot into his mouth and leaned back against the exquisitely carved, high-backed, ebony chair and belched.

"Ravensmoore might be right," Witt said. "Because I discovered Stone in the dense fog of the park, it's unlikely that anyone from outside the palace would be suspicious." Then he thought of Lady Victoria and her maid and the driver. What if one of them told what they had seen? "Still, the lords themselves may present the greatest possibility of panic. A couple of drinks and loose tongues, and it won't take long for word to spread."

Ravensmoore drank deeply. "You're right, Witt. The greatest panic will come within the House of Lords, and then it will spread within their families. Even though the regent warned the few who were summoned to the palace not to discuss the details, it won't remain quiet for long. We need to talk to them. All of them...all of us...together."

The regent sat back in his chair and let out a sigh. "I will notify the Lord Chancellor when the next meeting of Parliament will resume. Until then," he pointed to Ravensmoore, "you will care for Lord Stone, and you, Witt, will determine the best course of action to present to Parliament."

"I will send word to my sister that she should recover from her travels this evening. She won't be happy, but I will make it up to her later."

Witt tried to push away thoughts of his complicity in the situation. Even so, he still felt responsible because he had encouraged Prinny to call in Ravensmoore. It was further complicated by the fact that he'd been spying on Ravensmoore's actions in town to acquiesce Prinny. He and Ravensmoore had never been on friendly terms, but he wished him no harm—with his relationship with his sister or, even more importantly, from the unknown danger that seemed to lurk just beyond the walls.

Prinny sat back and rested his hands across the considerable bulk of his stomach. "You've no need to fret, Ravensmoore. I want you to attend to Stone. Witt will lead the investigation of this heinous act. Beginning tomorrow night." He smiled, looking smug. "He'll take your sister to the theatre tomorrow evening." When Ravensmoore started to protest, he held out his hand. "Rumors will likely be flying by then. There's nothing like gleaning information from the masses when they least expect it."

Witt's eyes widened as Prinny went on. Not so much because of the plan, but because of who his partner would be. He held his wine glass out to the footman to fill.

Ravensmoore looked like he'd been punched in the gut. He stood and paced to the window and back again. "If it is your wish, sir," he said, his lips tight. Then he turned to Witt. "My sister will not be pleased with the situation. She expected me to take her about London." He glanced at Prinny again. "Sir, the dangers...this...stranger...are you certain—?"

"Certain as hounds chasing a fox," the regent said, sipping his drink. "Have no concern about Lord Witt. I will hold him responsible for your sister's well-being. If he allows her to get even a sniff of danger...or if he should make any untoward advances...then I will simply have him executed."

Witt stifled a breath and straightened in his chair, warding off thoughts of his demise. He could see Ravensmoore's temper simmering just below the surface. He couldn't tell if it was directed more precisely at himself or Prinny.

"I will send word to my sister, Witt. I will have your word that you will treat her with the utmost respect and keep her out of danger…even as you act as Prinny's spy. She's not accustomed to the ways of the city and has no experience with this sort of thing, or men of your sort." Ravensmoore paced back to the window and stared outside.

"I will treat her like my own sister."

Ravensmoore stared at him. "You have a sister?"

"No, but if I did, I know I would want no harm to come to her. I give you my word that she'll be safe." Witt tried to smile reassuringly.

"It's agreed then, Witt. You will entertain my sister tomorrow evening, and I will attend to Stone's needs."

"Come, Ravensmoore," the regent pressed. "There's much to do. Send word to your sister and be done with it. You can make it up to her another time. I'll think of something stupendous that will win her back to your good graces." He dabbed at his mouth with a napkin. "Think of it too as a sacrifice you're both making for the good of society…and your regent."

"Very well, sir." Ravensmoore walked over to Witt and stood close enough for Witt to see the bloodshot whites of the physician's eyes. "We have an understanding. Do not disappoint me, or there will be much to pay."

"Of course."

Minutes later Witt strode to the carriage that waited outside the palace. He climbed in and blocked out the world as he examined the events of the day, turning them over and over in his mind.

What was this attack about? Would there be another? Why the lords of Parliament? They were the target. So in the mind of the attacker, had they committed some grievous act? *You have been found guilty of conspiring with sinful men for sinful purposes. I will now handle the situation as I see fit. Stone is only the first.*

*Repent, you lords of parliament.* How could he find out the reason for this savagery?

He concocted a mental list: revenge, terror, rage, the need to inflict pain and suffering, along with the possibility that perhaps the attacker himself had been maimed, scarred, terrorized, and could not or would not show himself in public.

If the attacker wanted to kill members of Parliament, why not simply shoot them? Pick them off one at a time. No, that would be too fast and too easy and not cause the suffering and fear this man obviously hoped to create.

Rage. Whatever the reason for this assault, rage factored into it. The horror of Stone's attack would send panic through the city. The longer the ordeal could be kept silent, the better, but he held no hope that the lords themselves could keep this quiet or from their wives. Fear had a way of making a man evaluate his life. Who could loathe human life so much as to torture a man so? Just as he'd always sensed a sniper in battle, he also sensed this type of sniper could be his most difficult to track.

The skin on his neck prickled, and he tried to shrug off his anxious thoughts. But he was so lost in thought that he started when the footman opened the door and he found himself at home. At least he took some comfort in the red brick townhome just behind the man. He clambered from the vehicle, gave the footman a nod, and then walked toward the entry. He'd barely let himself in the massive white door with its gold and red trim when the scent of something cooking drifted toward him. The rattle of pots and pans told him Mrs. Upton was cooking.

But as before, when Prinny invited him to sup, he had no appetite. Not today. Not after what he'd witnessed.

A young man appeared, blond and stiff in his butler's uniform. "Good evening, your lordship. Dinner will be ready soon." He helped Witt shrug out of his coat. "Long day, sir?"

"That's one way of putting it, Myron. I've been at Carlton House most of the day." Witt headed for the stairs.

"You must be tired. What do you require this evening?"

"A long, hot bath, Myron. And a stiff drink. I'll be going out tomorrow evening and entertaining a young lady. I'd appreciate your assistance in turning me out well."

"Shall I bring your meal to your room, sir?"

Witt thought about all he'd witnessed this day. "No. I'm not hungry. My apologies to Mrs. Upton. But I do need to send a message to the young lady."

"Very well, sir. I'll send it as soon as you're ready."

His thoughts churned through the events of the day yet again as he relaxed in a steaming tub of water and sipped his brandy. He forced his mind from the shadows and imagined Lady Victoria opening his missive. Perhaps tomorrow evening would serve well to lighten his dark mood.

Though he was following Prinny's directive, he certainly was not averse to getting to know Lady Victoria. There was something intriguing about her, and Witt couldn't remember the last time a woman had intrigued him.

He sat up as a new thought hit him. What if she didn't accept him as her escort? Or worse yet, what if she brought that beast of a mastiff with her as chaperone?

He almost chuckled. And then he remembered the real reason Prinny wanted him at the theatre. And he remembered the danger that he might be putting Lady Victoria in . . . again.

❧

Mist swirled outside the building that detained distraught souls. Talon hoped it would be as easy to enter Bedlam this evening as it had been the last time. He scanned the structure and squinted past the lamplight into the darker crevices that could hide those he wanted to avoid. "That's it. The signal." Talon grinned, and his heart beat a little faster. He clenched and unclenched his gloved fists, wishing he could simply fly up to whatever part of the building he wished to enter. Hawks certainly had some advantages.

Talon walked the entrance he chose to use, an entrance where only he knew who awaited him. The door opened, and a sliver of light spilled onto the walkway, frightening the mist as he entered the building.

"You found her? She is unharmed?"

The guard nodded.

Talon stuffed the bills into the other's hand. Only then did he receive the key that would unlock the entrance to the first ward.

The odor of urine-drenched straw made him gag. Poor souls. What had they done that was so awful? Ah no, a cry. Was she injured? Talon turned in the direction from which the small, sad whimper had emanated and caught his breath.

A young woman not much older than himself shivered in a dark corner, but it was not the one he sought. Blast! That man Toby would pay for this. She did not belong in this section of the building. He knew well why she was here, and it was unconscionable.

"Are you afraid?" Talon reached out and touched her shoulder.

Her head snapped up. The wild blue eyes that looked into his were filled with silent screams. She scooted backward, deeper into the darkness.

"You mustn't be afraid of me. I will not harm you. Are you hungry?" Talon withdrew a small package from within his overcoat and tempted the woman with a piece of chicken.

Long, thin fingers reached for the meat. Suddenly the morsel was snatched from Talon's hand by others. Anger welled. Talon turned on the intruders, slashing them with the special talons that Celeste had made for him, razor-sharp and deadly.

Their intrusion had ruined his plans for the night, and he tossed a sympathetic look at the woman, knowing he would have to leave her in this dreadful place. He raced back the way he had come, but the guard shoved him against the wall just as he reached the outer door.

"What mischief have you brought with you? They'll be asking questions now."

"You sluggard! You said you'd found her. Did you trick me on purpose, Toby? For if you did, I will find a way to redeem what I've lost at your expense." Talon's claws, wet with blood, grasped the man's neck. "I don't pay you to make mistakes. If you want to keep earning extra blunt, you'll keep your mouth shut. Understand? And next time you won't make a mistake, and you won't bring any women into the men's ward. Is that clear? If you dare to bring her to this area, make no mistake that you will die. You may have to die anyway for the mistreatment of that poor young woman."

The guard nodded, eyes bright with fear. But as soon as Talon removed his hand from around the man's neck, the man's angry and disapproving scowl returned. "Ye won't be comin' back now till the questions get answered. There's always questions."

"Tell anyone who asks that these things happen among the inmates. No one really cares. I'll double your pay next time. But don't disappoint me, Toby."

The guard pushed the door open. A toothless grin appeared in the dim moonlight. Talon knew his nocturnal visit was safe for now. He wound his way through the streets until he came to the hansom cab he'd rented and asked to wait for him. The driver bolted upright at his growl of orders.

"Yes, sir. I know the place."

Talon slipped into his seat and sat back against the musty cushions, damp with the evening mist and smelling of drink and women.

This was not the outcome he'd hoped for. He'd create another plan, another way to reach the woman he'd hoped to see this night, and he prayed she fared better than the frightened, abused woman he'd defended from greedy hands.

# CHAPTER 4

The very first moment I beheld him, my heart was
irrevocably gone.

—JANE AUSTEN

ICTORIA PEERED OUT from behind a lace curtain at the
parlor room window. It was an unusual occurrence for
two carriages to rattle down the cobbled street toward number
three Grosvenor Square, one behind the other, at this time of night
when no guests were expected. She watched them halt in front of
her brother's home and gasped when she noticed the royal crest on
one carriage and another crest on the second carriage she did not
recognize.

Lazarus barked with enthusiasm, his nose plastered against the
window, as they watched two footmen, one from either vehicle,
approach the entrance. Pleasantries were exchanged with Henry
at the door, and then Henry brought the notes to Victoria upon a
silver tray.

It might have been her imagination, but Lazarus seemed disappointed he wasn't bringing her the mail, as he sometimes did in
Yorkshire. He slumped to the floor at her feet as she opened the
crème colored envelope sealed with a large *W* in its wax design. She
hurriedly scanned the page in the unfamiliar handwriting. Then
her eyes moved upward to the beginning of the note again, and she
savored every word.

The corners of her mouth lifted upward, and her heart beat a bit faster. She read:

> *I want to make up for the horrendous way your visit to London began. I assure you that London is not always so dreadful. I want to introduce you to a lighter and friend-lier town. Your brother has been detained at the palace to attend Lord Stone. I hope you will accept me as a suitable escort for tomorrow evening.*

She dropped onto the green damask-covered settee near the window and, with a sigh, held the letter close to her heart. She'd dreamed of a moment such as this since she was a young girl, and now it was about to happen. But where was she being escorted to? She turned her attention to the missive again.

> *I am requesting the honor of your presence so we may attend the theatre for a presentation of the Taming of the Shrew. His Royal Highness insisted you not suffer boredom on your first excursion to town because he needs your brother's assistance at Carlton House. I will call for you at seven if you are willing to begin your grand adventure in London. I await your response.*

Smiling, she read the note again, almost forgetting there was a second letter waiting to be read. A gentleman would be escorting her to the theatre, a place she'd never been in her entire life. How absolutely wonderful and exciting.

"Now, that would be the look of a woman in need of a chaperone."

Victoria jumped. "Nora! You must not sneak up on a person like that. You nearly scared me out of my wits." In truth, she couldn't help the smile that covered her face, and if Nora hadn't interrupted, she likely would have read the lovely letter once more.

Nora crossed the room, carrying a tray that she placed on the dark cherry table beside the settee. On it was a warm cup of milk, a tiny pitcher of honey, and a plate of toast with a side of orange marmalade.

"What is it yer up to, my lady? I've brought you a bit of something to help you relax before bedtime."

Victoria smiled her thanks. "I love warm milk and honey." She poured some of the honey onto a teaspoon and stirred it into the cup of milk, raised it to her lips, and sipped. "Sinfully delicious."

Nora looked pleased and took a seat opposite the settee. "I recognize that look of yers from all them adventure books and penny dreadfuls ye read. Trouble is, yer not at home, and there's way too many adventures to be had in a town as big as London."

"You fret too much, Nora. Really you do. It's not healthy. Must I read Philippians four, six to you more often?"

"I'll be concerned to what yer about, that's what I'll be." Nora huffed and cracked her knuckles. "Yer so taken with the first one, I believe you've forgotten the second."

Her maid was right. Truly she had. Victoria bit back a smile and ripped open the second envelope, clearly written in her brother's familiar handwriting. As before, she scanned it first, and then read it again, frowning.

> *Dearest Snoop. Forgive me. I must remain at Carlton House at the regent's request. I will make this up to you later. I promise. Lord Witt will escort you tomorrow evening in my place. This was Prinny's idea, not mine. If you are uncomfortable with this, just let me know. If you wish to go, you have my blessing. I've also sent a note to Nora informing her of your needs. And that means rest as well.*

"Nora, you sly fox. You already knew." She folded the notes and held each in her hand. "Something's amiss at Carlton House. I surmise that Lord Witt did not tell him of the incident in the park this morning." She looked up at Nora and saw by her expression that she agreed. "At least, he didn't tell Dev we were involved or my brother would be standing in this room right now, lecturing me about the danger I put myself in and how I must be more cautious."

"There will much to pay when your brother discovers that we have kept the truth from him. I don't feel well about this at all. 'Tis not right."

"I know. Truly, I'd planned to tell him by now, but there's been no opportunity. It hasn't been intentional—"

Nora narrowed her eyes at Victoria, who sighed and started again. "Well, not entirely intentional. I do feel guilty for keeping it from him." She leaned forward, her voice dropping in her earnestness. "But he would overwhelm me with his concern. And he probably wouldn't let me out of the house. Ever."

"And when he discovers that Lord Witt did not reveal your secret, what then, dear one?"

Victoria chewed her lower lip. "I'll worry about that later. I think I can make him understand."

"It will not be pleasant. Untruths never are, whether willfully told as lies or simply truths left untold. What time is Lord Witt calling on you tomorrow?"

"He will arrive at seven. You won't give him trouble, will you, Nora? Giving him orders about how to take care with me, telling him about my illness or such? I want tomorrow evening to be a night to remember."

"That it will be, dear one." She smiled. "One way or another. Now finish your food and drink and let me draw your bath. You must get to bed so you can be well rested for your adventure tomorrow evening."

After her bath Victoria studied herself in the mirror to assess her progress. Since her brother had judged her to be well, she spent a few moments each day assessing her progress. She ran her fingertips under her eyes. The shadow of dark circles remained, but they were lightening up a bit. Her hair still felt like straw, her figure so thin she thought herself too unattractive to ever attract a beau.

Yet Lord Witt had not seemed discouraged by her appearance. Perhaps anything truly was possible.

"Lady Victoria, Lord Witt has arrived," Nora announced from the doorway of Victoria's bedroom. "Henry has shown him to the drawing room."

Victoria peeked down at the street as she held the drapes slightly away from the window. "I know," she whispered without looking at her maid. "I've been watching for him and saw him arrive."

"I hope he didn't see you spying on him." Nora entered the room and forced the drape shut. "You are impossible to guide in the ways of the world." She attended to a stray curl that had escaped the perfectly arranged style that Victoria loved. Her hair had been swept off her neck, and strands of flowers and pearls were woven throughout.

"Now, let me have a last look at you before you go down."

Victoria stood at attention and could see herself in the mirror behind Nora. "I believe you did well. I love this blue gown, and I never wear gloves at home." She ran a hand up the side of one long glove that matched her gown. "I feel like a princess." She smiled and could barely keep from twirling about the room.

"Indeed you are." Nora smiled in return with a look of pride.

Lord Witt stood and bowed as Victoria and Nora entered the parlor, Lazarus padding along behind. "I was so glad to hear that you had been assigned to my well-being, Lord Witt." Victoria curtsied. "Never fear, I won't plague you with idle chatter, as I'm sure many a young woman does in your presence."

"I seriously doubt any discussion with you, Lady Victoria, would be considered idle chatter."

She felt the heat of a blush rise to her cheeks and tried to cover her nervousness with words. "My brother tells me the regent asked you to escort me this evening. I apologize for this unexpected and probably unwanted intrusion upon your time, but I must admit that I am most excited. I will try not to be a nuisance."

"Ha, that I'll be lookin' forward to seein'." Nora bustled past them saying, "I'll just get my wrap, and then I shall be ready to accompany you."

"Be forewarned, Lady Victoria," Witt said. "The men will admire you, and the women will envy you. Your blue gown will make heads turn at the theatre tonight."

"I assure you, sir, that you do not have to compliment me. You are simply my escort for the evening, and I appreciate your willingness to help me further my adventures." She tried to sound convincing, though her heart beat with excitement.

"You do yourself a disservice. The ton will marvel and gossip about you, even if they don't welcome you with open arms. The women never welcome rivals."

Victoria felt her cheeks warm at the compliment. "I'm hardly a rival, sir. I'm practically a country bumpkin."

Nora bustled in with Victoria's long, dark blue pelisse. "Bah. When will you accept your beauty for what it is?"

"Allow me to assist you with your wrap." He took the garment from Nora. His fingers grazed her shoulders as he helped her into the wrap, and she wondered at the tingling sensation that slipped over her freshly bathed skin. "Are you ready to depart?"

Lazarus rose like a grumbling mountain and drooled his way toward their guest.

"Lazarus has not yet met you formally, Lord Witt. It appears he wishes to be introduced. He's a bit melancholy about being left behind. And because of the unhappy circumstances in the park, it might be best to begin anew."

Victoria knelt and looked her dog in the eye. "Lazarus, this is Lord Witt." She took Lord Witt's hand and rubbed her hand over his, which induced another pleasant sensation of tingling. "He's to show me about London this evening." She then hid a treat within Witt's hand and looked up at him.

"I haven't an affinity for canines, Lady Victoria."

"Oh, but Lazarus has an affinity for you, sir. I can see it in his eyes."

She withdrew her hand and allowed Lord Witt to offer the treat to Lazarus, who gobbled it down. "Good dog." She ruffled his ears. "You cannot accompany us this evening, but I am safe."

Lazarus then looked Lord Witt up and down, sniffed, and then drooled on his highly polished black Hessians. When he'd finished his perusal, he returned to his favorite spot in front of the fireplace.

"I don't think he sees quite as much in me as you believe he does."

"I'm sorry. He's not used to the ways of the city."

"Not to worry. They're only boots. Now, allow me to assist you and your maid into my coach."

Victoria liked him. She decided she liked him the moment he accepted the treat into his hand for Lazarus and the glint of humor in his warm gray eyes when she'd looked up at him. No longer were his eyes icy, but warm like a calm gray sea. So different from yesterday morning when he'd come to her aid in the park. *Had that only been yesterday morning?*

She thought she was prepared for her first adventure out with a gentleman, but perhaps she wasn't as confident as she'd hoped. This evening could prove a bit more complicated than she'd first imagined because she liked Lord Witt very much indeed. She liked his warm eyes, his warm hands, and his warm smile.

Witt studied her from his vantage point in the coach. The woman was gorgeous in an extraordinary kind of way. Fresh. Not touched by the worldliness of the city. Not cynical like him. She positively glowed with optimism as though nothing bad could happen. He wondered why.

"Why have you waited so long to come to London, Lady Victoria? Most young ladies have a season and are married off to the first young buck who shows interest and has a title worth flaunting."

"She is not like most young ladies, sir." Nora lifted her chin and squared her shoulders.

"Nora." Victoria sent her maid a warning glance.

"'Tis true." Nora crossed her arms and looked out the window as though her feelings had been injured.

A secretive smile told him that Victoria was thinking about her answer. That in itself was refreshing. Lady Victoria, true to her word, did not talk incessantly like many of the young women who'd tried to capture his attention and his title in his younger days. Later on, after his time in the war, he guessed they considered themselves lucky to escape marriage to a difficult man who had no interest in parties and social gatherings.

"I've had the opportunity to experience a different life. Mine was mostly a life of the imagination."

"You talk in riddles. What does that mean?"

"That, sir, is complicated in a simple kind of way." She tilted her head to one side and studied him. "I've been ill for most of my life." She found herself quite comfortable sharing this information, which she thought to hold in reserve.

Witt felt his heart tug and his pulse quicken. "I'm sorry. I didn't mean to make you uncomfortable."

She stared into his eyes, making him want to look away. But he didn't. He contained his uneasiness.

"Nonsense," she said. "I'm not uncomfortable in the least. Not everyone knows what to say when I tell them. I took an unexpected risk. I thought you might understand."

"And what makes you think that?" He smiled, thinking she had no idea how complicated his own life had become a long, long time ago.

"You're not squirming, for one thing. And you don't look as though you've just been saddled with an evening of torturous conversation about ill health."

"I doubt that any evening with you would be considered torturous."

"Ask my brother about that sometime. His answers may surprise you. Why, he's even been known to call me a hellion."

"I'm certain that is because the relationship that brothers and sisters share is not always easygoing or complimentary."

"My brother is responsible for saving my life, Lord Witt, and I didn't make it easy for him. In my pain I would scream the foulest things at him, and yet he stood it and loved me and ultimately healed me. None of which would have been achieved if I hadn't come to know God."

Witt lifted a brow.

She grinned. "Ah, now you're squirming."

"I've no doubt your brother and his skill healed you, but God? I'm afraid I don't share your enthusiasm for God."

"I hope someday you will. If you do come to know God, your life will be changed forever."

Witt thought how convenient naïveté could be. But in fairness, the woman had no way of knowing that his life had already been changed forever.

He looked out the window of the coach. "I've never been fond of change." He studied the people passing by on the street. The theatre came into view as they approached their destination. "That's why I like living in the country. No one bothers me there."

"Then why are you here in town?" Victoria's voice, gentle as a butterfly's touch, niggled at his conscience.

"I'm here because the regent ordered me to come."

"Ordered you to come?"

"Asked in a way that I could not refuse."

She tilted her head, looking puzzled, but she asked nothing more about the regent's orders.

The coach stopped in front of the theatre.

"We have arrived," he said, glad to change the subject. "Let me be the first to introduce you to the Drury Theatre. A feast for the imagination, a treasure for the soul."

"Magnificent," breathed Victoria, looking through the carriage window, her eyes wide with wonder. "I've never imagined to be so blessed."

A moment later the footman opened the door and handed her out of the coach. Witt offered his arm, and Victoria accepted. Nora followed close behind.

"So many people," Victoria whispered. "So elegant and beautiful. Yet it seems they don't recognize the wonder of being able to go out at night and enjoy such a thing as a play. You can see it in their faces." She paused. "Surely that isn't boredom I see."

"They've been doing this all their lives, Lady Victoria. They see it as a social responsibility."

"They should never take such opportunities for granted. I've waited for this kind of experience all my life. And now that it's arrived, I'm going to savor every moment of it like a meal of many courses."

As they ascended the stairs to the entrance of the theatre, Witt took delight in Victoria's wide-eyed observation of everyone and everything around her. Nothing escaped her notice. Honor and pride swelled in his chest to have her on his arm, and then the slightest bit of guilt crept in when he thought of her brother caring for the tortured body of Lord Stone. And what his real purpose was to be this evening and that Prinny wanted him to use the beautiful innocent Victoria as a cover for that purpose.

"Look." She pulled on his sleeve like a child trying to get another child's attention. "It's the name of the play, *The Taming of the Shrew.*" Large letters glimmered in the light that bounced off the lampposts that dotted the walkways. "Isn't it marvelous?"

He'd been here a hundred times, yet this evening he felt something stir in his spirit that made him glad, like setting his feet on solid ground after being at sea for a long time.

Victoria caught her breath as they entered the theatre. Dazzling chandeliers cast off a glow as bright as sunlight. Beautiful women and their escorts strolled throughout the elegant establishment as though walking through a park. She easily eavesdropped on bits of conversation. *Did you hear about ... Magnificent ... I don't know why she won't take my advice ... Why, isn't that Lord Witt? Who is that with him? Haven't seen her before.*

Victoria whispered in his ear, "I'm far too plainly dressed, sir. You should have warned me."

"Nonsense. Your smile and the light in your eyes are more than enough to outshine any beauty here this evening."

The warmth of a blush crept up her neck and into her cheeks.

Nora leaned close to her and whispered low, "Beware sweet words, miss. He may be leading you astray."

Victoria muffled a laugh and gathered her manners. On the inside she flooded with excitement and absorbed everything around her as if she'd never get another chance.

"Thank you, Lord Witt, but I don't have to look in the mirror to know that I don't even come close to the women in this room. They're so sophisticated and experienced and—"

"Jaded. Most of these women live a life going from one party to the next, trying their best to be who they aren't. As I said, jaded."

Victoria looked at him, surprised at his tone. "Oh, I'm sure you judge them too harshly, sir. They just want to enjoy life and not spend their time alone. It's hard being alone."

Nora squeezed her hand. A sign to be cautious. She hadn't meant to share so much of herself. She too had wanted to pretend she was someone else all the years of her illness, just for a little while.

Lord Witt expertly maneuvered through the crowd to the box above the stage. Victoria glanced at Nora, who appeared to have grown suddenly fond of Lord Witt as she seated herself in the rear of the box. And no wonder. The man had just slipped Nora a small box of chocolates.

Witt seated her in the front row of the box. Perfection! She watched the couples in the other boxes ogling each other. Women appeared to be gossiping as they hid behind beautifully decorated fans. She didn't even own a fan.

The crowd settled in as the curtain raised.

"How wonderful," breathed Victoria as she studied the actors. Act one was spent in wide-eyed wonder; in act two her wonder turned to laughter as the humorous lines drifted to them from the stage. Witt seemed as delighted as she, and even Nora laughed out loud.

During the intermission, Lord Witt introduced her to several friends and acquaintances who stopped to talk. As one couple approached, however, Victoria detected a slight frown darken Witt's features.

"Ramsey. I didn't think you enjoyed comedy," Witt said when the gentleman stopped in front of him.

"Oh, Witt. Sorry. It's far too crowded in here this evening. I'm not fond of the theatre, but I promised my sister I'd bring her to see this play. A birthday present." He turned around. "She was just behind me. Now, where—"

"Here I am, brother. There's such a crush." She blushed, seeming embarrassed that her brother had used a chastising tone. "I'm sorry. I didn't know you'd met up with friends."

"Lady Phoebe. I'd like you to meet Lord Witt. And I'm afraid I don't know this lovely young woman who has the daring to accompany you."

Witt bowed. "A pleasure, Lady Phoebe. This is Lady Victoria. She's just arrived in London, yesterday. Lord Ravensmoore's sister from Yorkshire."

"The Lord Doctor. I've heard of him."

Victoria didn't miss the quick glance that passed between Phoebe and her brother.

Phoebe studied Victoria from large brown eyes. Sun-kissed bronze tresses were pulled into a neat chignon that flattered her slightly round but pretty face. She dressed in pale yellow muslin with embroidered daisies trimming the neckline.

Phoebe said, "You've only just arrived? Perhaps we will see each other again before you return home."

They exchanged pleasantries for a few moments, and then the signal to return to their seats prompted them to end their conversation.

They found their seats quickly and settled in for the rest of the play. Victoria wondered why Lord Witt did not care for Lord Ramsey.

The ride home from the theatre was bittersweet. Victoria didn't want the evening to end, yet in the darkness she fought a growing worry about the events of the past two days. As they passed near the park, she was reminded again of the man they'd found.

"Lord Witt. Who was that unfortunate man we discovered yesterday morning? And what exactly is Devlin doing at the palace? The regent has his own physician at Carlton House who could help. Why would he have need of my brother?"

For several long moments, Witt didn't answer. The carriage bumped along in the dark, swaying now and again as the driver swerved to miss other carriages, drunks, and any assortment of society that apparently crossed their path. At least that's what she gathered from his rather colorful shouts of warning.

Finally he said, "That is something you will have to ask your brother. I am not at liberty to discuss the situation."

Victoria stared at him, barely able to make out his features in the dark. "I knew it. He's involved in something secretive. I truly believe if I hadn't been born female, I would have been a detective for Bow Street. A street runner or some such position that would have afforded me all kind of opportunity for spying."

He gave her a curious look. "A spy? You?"

"Is that so hard to imagine?"

"Mysteries can sometimes turn dangerous. They aren't safe for women to involve themselves in, Lady Victoria. There are so many other more gentle activities for women. No need to get involved in men's work."

"First of all, sir, let me assure you that I am as capable as any man when it comes to the art of detecting. I've spent most of my life studying human behavior because there was little else I could—"

Witt held up his hand. "Lady Victoria, I meant no offense. It's just that I've never heard of a woman being interested in detective work."

"Why is it that men always think women so unimaginative? When I was at Ravensmoore, I read voraciously and talked to everyone my brother brought to the house, including Constable Barton, a Bow Street runner himself. He came to Ravensmoore last year when sent by Sir Nathaniel Conant, the police magistrate here in London, after he'd heard of the crimes at Ashcroft Asylum."

"My Lady Victoria, simple inexperience could get you killed."

"Excuse me, sir. I am not finished. Sir Nathaniel told me many tales of Bow Street and its runners. And I've studied everything I can get my hands on regarding criminals and the like. I spent hours reading and re-reading Henry Fielding's *Inquiry into the Causes of the Late Increase of Robbers* that he wrote in 1751. It's positively riveting. So you see, I was exposed to gentlemen with great intelligence and experience." She took a long deep breath and tried to calm her ire.

"Beg pardon." Lord Witt arched a dark brow. "You are obviously different from other women."

"Oh, you don't know the 'alf of it, yer lordship," Nora blurted. "Given 'alf a chance, she'd try to replace that there magistrate of Bow Street himself."

Victoria and Lord Witt burst into laughter.

❧

Exhausted and happy, Victoria lay in her bed thinking of the day and reliving the night at the theatre. She listened to the sound of Lazarus breathing on the floor beside her bed. She rolled onto her stomach and gently laid a hand on the big dog's head and rubbed the hair back and forth in a comforting motion. He let out a contented sigh and continued sleeping.

Victoria smiled and whispered, "Thank You, God, for this great adventure. I would be most grateful if You would protect my brother from harm and bring him safely home after attending the gentleman at Carlton House. And God, protect Lord Witt and guide him, please. He is a mysterious man. I think he relies on himself overmuch and isn't so sure about You. Help me help him if I can."

She tried to stay awake, waiting for Devlin to return home, but her eyelids grew heavy, and soon she dreamt of a gray-eyed man and the words from the mouth of the stubborn Katharina in *The Taming of the Shrew*, saying, "Why, sir, I trust I may have leave to speak; And speak I will. I am no child, no babe . . ."

And then a mist filled her dreams and the face the man in the park became Lord Witt's face. She reached out to him, but he turned away from her, and she was lost.

# CHAPTER 5

There is nothing I would not do for those who are
really my friends. I have no notion of loving people
by halves. It is not my nature.

—JANE AUSTEN

*R*AYS OF EARLY morning sunshine slanted through
the windows of Carlton House as Witt walked up the
marble staircase to the second floor. He didn't want to let go of the
wonderful evening he'd had with Lady Victoria. He didn't want to
think about what awaited him upstairs. He slowed his steps, wondering if Stone still lived.

Guilt sliced through him as he thought of his evening com-
pared to that with which Ravensmoore had been forced to deal.
Witt turned the corner, nodded to the guard still watchful of Lord
Stone's chamber, and entered unannounced. He walked through
the parlor, where a nursemaid sat dozing, and then continued past
her and into Stone's bedchamber, where Ravensmoore bent over
his patient, apparently listening to his heart. "He's still alive?" Witt
took in the scene. Stone, if he lived, was covered with bandages.
Even his face had been wrapped.

Ravensmoore placed one piece of the wooden stethoscope inside
the other and set it in the black bag on the floor. "Yes."

Dark shadows nestled under the doctor's eyes. "You look like you
could use some sleep."

"How is my sister?" he asked. "Tell me all is well."

Witt dropped into a well-cushioned armchair. "She had a delightful evening. I took her to see *The Taming of the Shrew*."

"I'd hoped to be the one who took her to see that play." Ravensmoore scrubbed his face with his hands. "Hopes are sometimes delayed. What did she think of the theatre?"

"Nothing escaped her attention. She literally glowed with excitement. I'm certain she'll look forward to her next play at the Drury with you."

"You look rested." Ravensmoore gave Witt a cautious look. "Which tells me you ended the evening early." His expression said that pleased him.

"Ah, yes, indeed, as was proper for your sister. But I also admit that I haven't enjoyed town for many years. Last evening made me think I should visit more often."

Ravensmoore's demeanor darkened. "Remember that you only escorted my sister last evening because Prinny made it impossible for you to refuse. I don't want you putting ideas in Lady Victoria's head. She has far too many ideas swirling around her mind as it is. And she's been far too sheltered to fully comprehend the ways of society."

"You don't give her the credit she deserves. And have you forgotten my primary aim, according to the regent?"

"And was that part of your mission successful?"

"I heard nothing of importance."

"Not that you would tell me if you did—"

They were interrupted by a deep, guttural moan. "Where?" Lord Stone rasped.

Ravensmoore moved to the head of the bed and pulled the bed drapes back further. "You're at the palace. You were attacked, but you're safe now."

Stone looked at his hands. "No." His brown and bloodshot eyes widened. He tried to sit up but then fell back on the pillows help-lessly. "Let me die."

Witt stepped forward. "You don't know what you're talking about. Give it time, Stone."

Ravensmoore caught Witt's attention and shook his head. "You've had a shock and need to rest." He picked up a bottle from the side table. "This will help you sleep. Do you remember what happened to you?"

Silence slipped through the room, cutting a path of despair. Stone lay on the bed with his face turned away from them. Witt couldn't tell if he was conscious any longer. After what seemed minutes, Stone, his eyes full of dread and bright with unshed tears, turned toward Ravensmoore. "Help me."

Ravensmoore measured out the liquid into a small cup. "Drink this. I plan to help you, but you've got to fight to live." He held the cup to his patient's lips. The man could barely swallow. Finally he got the laudanum down.

"My wife?"

"She was here all night. She left only an hour ago."

Tears slid into the bandages that covered his cheeks. "She shouldn't have." He closed his eyes, yet the silent tears continued to flow until he slept.

A shudder of memory suddenly attacked Witt from the past, and he could see and hear the dogs. Rain pelted him as the first dog…he shut the memory out before it could hurt him. Witt studied Lord Stone's still form, the bandages, the foul smell of the wounds, and the bitter tears of fear and powerlessness. Then he looked at Ravensmoore. "What now?"

"We wait."

"I believe that brief statement is the most frequently used of any physician."

Ravensmoore nodded. "And the most frustrating." He emptied

water into a basin, rolled up his sleeves, and washed his hands as he continued talking. "Don't forget the note pinned to his clothing. There will be more, but who? How can we protect the next intended victim?"

"I think we should visit Bow Street."

"I agree."

A rustling sound alerted them.

"Wake up, woman," a female voice ordered from the other room. "My husband could be dead and you'd never know."

"Oh, yes, madam. The doctor's with him, my lady."

"Doctor indeed," Lady Stone grumbled as she stalked into the room. Her body jiggled, setting off a rippling effect that caused her dress to rustle with activity. Pulling the poor nursemaid behind, she fairly flung her into the room. "Sit in that chair next to my husband and don't fall asleep."

Witt resisted the urge to roll his eyes. "Lady Stone."

She nodded. "Lord Witt. The regent assures me that you will capture the man who committed this atrocity."

"I don't think I will be accomplishing that single-handedly, madam."

"I don't care how you do it. Just do it! I want to attend the hanging."

"I was just leaving to attend to business, Lady Stone. If you will excuse me." He quickly walked to the door, grateful to be past her as she moved on to assault her next target.

"Well, Lord Ravensmoore? If you are going to be a doctor, you had better learn how to deal with the family. Give me your report. How fares my husband?"

Witt grinned and saluted Ravensmoore as he hurried from the room, relieved to be away from Stone's wife. No doubt the stories of Stone's infidelity were true. Witt closed the door behind him, but the nagging sound of her shrill voice followed as he walked away.

Victoria relaxed at the table in the breakfast room and stirred a teaspoon of sugar into her cup. She reviewed the events of the last evening again and smiled.

Nora bustled into the room. "And what is it you've got on your mind, Lady Victoria? I can see you're thinking. Did you enjoy the Sunday morning service?"

"To tell you the truth, Nora, I was so tired I could barely keep my eyes open, but I did enjoy the parts of the sermon I was awake for." She set the cup down after a deep, satisfying swallow. "And you? Did you enjoy the sermon?"

"Indeed I did. One can never tire of hearing about our Lord's grace. So undeserving we are. And He so understanding of our needs and weaknesses."

"I couldn't agree more. And that brings me to another idea, Nora, speaking of needs. I met a young woman last evening. Her name is Lady Phoebe, and her brother is Lord Ramsay of Thistledown Hall. I wanted to invite her here to visit. Is that too forward, do you think?"

"You mean, is it too soon for you to find a friend? I think not. You must make your own friends and find your way in society. 'Tis not always easy, and you haven't had much practice."

"I'm a bit nervous."

"Then I suggest you sit at your writing desk and dash off an invitation to the young lady. If she agrees to come, you will have a chance to make a friend."

After tea Victoria followed Nora's recommendation. Several false starts eventually led to an invitation that she read aloud in the privacy of the morning room:

> *Dear Lady Phoebe,*
> *I hope that you are well and will not think me too forward since we've only just met at the theatre. But since I*

*am new to London, I thought it might be pleasant if we spent some time together, getting to know one another. My brother is at Parliament most days, and I assume your brother is as well. I invite you for tea, and I hope you will come tomorrow afternoon so we may indulge in those many things that women love to talk about.*

*If you would like to join me, we will come for you in the Ravensmoore carriage. Please do let me know.*

*In earnest,*

*Lady Victoria*

Victoria sat back, considering the letter. Her heart longed for a good friend, and she had enjoyed meeting Lady Phoebe the previous evening. She let out a sigh and chewed her lower lip. *Dear Lord, please let her accept this invitation.*

❧

The next afternoon Victoria and Phoebe, accompanied by Nora, rode through Berkeley Square in a carriage with the Ravensmoore crest upon the door.

"We must stop at Gunter's for some flavored ices or ice cream," Phoebe said as they rode through town. "I do believe you will enjoy the refreshment."

"That sounds wonderfully decadent." Victoria's mouth watered just thinking of the treat that awaited.

They entered London's exquisite Gunter's Tea Shop by walking under the sign of its famous pineapple.

They were greeted by a young woman who seated them at a table covered with a lime-green tablecloth. Other tables were covered in yellow. The moment they were seated, a young man appeared to wait on them with a pineapple pin on his shirt collar. Phoebe ordered the bergamot water ice, and Victoria was tempted to drool like Lazarus over the royal ice cream, with its hint of pistachio and orange.

"I will leave you two alone if you promise to stay here and stay together," Nora said as she stood. "I don't want to have to go chasing around London looking for you. I'll just take these lovely orange sorbets fortified with a wee bit of rum for our driver and meself." She winked and carried her treasures outside to where the carriage was parked under a nearby maple tree.

"I'm so glad you invited me in to town, Lady Victoria. I rarely get the opportunity." She smiled and shrugged. "Although I shouldn't complain. I could live in town, I suppose, if I wanted. My brother has a townhouse here, as well." She leaned forward and whispered, "Although I suspect he likes it for himself because he's a bachelor."

"Don't you get lonely in the country?"

"Sometimes." Phoebe spooned another bit of her treat into her mouth and sighed. "But the city is far too busy and crowded for me, although I do love the theatre."

Victoria indulged in another bite of her ice cream and sighed as it slid down her throat. "I do believe I could stay here till closing and not have enough of this wonderful delicacy. I'll have you to blame for the loss of my figure if I visit here too often." She laughed.

"That's probably another good reason not to visit town too often." Phoebe's eyes danced. "I insist you attend the full moon masquerade ball that my brother is hosting next month. It's always a wonderful ball, and it's held at our country home. Will you come? I'll be certain that your entire family is invited, and Lord Witt too, of course."

"I'd love to come. That will give me enough time to be fitted for a costume. I'll have to get permission from my brother, of course, but I don't think he will object. What a wonderful event to look forward to, Lady Phoebe."

The next hour passed quickly as the two women shared ideas

regarding costumes and what colors would suit each of them to the best advantage.

Before leaving, they bought several confections and then headed for the Ravensmoore carriage. "This feels wonderful," Victoria said as she studied the people they passed. "It is nothing like Yorkshire. I haven't seen a single sheep since I arrived."

Victoria and Phoebe laughed.

Phoebe said, "The only sheep you will see in London might be sheep in wolves clothing. Those gallant gentlemen pretending to be gentlemen." She sounded wise. "After you get to know them, you discover they are on the prowl, and they aren't looking for sheep. They are looking for young, naïve, vulnerable women or easily accessible widows who are so lonely they no longer care about being fleeced."

Every morning Talon rose early to care for his beloved hawks. When he entered the mews where the birds lived, he felt at home. He wondered what it might be like to be free. Really free. Perhaps that is why he loved to fly the raptors. Every time a bird took flight, he imagined he could see everything as the hawks see from their vantage point. *Talon.* He loved his name. Talons were razor-sharp and could inflict irreparable damage. He'd even trained one of his superior raptors to bring down a large deer. Unheard of, to his knowledge. It was one of the few times in his life that he felt proud. Proud of his skill. And proud of his kill.

"Good morning, Wellington." Talon walked up to the first cage and admired the great red kite, larger than any he'd ever seen, with its wingspread greater than five feet. He'd dared to save these hawks that were practically extinct in England. He knew them to be intelligent if well cared for and loved, not the vermin the government claimed. "I know you want to fly today. So do I. Let me care for the others, and then we will practice."

Talon worked with all five birds in the mews. He'd named them all. Each had to be weighed and fed unless it was their turn to train. If the hawk wasn't hungry, he wouldn't hunt. He looked forward to these days when he trained Wellington. Unlike most raptors who had no allegiance to their owners, this raptor had developed affection for him. He helped Talon achieve his goals.

"And Lord Byron. How do you fare this lovely morning? Written any good poetry lately?" Talon donned his leather gloves and opened Byron's cage. The hawk jumped to his fist. "*She walks in beauty, like the night, Of cloudless climes and starry skies.*" The bird looked at him with curious eyes. "Let's see what you weigh today."

Talon continued to recite the poem by Byron while he weighed and fed the bird and placed him back in his cage. "Now work on another poem for me, you old romantic." Talon grinned and proceeded to the cages of the other three birds. He called each by name as he cared for them.

"Ah, Pandora. When will you unleash your evils?" Pandora shrieked like a screaming woman. Talon covered his ears. "Stop that. I will not stand for that behavior. Your manners are atrocious. Has Wellington been teasing you again? I will fly you tomorrow. No food today, dear one. Tomorrow you will practice what you have been trained to do. Your speed and power will be an asset."

"And last but not least. Goliath." True to his name, Goliath sat on his perch, large and still and quiet. He overshadowed Wellington by two feet and his wingspread by two feet longer, to a full extent of seven feet. Powerfully built, but not fast.

Talon heard the door of the mews open and turned. "Ah, Celeste. I was just talking to my beloved hawks. What have you been feeding them? Goliath is as large as an eagle."

A woman stood in the doorway mirroring Talon's smile. "I

thought you'd never tell me you were satisfied with their progress." Celeste lowered her copper-colored cape to reveal black locks, almond-shaped eyes the color of the sea, and a low-cut aquamarine gown.

"Have you been conducting experiments again?" Talon pulled open Wellington's cage and the bird fisted his leather glove. When the bird cleared the cage, Talon placed the hood over Wellington's head to prevent him from seeing until they were at the spot where he wanted him to fly.

Celeste removed the long jesses hanging from the bird's feet and replaced them with short ones so as not to impede flight. "There you go, Wellington. Fly high for Talon. He does love to see you soar."

"Attach the leash, Celeste. I don't think he'll try to fly with the hood on, but it is a good precaution."

Celeste attached the leash to the thong of the glove.

"Walk with me to the clearing, Celeste, and tell me what you've been working on so diligently of late." He held the hawk on his left hand. The two of them left the mews and walked into a wonderful spring day full of birdsong and luscious scents of flower and dewed grass.

"I've been working with the hives. There's nothing like the taste of fresh honey. I have some thoughts to share with you about the bees and about the ultimate use they might serve. I've also been working in the laboratory and concocting a brew that might serve our purpose." She slanted a look toward him, and his eyes darted between her and the hawk.

"What is it? You sound very mysterious."

"I need to test my plan on a subject. A person who will not be missed. I hate to use an innocent, but I can think of no other way. If it doesn't work, then it's not a risk we should take with the gentlemen of Parliament. Do you understand?"

Talon nodded as they entered the clearing. "Of course. So tell me what you want to do. I may be able to find someone who is not so innocent."

⚜

Victoria woke from a sound sleep. She blinked and rubbed her eyes, trying to place the sound she'd heard. Then swinging her legs over the side of the bed, she lit a candle and padded across the Armenian carpet, ornately decorated with dragons and eagles, to one of three sets of gold silk drapes. She edged back a drape to see what stirred outside her window. The moon dipped in the sky and played tag with the clouds in a light breeze. Her gaze followed the path of the clouds and the beauty of the diminishing full moon.

Lazarus slept in a heap at the bottom of the four-poster bed, his snores a sure sign that his stomach was full and he dreamed of things that flickered across the minds of such beasts.

She heard the sound again. Men's voices. Or something else?

As she peered through the window, a soft exhalation of breath brought a low rumble of concern from Lazarus. She turned to look at him. "No worries, old friend. It must be the wind."

Lazarus opened one eye to study her, rubbed a giant paw over his nose, and went back to his dreaming. Victoria was about to let the drape close when movement in the gardens behind the townhouse caught her attention.

She blew out the candles on the table beside her and rubbed the condensation from the window pane. Lazarus growled. "Quiet," she whispered. He was beside her in an instant, his large paws on the windowsill and his nose smashed against the window. He stared into the gardens as she did, looking for what might be out there.

Something moved again, but she could not decipher the shapes. Then the shadowy forms broke free of the clouds, and she saw two men. Her brother must surely be one. Lazarus growled and pushed his nose against the window. Victoria changed her position to see if she could make out the other, for she could see that he was talking in earnest and moving his hands in quick bursts of silent speech all their own.

"Lazarus, do be careful. You're drooling on me." She looked back out the window and gasped.

The shadow of a large bird soared past the house.

Lazarus barked and stood on his hind legs. His breath steamed the window. If Lazarus hadn't barked, she would have thought herself overtired. But she did see a large bird, perhaps a hawk, but its wing spread...its wing spread...a chill ran up Victoria's arms...was huge.

The Apostles clock in the hallway began its midnight chime. The house staff would be abed. She and Lazarus tore down the stairs, into the kitchen, and out through the rear door of the house. Her bare feet hit the cold terrace. "Devlin!"

Devlin and Witt met her halfway.

Lazarus barked and nearly ran over Lord Witt.

"What's happened?" Devlin asked. "Easy, Lazarus. Quiet."

She ran straight into her brother's arms. "A huge bird. A hawk, perhaps, skimming over the rooftops and then near the house. It flew past my window!"

Both men looked to the sky and then at each other. Victoria saw them exchange a glance, a meaningful glance.

"I don't see anything now," Witt said. "Are you certain?"

"Of course I'm certain." Victoria's back stiffened, and she pushed away from Devlin and turned to Witt. "I'm not having visions, and Lazarus saw something too. That's why he barked."

Lazarus barked again and nuzzled Devlin's hand.

"If you got excited or scared, then Lazarus would react to your emotions, just as he did now. I'm not saying you didn't see something. I just don't know if—"

"I saw the look the two of you just exchanged. You don't believe me." She looked from one to the other in dismay.

"Lady Victoria." Witt stepped closer to her in the darkness.

Lazarus growled and nudged his way between them.

"What's going on?" Devlin asked.

"I think we better go inside." Victoria gathered her courage for the discussion yet to come. "I'd like to know why you two are talking in the gardens behind the house this time of evening. It's near midnight and—ouch!" She grabbed Witt's arm to keep from falling. "I'm sorry. I stepped on a thorn or perhaps a stone."

Lord Witt picked her up in his arms. "It would seem you have another patient, Ravensmoore."

Her brother sighed. "Follow me." He led the way into the house.

Victoria forgot all about her foot as she leaned her head against Witt's shoulder for the second time in two weeks. Victoria's heart beat faster. She thought she could get used to being in his arms.

Nora met them as they entered the house. "What's amiss? Lazarus has awakened the staff and—oh, my lady. What have you done?"

"It's nothing, really, Nora. Go back to bed. I stepped on something when I ran outside without my shoes."

Henry came into the parlor carrying a candelabra. "I thought you may be needing some light, your lordship."

"Thank you, Henry. And Victoria, you need to lie still. It will be easier for me to examine the bottom of your foot. Now let's see what you've stepped on."

Devlin grasped the heel of her foot, after Witt had lowered her onto the settee, with Lazarus looking on as though he were an assistant.

"A simple thorn, but it's —"

"Ouch! That's not simple at all."

Lazarus slumped to the floor with a whimper.

"I'll be fine, Lazarus."

Witt knelt next to her and took her hand in his. "Squeeze hard on his next attempt."

She did.

Witt said, "Ouch!"

Devlin held up the thorn. "A nasty little barb."

"The hazards of gardens," Nora said.

"Thank you, brother," she said avoiding his eyes, afraid he would see too much. "And Lord Witt, I hope I didn't hurt you too much. I didn't mean to squeeze your hand so hard. Now that's taken care of, I think I shall retire for the evening. Nora, if you would be so kind to—"

"Aren't you forgetting something, my sister?"

She looked up and saw that he already suspected something. Then he arched a brow in that way that made him seem so superior.

She huffed. "Perhaps another evening. I know you must return to the palace. And I wouldn't want to be responsible for—"

"I don't think so. Nora and Henry, excuse us while I have a much-needed talk with my sister and Lord Witt."

Victoria glanced at Nora and mouthed the word *please.*

Nora frowned. "You may wake me if you be needn' me later, Lady Victoria." Nora mouthed the word *courage.* "I'll be returning to my bed."

Nora and Henry left the room. Victoria prayed for escape.

Devlin stared hard at both of them, but his eyes rested on Victoria. "As I asked about half an hour ago, what's going on?"

# CHAPTER 6

Where the law ends, tyranny begins.
—HENRY FIELDING

VICTORIA SCOOTED TO the edge of the couch and gently tested her sore foot on the floor. "That's much better."

Devlin crossed his arms and waited. "Victoria? I believe you have something to tell me."

Victoria glanced at Witt. "Lord Witt, would you care to sit down?"

"I believe I'll remain standing, thank you. There may be need for a quick escape." He grinned but then sobered when Devlin glared at him.

Devlin took a deep breath. "I'm waiting."

"Do you remember the day I arrived?" Victoria straightened her back. *Lord, I require Your assistance at this moment. Please guide my words.* "I never really explained to you that I met Lord Witt in the park that morning."

Devlin stroked his chin. "I'm not sure I understand. That's the morning that Witt discovered Lord Stone in St. James Park."

"Yes." She squirmed under her brother's scrutiny. "I, or actually, Lazarus, discovered Lord Stone first."

Devlin froze. "You were in the park. You discovered Lord Stone. You saw his condition?" He looked first at Victoria and then at Witt. His eyes turned molten green, and he looked like a panther about to pounce. "And you didn't tell me?" He dropped his arms to his sides and started to pace the parlor.

Victoria's heart clenched and tears sprang to her eyes at the last words. "I'm sorry." And then she added, "What do you mean by 'his condition'?" She paused. "All I saw was that he was injured. There was blood…and then Lord Witt turned me away before I could get a closer look."

Her brother held up a hand. "You should have told me."

"Ravensmoore. I think I can explain."

"Now you want to explain, Lord Witt? Two weeks after the attack on Lord Stone, you want to tell me what happened? Please, don't keep me in suspense."

"The mist caused the coach your sister rode in to move slowly. I was out for a walk before the session at Parliament was to begin. We think that Stone ran blindly into the coach and then fell."

"The driver stopped immediately," Victoria said.

Devlin nodded. "Go on."

"I jumped from the coach when the driver said we might have run someone down, and I sent Lazarus to find whoever it might have been, and then I followed him into the mist. That's when Lazarus found Lord Stone." She hesitated, and then asked again, "What do you mean by 'his condition'?"

Witt and her brother exchanged a glance, and then ignoring her question, Witt said, "Your sister allowed us to use the coach to get Stone to Carlton House."

Devlin quit pacing and shook his head as if trying to wake from a nightmare. "What in the name of all that is honest prevented you, either of you, from telling me this when it occurred?" He gave Witt a hard stare. "And you, once you saw the…disfigurement…why did you not tell me then? When I think of the danger…" He let his voice drop off.

Victoria tiptoed across the carpet, protecting her heel. She put her hand on her brother's cheek. "Forgive me, Dev. It's my doing. I asked him not to say anything until I told you. Then I thought you would be afraid for me and that you wouldn't allow me out of your sight, and I didn't want to be confined to this house on my first adventure to London."

She noticed that Devlin clenched his teeth so hard that a vein on the side of his temple stood out and looked about to burst.

He moved away from her and stood directly in front of their visitor. "And you, Witt?" Devlin asked.

"As you mentioned, it's been two weeks since the incident, and I honestly didn't know if she'd told you what happened that morning. All along I've thought it her place to do so. I was trying to protect your sister."

"From me?" Devlin asked, incredulous. "That is—"

Victoria pushed between them, facing her brother. "Not as ridiculous as you might think, Dev. You are too protective. I love you, but I'm a full-grown woman now, and I want to live a full-grown life. I was afraid you'd send me back to York if I told you the truth."

Devlin opened his mouth to speak and then changed his mind.

"I only meant to delay telling you the truth a day, and then you were called away to the palace. There just never seemed to be a good time."

"This makes it very difficult for me to trust either of you under these circumstances. However, I actually think I understand what you're both saying, which is a bit disturbing. Still, Victoria, you've always been honest with me. I'm disappointed that you couldn't trust me with what happened to you that morning."

"I know, Dev. Forgive me. I won't keep the truth from you again."

"You're forgiven. And I do and will worry about your safety, but I'll try to be more understanding of your need for freedom. I vow, though, it won't come easy."

Devlin turned to Witt. "Thank you for assisting my sister the morning of her arrival, Witt. I'm glad to know you were there and able to help both Victoria and Lord Stone. But don't keep secrets any longer when it comes to my sister's safety. That's the one thing that I will not tolerate. Understood?"

Witt looked at Victoria and her brother. "Understood."

Victoria turned from her brother and stood before Lord Witt. "And speaking of secrets, why are you here, and what were you and my brother discussing out in the garden? Late at night and in danger of being attacked by a large bird? Is that what attacked Lord Stone?" She frowned. "I did see a bird. The wingspread was enormous. It was no ordinary bird of—"

Devlin stepped between them. "I think it's time you returned to bed, little sister. We'll talk of this further tomorrow. I must return to the palace and attend Lord Stone. He's in and out of consciousness but unable to speak yet about what happened to him." He kissed her on the forehead.

"You can send me off to bed, but I know what I saw, and that creature was hunting." She shivered. "Something or someone."

⁂

Bow Street loomed in a cloud of mist in Covent Garden. Light filtered through the grimy windows, an illusion of warmth that cast its beams onto the cobblestone streets outside the infamous building of crime solvers and professionally organized thief-takers known as the Bow Street runners. Witt's thoughts turned to Victoria and how she would have loved to be with him and her brother at this moment. If the woman wasn't careful, she would find herself in serious trouble someday with all the thoughts she entertained of detectives and snooping. He grinned.

"What do you find so amusing, Witt?"

"Your sister." He opened the door and entered the building before Devlin could comment.

The magistrates' court functioned within 4 Bow Street. Witt peered into the large smoke-filled room. Witt spotted his old friend talking to a group of runners and studied him briefly. He still held a cheerful disposition in a place that dealt with crime and its ugly outcomes. His friend caught sight of him.

"Witt!"

Sir Nathaniel Conant, chief magistrate of Bow Street, gripped Witt's hand. "It's been too long. About time you came out of that cave in the country. How are you?"

"I'm well, Nate."

"Then why haven't you been in London? I figured you'd at least be here during the season to find a pretty bride to keep you company and help you raise a dozen children."

"Because I've been raising horses instead."

"They're a poor substitute for children, Lord Witt."

"Not that I want to change the subject, but I'd like you to meet Lord Ravensmoore."

"Your lordship." Nathaniel bowed. "I've heard much about you. Helping the sick in Southwark and tending to those in Bethlem. You've taken on quite a burden in addition to your other responsibilities."

Devlin nodded. "Sir Nathaniel. A pleasure. I appreciate you sending Barton up to Yorkshire last year."

"And I appreciate you sending Simon Cox to me. He's worked out quite well here and has a way of garnishing information that few of the runners can rival. Stirs up good, healthy competition."

"I can't think of a better place for Simon," Devlin said. "He's quite proud of assisting the runners."

"Indeed he is. He surely did kick up a storm, though, about not being able to call himself a runner because of the height requirement. All the runners need to be at least five foot and eight inches tall for safety reasons. But I imagine you're not here to discuss these kinds of issues. We learned of the attack on Lord Stone in St. James Park. I knew it only a matter of time before someone called us into this situation."

"We need your help," Witt said.

"Let's go to my office and share our information. Then we'll devise a strategy to catch Lord Talon."

The three of them settled into straight-backed chairs around a solid table stained from years of use. Witt studied the small office. *The Times* was strewn and open to the story about grave robbing. Framed portraits of previous magistrates Henry Fielding and his brother Sir John Fielding, the Blind Beak of Bow Street, decorated one wall. The novels and periodicals of Henry Fielding, including *The History of Tom Jones, a Foundling* and *The History of the Adventures of Joseph Andrews and of His Friend Mr. Abraham Adams*, graced two shelves of a bookcase. A framed copy of Sir John Fielding's *Quarterly Pursuit* and also the *Weekly Pursuit* hung side by side on the wall above the bookcase.

"Your office is one that reveals your character, Nate."

Sir Nathaniel smiled. "And all those who come after me."

Devlin leaned back in his chair and stretched long legs in front of him. "How did you hear of the attack, Sir Nathaniel?"

"We have our sources, Lord Ravensmoore." He flipped through some notes. "But I must admit that in this situation, our biggest resource was our smallest assistant, Simon Cox."

"Simon? How did he find out?" Devlin asked.

"Unbeknownst to you, Witt, Simon saw you enter the rear of Carlton House with Lord Stone the morning of the attack. He spied on you and the guard and young Thomas, the page that was sent to notify the regent."

Witt heard something scrape outside a window and looked up to see a face pressed against a window. He flinched in surprise, but when the others turned to look, the face had disappeared.

"What is it?" Sir Nathaniel asked.

Witt stood. "I believe we have a spy." He walked toward the door and opened it. A dwarf fell into the room.

Witt picked him up by the collar of the coat and righted him. "Who have we here?"

"You have caught my friend Simon." Devlin stood. "You can release him now. He's quite capable of crippling your shins if you're not careful. I know from experience." Devlin grinned.

Witt let go, and Simon brushed off his black overcoat with a red waistcoat beneath. His unfashionably long gold hair was tied back with a black ribbon.

"Lord Ravensmoore. A pleasure to see you, though I can't say as much for your new associate."

Sir Nathaniel sat forward in his seat. "Simon, I want you to meet a friend of mine, Jonathon Denning, Lord Witt. And Witt, this is our very capable Simon Cox wearing the uniform of the horse guard. Even though he is not technically a runner, he's been given permission to ride due to his stature. It increases the likelihood of his success when dealing with the criminal element."

Simon bowed. "Lord Witt. I understand from Sir Nate that you were a spy during the war. You must consider me the spy's spy." He grinned a yellow, broken-toothed grin.

Witt arched a brow. "I'll remember that, Mr. Cox."

"Join us, Simon," Sir Nathanial said and pulled another chair close.

Simon boosted himself onto the seat and grabbed *The Times.* "The grave robbers are getting worse. Too much money to be had at the hands of the anatomists, but much risk to themselves if they are caught. The grave robbers think it's worth that risk."

Devlin nodded. "The need for cadavers for students of medicine is great. But robbing graves is a ghastly business. Have you discovered anything, Simon?"

"I've been visiting the pubs and listening, asking questions. Nothing so far. Everyone's talkn' 'bout the attack on Lord Stone, but I've no leads. Most unusual."

Sir Nathaniel rubbed a hand through his thinning hair. "Simon, I want you to assist Lords Witt and Ravensmoore any time you can and add their requests to your duties. Continue to make rounds at the pubs."

Witt nodded. "I'll keep an ear out at the clubs, and tomorrow Parliament is in session. Ravensmoore and I will both be there."

"And I will keep alert to rumors in Southwark. The poor and others with criminal intent frequent the area. I doubt if any souls at Bedlam can help in this instance."

"Then we begin our work together. Lord Witt, I will count it a favor if you inform Prinny. He won't be happy, but tell him we will be discreet. I'll have all the runners on alert for any sign that may lead to the capture of Talon."

⚜

Witt ducked into his seat at Parliament as the session started on the sixteenth day of April. The Lord Chancellor addressed the lords in attendance.

"We've much business to discuss this day. The problem before us is the need for asylums to be more closely monitored and for more room to be made in asylums for those who are criminally insane instead of rotting in prison. Lord Ravensmoore brought this to our attention last year. If it had been up to me, I would have ignored the situation."

Ravensmoore stood. "Then thank God that it was not up to you alone, Lord Chancellor."

Witt laughed with the others and admired this man who'd taken on Parliament to help conditions improve within the asylums, and ultimately within the prisons, by getting those who need treatment into asylums.

Lord Davenport smirked. "I heard rumor that you attended the last costume ball for the regent dressed as a physician, Lord Ravensmoore. Ah. My mind escapes me. You *are* a physician. What a pity that you've no higher ambition."

Witt's anger flared, and he jumped to his feet. "Sir, I think you are right. *Your* mind has escaped you. Perhaps Ravensmoore can write a receipt for you to take to the apothecary this day." He bowed, keeping his eyes on the so-called gentleman, whose face mushroomed into a crimson cloud. A deep sense of satisfaction swelled in Witt's chest.

Ravensmoore nodded in appreciation. "Lord Witt, your support is noted." A rumble of displeasure filtered through the room. "Unfortunately, not all of Parliament is so approving of my calling. You'd think those of us in Parliament would be more mindful of the needs of those who are not in control of their minds or actions."

Lord Winston pounded a fist into his open palm. "The issue of asylum law has been disputed many times throughout the years, and there is the more pressing issue at hand! Why don't you tell us who has committed this atrocity against Stone and who threatens the good men of Parliament? That may make your 'calling' more valuable. Not a man here wants to be the victim of this criminal who has chosen to disfigure and possibly murder. You've seen Lord Stone's face, the brutality, yet you can do nothing to prevent further attacks nor restore a savaged face!"

"Enough!" Ravensmoore rushed down the steps to stand on the main floor before Parliament. "We call ourselves men of justice, capable of making decisions that affect all of the this country. Each of us brings special skills and talents to this place. Let us act on behalf of God and country." He raked a hand through his hair and then stood with his hands clenched into fists at his sides.

"The prisons are overcrowded with those who should be in Bethlem. Some of the women I am treating in a ward at Bethlem may have the opportunity to return to their homes and make room for those who are very ill, including the criminally insane. This cannot happen without your help.

"Wynn's Act passed in 1808 and made recommendations for county lunatic asylums. Since 1815, horrid abuses have been discovered in York and Bethlem. Not nearly enough has been done to help cure and manage madness, and now Bethlem sits in St. Georges Fields in Southwark."

"Surely the plight of the mad is not nearly as bad as you claim," Ramsay stated. "Perhaps you've spent too much time in the madhouses."

Laughter echoed off the walls.

"Do you forget that even Samuel Whitbread committed suicide by cutting his throat with a razor when Napcleon abdicated? A member of our Parliament, melancholy and deluded, killed himself! We must continue to address the changing needs of the asylums in order to help those who cannot help themselves, whether they be aristocrat or commoner. I pray you don't wait too long to consider these changes, Lord Ramsay, or perhaps you and the others who side with you will suffer the consequences of your apathy. "

Witt examined the faces about the room. Some scowled while others appeared relieved that Ravensmoore spoke words of honor. Witt rose to his feet again. "Let us discuss this attack now. It is what is in the forefront of every man's mind who is present. Stone's empty seat cannot be ignored, but keep in mind that what we put off may very well be related to what is to come. Certainly the person who attacked Lord Stone is not in his right mind."

"Here, here," roared a section of those present.

Others jumped to their feet. "You don't know that, Lord Witt!"

Witt joined Ravensmoore on the floor of Parliament. "Plans must be made, possibly a trap set, to catch this…this…*chameleon* that walks among us and has such ready access to our whereabouts that he knows when and where we will be most vulnerable and easy to reach."

The Lord Chancellor bowed out of the way, indicating with his outstretched hand that Witt and Ravensmoore should lead the discussion. A heavy silence sealed the room, and all turned their attention to them.

Ravensmoore looked Witt in the eye and studied him briefly. "You take the lead. I will answer the medical questions and concerns of what's been discovered."

Witt nodded and turned his attention to the others. "Stone is disfigured and near death. Pervasive fear runs rampant among the lot of us. Who will be next?" He held the note up. "This beside Lord Stone. Perhaps he can tell us something if he lives."

"But why?" Lord Templeton stood, a short, pudgy man who obviously took delight in overindulgence. "Why the members of Parliament?"

Another undercurrent of questions and a wave of anger washed through the room. The noise level rose to a pitch of near hysteria.

"Calm down!" Witt walked the length of the room. He swore to himself that he could smell the stench of fear in the room. "We must not let fear rule our minds or we will be susceptible to rushed decisions and wrongful thinking."

"Quiet!" The gavel hit the desk of the Lord Chancellor, demanding control within the room.

Witt smiled, despite the reason for the upheaval. The Lord Chancellor nodded for him to continue.

"I want you to hear Ravensmoore's thoughts on this matter. I don't care if you approve of his choice to practice medicine. His experience may be what stops this beast." He nodded to Ravensmoore.

Devlin nodded. "As Witt said, we must not allow fear to fester and grow among us. There will be plenty of fear within the city if there is another attack. For now, it can be kept under control. I suggest we focus on why Parliament members, as Lord Templeton mentioned. Why us, indeed?"

Now it was his turn to pace the floor of Parliament. "Why would someone do this? Perhaps they don't like what we're doing. This person is angry, out for revenge, in my opinion."

"Revenge for what?" Lord Weatherby stood, his cane providing a certain amount of stabilization for his aging body. "What have we done that is so awful?"

"We may not consider it something awful, Lord Weatherby. Please sit down before you fall down." The gentleman next to Weatherby caught him before he tumbled forward.

"But I do think this man who is wreaking terror on us believes we have committed the unforgivable and wants us to suffer like he or his family has suffered. I believe that is what we must look for. We have to think like this person is thinking."

Weatherby pounded the floor with his cane. "Ha! And how do we go about thinking like a madman, Ravensmoore? Why don't you share some of your experiences since changing Ashcroft Asylum into Safe Haven? How does a madman think?"

"More narrowly in some instances, Lord Weatherby. It's not all about what they choose to think but how their minds are possibly different in some physical way than others without these maladies."

Lord Malvern stood. "Demon possession and unholy living, Ravensmoore. You make too much of these things. This monster is not sick like one who suffers from gout; he is evil and plans our demise while you talk about his mind as if he should be given a reprieve for ripping off the faces of our peers. Hogwash, I say."

"Lord Malvern. I am not talking about the one who stalks us. You questioned how madmen think. I provided you one idea. We cannot know if this man is evil or mad."

Malvern huffed. "There's no difference. Evil men are mad, and madness begets evil."

"No! I reject that belief." Devlin raked a hand through his hair and targeted Malvern. "Madness may beget evil deeds, but evil itself is not madness. Evil is from the bowels of hell, and don't be misled. We don't know who Talon is and why he's chosen this awful road. I merely suggest we withhold judgment and search for a way to stop these attacks. The law will take care of the rest."

Templeton shouted from his seat. "The law is not able to protect us until this murderer is caught. What do we do in the interim?"

Witt walked to the railing below Templeton. "Do not go about the streets of London by yourself. Travel in pairs at all times. Be watchful."

"That is not to be tolerated." Templeton wiped his brow with a lace handkerchief. "We are not women. We are men, and we will not hide from this fiend, Lord Witt. Do you plan to walk the streets of London in the company of someone else at all times? I doubt it."

"Perhaps not, Templeton, but it is a way to be more cautious. I would not recommend roaming the clubs at night without a thought for your welfare and deep in your cups. That is just the sort of prey that he seeks. Someone easy and unaware of his surroundings."

Ravensmoore cleared his throat. "One of our peers was savagely attacked about the face and neck. There were no other wounds except upon the hands, which he used to ward off his attacker."

Witt decided this was the time to share what only he, the regent, the regent's physician, and Ravensmoore knew, and of course the one who attacked Lord Stone. "The man calls himself Lord Talon. It does not take much imagination to consider these attacks carried out by someone who may own or train falcons."

Voices erupted in shock and confusion. "And when did you learn this bit of news, Lord Witt?" the Lord Chancellor roared above the others.

Templeton smirked. "That narrows our search to about eight in the area, perhaps more. How many of us will be disfigured or perhaps killed while the falconers are investigated?"

Witt pound his fist on a nearby table. "We'll find a way," he yelled. "We *will* find a way. If we don't, we will suffer the consequences."

Parliament buzzed. A hornet's nest of arguments ensued about what should be done, what shouldn't be done, and the horrible results that would float to the top of their society if the wrong steps were taken, their decisions made ineffectual or worse.

Witt listened to the cacophony grow to unbearable pressure inside his head. How difficult men can make the simplest of decisions by worrying overmuch about what others will think. A waste of time and money. He held his hands to his temples and massaged the skin there; then he rubbed his hands over his eyes, praying for relief.

He stood, waiting to be acknowledged. "I ask your indulgence. We seem to be getting nowhere. I suggest we tackle this problem in a different manner."

Shouts and the stomping of feet and canes rained down on him. "I beg your indulgence, gentlemen. I've been listening to you, and though you each have some excellent thoughts, we need to focus in on what will work best."

Witt remained standing until he'd gained the attention of each lord. "We must outsmart Lord Talon. Bow Street is on this, and they are capable, but I think we must search among ourselves to think of every possibility, no matter how small or unlikely we think it may be, that could contribute to the crisis we find ourselves in today. It must be something related to what we are doing, have done, or are contemplating. Or perhaps one of us has brought this down upon the rest of us."

Templar stood and shouted across the floor from one of the upper sections. "Do you mean to have each of us air our dirty laundry,

Lord Witt? What good would that bring any of us but embarrassment, and even ruin in some cases?"

Witt looked at his peer and smiled mischievously. "You have dirty laundry to air, Lord Templar? Please share it with us now. You have our attention."

"You know full well what I mean. Not me, necessarily, but perhaps others who might have gaming debts or...how shall I say this? Affairs of the heart they don't care to make public. Even you, sir, must have secrets you don't care to have unearthed. Secrets from the war perhaps, or of a more tender nature?"

Witt fumed inwardly and steeled himself so as not to make a remark he would regret. "I do not suggest the airing of dirty laundry or public declaration of concerns or knowledge of something that may be helpful. I ask for your trust. That each of you would arrange to meet with me personally and discuss anything you think could have caused someone to become so angry at the lords of Parliament that they chose to start killing us rather than utilize the House of Commons to make their needs known through channels that work for the public at large."

Another shifting of bodies and raising of voices rippled through the House. "Why should it be you and not the Lord Chancellor?" Lord Marley asked, tilting his head in the direction of the Chancellor.

"Because—"

"Because I want him to." The voice of the prince regent boomed through those assembled, and everyone stood. "I asked Lord Witt here on another matter before Stone was attacked, and now I want Witt to lead us to the answer along with whatever help he can get from Bow Street. He was one of our best during the war, and I think we should allow him to use his skills and capabilities to lead us now. I demand that each of you report to him as he has requested and that you begin as soon as this session has ended for the day."

Witt stepped forward. "I would like each of you to report to Carlton House when you are asked to come. We will send messengers to alert you beforehand."

Lord Bellinger stood. His jowls trembled, causing his face to turn various shades of red and purple. "Unheard of. Preposterous! You cannot be serious in this endeavor."

"Would you feel the same way, Lord Bellinger, if you knew without doubt that you were the next to be targeted? I don't think so."

The elderly lord shook with rage but resumed his seat. The members of Parliament shook their heads in disgust and grumbled amongst themselves, but no one else protested.

Witt studied the faces of the men in the room and tried to imagine who might be next and why. What was this madman thinking, and why so much hatred to take such risk? "I am also one of you. I don't plan on allowing anyone to take my life if I can prevent it, and I'm guessing you all feel the same."

Frustrated nods of agreement.

"So if any of you have an idea that you think will work better, by all means, speak up now. We cannot afford to be at odds with one another. It will take strength and working together to find out why these attacks are happening and why Parliament is being targeted."

Witt saw Simon from Bow Street motion to Ravensmoore from a hallway.

"One moment," Ravensmoore said. All eyes watched as the dwarf delivered information to Ravensmoore and then left.

"I'm afraid I have more news, and it's not good. If anything, it confuses the matter before us. I've just been informed by Simon Cox of Bow Street that two patients at Bedlam were brutally murdered last night. Their throats were slashed by what appears to be the talons of a hawk."

Celeste loved her laboratory enclosed and secreted in an area no one would think to look. She'd discovered the hidden room years earlier. Now she worked at a table, but the room also contained a desk, microscope, jars of honey, herbs, and mortars and pestles of various sizes and colors.

This might be just the formula she'd been trying to come up with for the past two months. It was now the eighth of May. Celeste poured a brown liquid into another tube and watched the colors ignite. Talon would be thrilled if it worked, but there was so much to do. She couldn't afford to make a mistake, because then Talon may not allow her another opportunity to play the game. This had to be perfect. Perhaps—

Talon burst into the room. "Is it finished?" He leaned in close and looked at the colors shimmering in the test tube. "Beautiful. It's beautiful, but will it work? We have to make sure it works, Celeste. Are you up to an adventure this evening? I have another falcon to train. You know what must be done. Have you made the arrangements?"

"The bait is prepared, waiting for us at the designated spot. We will train this evening."

"Perfect. The moon is high and will provide enough light, so we don't risk the torches. If the illumination works, then we'll find out tonight, and that could make all the difference. How did you get to be so good at this?"

"Don't forget that my father was a man of many skills. His education went far beyond the walls of the traditional classroom at Oxford. His mother was the one that taught him the power of chemistry and use of herbs. Now I have practiced long enough to begin to perfect my skills, and I can only hope to make my dead parents proud."

Talon led the way to the training site. "The molting continues this time of year, Celeste. The hawks need extra meat, the fresher the better." The branches and shrubs cracked under their boots as they tramped through the forest.

Celeste stepped forward. "The clearing. 'Tis a perfect night to train, Talon. You were right."

"The bait, Celeste. The hawk is hungry. Now is the time."

Celeste whistled low and long.

Nothing.

"Try again," Talon demanded.

Celeste repeated the whistle. This time they were rewarded with a whistle in return, and at the far end of the clearing two riders appeared. "You paid them?"

"Of course."

Talon grunted. "Signal them. The hawk grows annoyed."

Celeste whistled three times. Short and low.

One rider galloped forward and dropped his cargo in front of Talon and Celeste and then disappeared into the forest.

Celeste cut through the rope and threw back the blanket. "A fresh body."

Talon removed the hood from the hawk's head. "Time to practice, Wellington. We'll work with the hawk as long as possible. This is one corpse that will not make it to the anatomists' table."

## Chapter 7

Society is always taken by surprise at any new
example of common sense.
—Ralph Waldo Emerson

Three weeks later Victoria stepped into her brother's
phaeton for an outing in the park. The sun sparkled
through the treetops when they entered St. James Park. The clip-clop
of the horse's hooves on the road soothed a restlessness of spirit that
Victoria found disconcerting. She took a deep breath and prayed.
*Lord, help me to fit in with society. I fear myself too different from
those here in London.*

"Have you been enjoying yourself these past days, Lady Victoria?
You seem a bit preoccupied."

"Forgive me, Nora. I'm not ungrateful. I fear perhaps I've dreamt
of escape from my illness for so long that I've created a dream world
that does not exist. And Devlin is so protective that I'm finding it
difficult to have a real adventure."

"And what do you call this?" Nora waved her hands about like
birds flying to and fro among the trees. "I'm thinking this ride
in the park is a grand adventure." Nora grinned that wonderful
crooked grin and folded her hands. "Let that imagination of yours
run free."

Victoria grabbed her maid's hand. "I'm gratified beyond belief
to be in London, Nora, and you've been lovely as always but…I'm

lonely. I find myself straining at the bit like a horse who wants to run and does not wish to be controlled. If it hadn't been for the outing to the theatre and Lady Phoebe's recent visit, I'd be in Bedlam by now."

Nora smiled. "I know."

"You do?"

"Indeed. And your brother knows as well. In fact, he's taken the liberty to make sure that you are no longer lonely when he is unavailable."

"Whatever do you mean, Nora?"

"If you would be so kind as to study the woman sitting on that bench, I think you will begin to understand."

Victoria squinted into the sunlight and shaded her eyes with her hand. "I don't...oh my goodness. It isn't! Stop the horses." Victoria scrambled from the phaeton and ran toward the bench where the woman was sitting.

"Surprise!" Her sister-in-law stood. Chocolate curls danced beneath a gold bonnet.

"Madeline! Is it really you? I can't believe it. "

Victoria crushed Madeline close, tears stinging her eyes. "I didn't think you would be able to get away."

Madeline pushed Victoria back at arm's length. "Let me look at you. You've only been here a short time and already your cheeks and skin bloom. I do believe the polluted London air is healthy for you." She laughed.

"Madeline, I've missed your wonderful laugh. I'm so glad you came. Devlin will be thrilled to have you here too. Then again, with all that's happened, he may send us both back home."

"He won't be sending either of us away."

"What makes you so certain?" Victoria asked.

"Because he still can't say no to me and mean it." They laughed and linked arms while they walked through the park. "Now tell me what has happened."

Children chased each other while their nannies chased after them.

"It's a wonderful thing to be so carefree, isn't it?"

Victoria turned to see the woman who had spoken and her companion. "Hello," Victoria said. "It is nice to be so young. I agree. I don't believe we've met."

"No," the elder of the women said dryly. "But we should. I am Countess Stone. I believe your brother is caring for my husband at Carlton House. And this is my eldest daughter, the Lady Mary, Countess of Norbrook."

"Countess Stone. Lady Mary. I am so sorry for the suffering you must be experiencing now. I assure you Lord Stone is in the very best care. May I present my sister-in-law, Countess Ravensmoore."

"How nice to meet you." Madeline curtsied.

"I wish we could say the same," Lady Stone said, her voice thick with bitterness. "I don't know why the regent would allow Ravensmoore to play physician to my husband. It's unconscionable."

"How dare you," Madeline gritted out, shocked at the crude insult.

Victoria stepped forward. "Whatever are you talking about?" Victoria asked. "My brother is a wonderful physician. How can you even think such awful thoughts, let alone say them aloud to his wife?"

"Come, Mother." Lady Mary twirled her yellow parasol behind her head. "I wouldn't doubt that your brother is this Lord Talon and attacked my husband just so he could gain attention and pretend to save the day. I'm sure he's desperate to save his reputation. Imagine. A lord of England practicing a trade. How ghastly."

Victoria gasped and grabbed Lady Mary's parasol from her

hand, broke it in half over her knee, and threw it at the venomous woman's feet. "Liars! You should be ashamed."

"I'll see that you pay for that. One way or another," Lady Mary said, her features ice cold.

"You are the most—"

"Don't waste your breath," Madeline placed a hand on Victoria's arm. "I don't think I could have defended my husband any better."

Nora and their driver pulled alongside. "Ah, there you are. A wonderful tea is awaiting yer ladyships at home."

"Outstanding timing, Nora," Madeline said. "I am famished."

Victoria swallowed hard, and her cheeks burned with indignation. "I think I've lost my appetite, but perhaps it will return when we gain a different view of the park." She forced herself to turn her back on the rude females, for she certainly refused to think of them as ladies.

Victoria placed her hand in Madeline's as the phaeton carried them back to number three Grosvenor Square. "Devlin will be livid."

Madeline said, "Devlin will never know. Is that clear, Victoria? Nora? I will not have my reunion with my husband ruined by a foul-mouthed liar."

Victoria nodded and wondered what Devlin would do if he discovered that once again he wouldn't be told all as another of his family arrived in town.

❧

"I don't believe I can eat one more cucumber sandwich, Mrs. Miller." Victoria patted a napkin to her mouth.

"No room for a pudding?" Mrs. Miller asked.

"Perhaps later." Victoria grinned and patted her full belly.

The cook beamed and returned to the kitchen.

"And you said you'd lost your appetite," Madeline laughed. "That didn't last long. It is good to see you eat well, though. I remember when you would have fed that sandwich to Lazarus within the last year."

"I love eating now. Especially Mrs. Miller's food. I'm surprised that Lazarus hasn't lost weight."

Nora hurried into the room. "Lord Ravensmoore's coach has arrived."

"Both of you, kindly remember what I said. Not a word about what happened in the park. This is to be a joyous time, and I want nothing to interfere. Understood?"

Nora and Victoria nodded.

Lazarus barked and hurried to the front door.

Victoria took her spot at the entrance to the dining hall and covered her brother's eyes when he entered the room. "I bet you can't guess who is here?"

"I guarantee you, my sister, that I cannot guess who is here unless you remove your hands." He sniffed the air. "However, I believe I recognize that scent. Ah. Jasmine in bloom." He gently pulled his sister's hands from his eyes and stared into the face of his beloved wife. "Ah, Maddie."

"Devlin. I've missed you so much. Even though I received your letter asking me to come, you must know that I'd already decided even without your invitation. I just couldn't remain in the country any longer. Can you forgive me?" She threw her arms around his neck, whispered in his ear, and then kissed him for so long that Victoria felt her cheeks burn.

"I would forgive you anything. Even coming to London without asking my permission. You know how dangerous the roads can be, and I know you wouldn't have traveled with as many escorts if I'd not ordered it. Highwaymen abound, and they would not think twice about taking advantage of a woman with a small escort."

"That's the hazard of travel, darling, but nothing would stop me.

I love you very much, but you knew of my stubborn independence when you married me. Now you must pay the price."

"That is a price I am happy to pay every day for the rest of my life." He then put his arms around his wife's waist and turned to his sister. "I'm pleased that my wife and sister are here with me in London. Now I can keep my eye on both of you."

"Why, Devlin." Victoria put her hands on her hips." That works both ways, brother of mine. And now there are two of us to keep our eyes on you." She curtsied to her sister-in-law. "I will teach you the fine art of snooping, Madeline. I'm proud to call you sister."

"Thank you, Victoria. I knew I could count on you. I dared not leave my husband alone in London any longer with beautiful women everywhere." She turned and faced Devlin. "And with all the temptation London has to offer, you have been a true and faithful husband, have you not?"

"O ye of little faith." He smiled a mischievous smile and wrapped her in his arms and swung her around in a circle. "You will always be the only one for me." And he kissed her quite thoroughly again.

The butler appeared in the archway to the room and cleared his throat. "I beg your pardon, your lordship, countess. Lord Witt would like a moment of your time, sir."

Devlin arched a brow and looked directly at his sister. "And I suppose you had nothing to do with the arrival of Lord Witt, my dear? I'd much rather be alone with my wife than entertaining a guest this evening."

Madeline said, "Devlin, don't be rude. I'd like to meet Lord Witt. He's obviously a man you don't approve of, but from the blush in Victoria's cheeks, I'd say you are about to entertain a guest regardless of that approval. I, for one, am intrigued."

"Your wish is something I cannot deny, love." Keeping his eyes on his wife, he said, "Show him in, Henry."

Victoria's heart beat a little faster, and her palms grew moist.

What was it about this man that made her look forward to his appearance in the room?

Henry returned. "Lord Witt."

"Thank you, Henry."

"Witt. May we entice you to dinner?"

"I'd be honored," he said, all the while keeping his gaze on Victoria.

"And Henry, tell Mrs. Miller we have a guest for dinner," Ravensmoore ordered.

Henry bowed and left the room.

"Lord Witt, allow me to introduce my wife. My dear, this is Lord Witt, who was most impressive in his speech and manner at Parliament this morning."

Madeline curtsied. "It is always a pleasure to meet one of my husband's friends."

Witt bowed deeply. "Ah. The woman who heartens the man. I can see where your husband gets his inspiration. I too would be in a hurry to conclude my work for the day if returning home to one as lovely as you."

"My wife has surprised me with an unexpected but welcome visit from Yorkshire. And you know my sister, Lady Victoria."

Witt turned his full attention to Victoria now, and she felt her face flame when his intense gaze locked with hers. She curtsied and found it difficult to tear her eyes from his for that brief moment. She must practice concealing her emotions better, as the ladies of the ton are able to do so skillfully.

"It's a delight to see you again, Lady Victoria. Perhaps later we can take a walk, if your brother permits."

Victoria's hope leaped. "That would be—"

"Impossible," Devlin said. "This is not the country, Lord Witt, and you of all people know the current atmosphere in London. Besides, Nora is off this evening and there is no one to chaperone."

Victoria implored her sister-in-law with a quick glance.

"Surely, the atmosphere in town could manage a walk with the four of us, my lord."

"Not after dark. It's not safe."

"Since when did you become afraid of the dark, brother?" Victoria asked and immediately regretted her words. She placed her hand over her mouth in dismay.

"I fear not for myself but for those more vulnerable. And since Lord Stone's attack and the murder of the two male patients at Bedlam, I suggest we find another source of entertainment. "

Witt nodded, his face an unreadable mask. Victoria determined to ask him how he'd learned to do that. She couldn't tell if he was angry or in agreement. She hoped it was not the latter. The man showed promise.

Victoria straightened her back and inhaled deeply. "I believe Mrs. Miller has been experimenting again."

"I believe you are correct." Madeline smiled. "I do enjoy a good sweet. Devlin, let us not tarry here in conversation, but at the table where we can talk in comfort and enjoy our sister and guest."

Devlin stood near a window and appeared lost in thought as he gazed through the sheer curtains and out into the darkening street. "Yes, of course. I'll be with you in a moment."

Victoria swallowed a knot of concern and looked back at her brother as Madeline whisked her and Witt into the dining hall. "Mrs. Miller loves to experiment on my taste buds. If she can fatten me up, I think she'll swoon." The table glowed with candlelight and silver. An extra place had been neatly added for Lord Witt. A footman seated Victoria.

"Lord Witt, would you take the place across from Lady Victoria?"

"With pleasure, Countess."

Madeline looked at him and then at Victoria. "I'm so glad you are both here this evening. I hope you'll help me erase those frown lines burrowing into my husband's forehead."

"We'll do our best," Victoria and Witt answered together and then laughed.

Devlin entered the room. "What's this? Laughter? I hope it's not at my expense." He kissed his wife's cheek and held her chair, which earned him a smile of gratitude while the footman frowned but walked to the other end of the table to assist Devlin.

Victoria hoped that someday a man, a husband, would treat her with that same respect, with loving gestures and knowing smiles. She caught herself playing with the silverware, the fork in particular, a habit she'd acquired years before when she became ill, a habit that had made her younger sister Mercy say the most unladylike things under her breath when she'd catch her sister "fiddling."

Victoria let go of the fork and purposely forced her hands into her lap. She looked up to see if Witt were watching. His eyes glittered a brilliant gray that mirrored a molten reflection of the silver on the table. The lightest of butterfly wings flitted across her heart.

Devlin led them in grace and then raised his glass. "A toast." He waited for the others to raise their glasses. "To my beautiful wife, who never fails to surprise me." He took a long swallow. "And to my sister, Snoop. May you stay out of trouble long enough to find your adventure."

Victoria felt her eyes widen.

Witt coughed and sputtered and finally put his drink down to keep from spilling it. He said, "Forgive me, Ravensmoore. Did you just call your sister *Snoop?*"

"A family endearment, Lord Witt." Madeline slanted her husband a look that Victoria knew all too well. She'd wager that if he were close enough, Madeline would have kicked him under the table.

Witt grabbed his napkin and wiped at the corners of his mouth. "Indeed."

Victoria thought she caught the edge of a grin behind that napkin. "Pay him no heed, sir. He loves to tease. Brothers can be downright irritating, if you ask me."

"Well, I'm not asking, sister dear."

"No, you're—"

Mrs. Miller entered with a covered platter of silver. "Mmm," Victoria hummed. "What delicacy have you prepared us tonight, dear woman?"

The robust woman flushed from either heat or pride, probably both, and set her burden down in front of her brother. "Here you are, your lordship. In honor of Lady Ravensmoore's arrival. Be blessed." She removed the cover with a flourish and beamed at the compliments that lifted around her.

"Salmon." Madeline nearly crooned. "Broiled salmon with melted butter and lemon. Cook, you're amazing."

Devlin looked pleased. "Are you happy, darling?"

"You could say that."

Witt added his praise along with Devlin's. "I might have to send my cook Doris over to take lessons. If the salmon tastes as good as it looks, I may have to find more reasons to stop by unexpectedly."

"Lovely," Victoria added. "What's for dessert?"

"Some things never change." Devlin laughed. "My guess is that it's something decadent and perhaps not so good for one's nourishment."

"I made one of Lady Victoria's favorites, and thanks be to God, it's one of Lady Ravensmoore's, as well."

Victoria and Madeline looked at each other and smiled. "Cheese cakes," they said together.

"This was a grand night to return to my husband's side." Madeline looked at Devlin, and Victoria hoped that someday she would want to look at her husband in just such a manner.

She enjoyed listening to the easy banter between her brother and

Madeline and Lord Witt, who tonight fit in with the others like a long lost friend.

"I don't know when I last enjoyed such a meal." Witt sat back with the smile of a well-satisfied child after raiding the sweets jar.

"We are glad you could join us, Lord Witt," Victoria said.

"Yes," Devlin agreed. "But I must admit I'm tired, and I know my wife must be exhausted."

"I won't deny it." Madeline stood, and the men followed suit. "Please excuse us, Victoria, Lord Witt. I'm most anxious to spend some time alone with my husband. Tomorrow he will disappear early for some medical necessity or to Parliament."

"Victoria, why don't you take Lord Witt into the gardens. I'll ask Nora and Lazarus to chaperone from the terrace, and you can share ideas with each other."

"Share ideas?" Witt tilted his head in Victoria's direction. "That sounds revolutionary."

Devlin smiled, kissed Victoria on the top of the head, then placed his hand on the small of his wife's back, steering her toward the door that led to the staircase and the rooms above. "Good night."

Victoria stood and walked to Lord Witt. "Would you enjoy a walk in the garden, Lord Witt? I promise I won't allow Lazarus to slobber on you."

Witt smiled, and his hand reached toward his neck cloth. He edged a finger inside the silk and unconsciously ran the tip of it around the front portion. Almost as if he were nervous. Nervous about being alone with her.

"I'd like nothing more, Lady Snoop." He laughed and then grew serious. "I hope that's not too brash. Your brother's nickname for you is unique." He offered his arm to her.

A dozen different thoughts crowded her mind within a few seconds. "I believe I prefer Lady Snoop to Snoop, my lord. But perhaps that should remain between us. It does hint at a certain amount of intimacy, and I do believe we can consider ourselves friends, can we not?"

"I consider it an honor to be your friend." He placed his hand on the small of her back and ushered her out onto the terrace.

"Look, there in the corner, Lord Witt. It is the ferocious Lazarus and his caretaker, Nora." Victoria laughed as Nora relaxed in a comfortable rocker and Lazarus settled down to doze at her feet.

"Lord Ravensmoore has asked me and the dog to chaperone the two of you whilst you're in the gardens. Just remember that. I have very keen eyesight and can see more than most people might think."

"We appreciate your forthrightness, Nora. You can trust me to make no untoward advances." Witt squeezed Victoria's arm, and they descended the steps into a lush summer garden that smelled of roses and lavender and vanilla.

"I do so love this garden." Victoria inhaled deeply and admired every bloom. "Of course, it's not like the massive gardens at home, but it's the first garden I've been able to enjoy outside of Yorkshire, and that is a wonder in itself. Do you like gardens, Lord Witt?"

"That would depend on the garden." He shivered.

"What is it?" Victoria asked. "Is something wrong?"

"No. Not at all. I suspect the fact that I have been able to dine and laugh with you and your family this evening with all the events of late simply caught me off guard. I haven't walked in a garden for a long time."

"But I thought you lived in the country?"

"I do. It's just that I haven't taken to improving the grounds for some time. When I returned from the war on the Peninsula, I couldn't think much about gardens. I focused entirely on my horses, and then after a while, I couldn't gain a sense of satisfaction with them either. I sent most of my help away and brooded."

"And what did you brood about?"

"Things I would rather not recall at the moment when I'm with such a thoughtful woman. What about you? Did you like gardens when you were growing up?"

"I loved the gardens at Ravensmoore. It's one of the few enjoyments and entertainments I had when confined to my wheeled invalid chair." Victoria looked back at the terrace and saw that Nora's chin was resting on her chest and Lazarus's chin rested on Nora's knees. "They've fallen asleep."

Witt followed her line of vision and chuckled. "Nothing like a nap after dinner."

They came upon a stone bench and fountain surrounded by statues of cherubs pouring water into the fountain with buckets they held in their tiny hands. "The sound of the water can make that happen. It's a peaceful sound. Would you like to sit here?"

He stopped at the bench. "After you, my Lady Snoop." He held her hand until she'd situated herself on the bench, and then he joined her.

"As city gardens go, this is larger than most for a townhome. If you're interested, I'd love to take you on a walk in the gardens near the regent's townhouse at St. James. Would you enjoy that?"

"Carlton House? St. James? Is it possible?" She jumped to her feet. "When might we go?"

"I don't think this evening would be appropriate. Your brother wouldn't approve, Nora would have difficulty staying awake, and then there's Lazarus." He arched a brow. "I suppose you would want to bring him with us?"

"Of course. He does love new adventures. Almost as much as I do." She sat back down and sighed. "It does sound like heaven."

"Then heaven it is. Not tonight, though, but another time. When I can arrange a private showing." He grinned.

For a moment Victoria thought she saw the shadow of the boy he must have been in his youth: enthusiastic, full of energy, and perhaps even a bit of an imp. Could boys be imps? She had a feeling this one had been, and for some odd reason she hoped that he might become a bit of one again.

The sun lowered in the western sky as the water in the fountain splashed onto the surrounding budding white roses. Witt took her hand in his, raised it to his lips, and planted a soft kiss within the naked palm. "Tomorrow, I have a surprise for you."

# CHAPTER 8

Come unto me, all ye that labour and are heavy
laden, and I will give you rest.
—MATTHEW 11:28

VICTORIA WANDERED AMONG the beautiful plants and rare flowers in the townhome greenhouse, pondering a new emotion that had crept into her heart. Once she'd thought it impossible to leave their home in Yorkshire, let alone be able to travel, shop, eat, and sleep like normal people do.

And now, here she was in London, experiencing things she'd once thought impossible: the beauty around her, Lord Witt, and his promise of a garden walk and talk of some surprise.

She stopped to inspect a simple blossom of unusual color and slender stem that stood out from all the others in the greenhouse.

Her heart should be dancing. Instead, the growing worry that she didn't fit into London society, and perhaps never would, nagged at her. She wished to be chameleon-like, to blend in with the other women, the elegant and experienced. Not like this simple flower that seemed to be alone and set apart.

She blinked back her tears.

Madeline knocked on the door and entered the doorway of the greenhouse.

"Victoria? Are you all right?"

"No. I don't think I am."

"What's wrong?" Madeline grabbed Victoria's hand. "Come, sit with me."

Madeline pulled her down to sit in a chair and took the seat next to her sister. She kept Victoria's hand gently cradled in her own.

"I don't know how to fit in. Not really." Victoria tried to hold back the flood of emotion that had been building for days, but she just couldn't find the strength. She turned to her sister-in-law, laid her head on Madeline's shoulder, and sobbed out the fear that had been threatening her for days. "I don't fit in." She felt so foolish saying it aloud, but there it was.

"Oh, Victoria, my dear, that's not true. You judge yourself too harshly. You've made friendships with Lord Witt and with Lady Phoebe. It is not easy to understand London and the ton. You've not been exposed as the rest of us have to society and all its layers." Madeline wrapped her arms around Victoria. "There, there. Let it out. That's it, just let it all out."

Victoria pulled a handkerchief from her sleeve and blew her nose. "What am I to do, Maddie? I thought this would be such a grand adventure, and it is in many ways, to be sure, but there is so much I don't understand. Those awful women in the park. Lady Stone and Lady Mary. They were dreadful. And I made a complete fool of myself."

"Is that what this is all about?" Madeline took Victoria by both shoulders. "You mustn't allow such hard-hearted women to hurt you. They are angry and looking for someone to blame for Lord Stone's misfortune, so they blame Devlin. Therefore, we are at fault, as well, because we are his family. There will always be people in the world who hurt others."

Victoria sniffed "But why? It's so pointless."

"They forget that God is bigger than their fears, so they torture others so that they may feel better. That has nothing to do with you not fitting in. That's their fears speaking."

"I don't know how to get past that. I've prayed, but to no avail. I can't hear what God wants of me."

"That will change. You must find out who you are and what God's purpose is for your life. Give yourself time to grow, to explore, and to experience London and your new life. Yes, there is much good, but there is also much evil. You survived your illness for a reason. God has a plan, my dear, and I know it's frustrating beyond measure when He doesn't share that plan with us, but it's just the way life is." She sought her own handkerchief and dabbed at her tears.

Victoria wiped her tears away with the back of her hand. "I'm so sorry, Maddie. I don't know what came over me. An episode of melancholy, perhaps."

Madeline attended to a stray wisp of hair that had escaped Victoria's ribbon. "We are all subject to bouts of melancholy, but we must do the best we can to fight them off. I've discovered that helping others is sometime the best cure for my own moments of despair."

Victoria dug deep inside and tried to pull herself together. "So what do you think I should do?"

"Not you, darling. We. You and I and Nora and perhaps Devlin will go to Bethlem and minister to the unfortunates there for the day if you are willing to try. Are you?"

"Bethlem?" Victoria sat back in her chair and thought for a moment. Then she took a deep breath. "I'll do it, Maddie. Others have taken care of me all my life. It's time I tried to do something for someone else."

"I will have Nicholas ready the carriage after we've something to eat. We'll take some food along and see how we can be most helpful."

Bethlem Hospital. Bedlam. For all her talk of bravery, the place made her skin crawl. From the carriage Victoria studied the massive structure and wondered just how dreadful it was from within. "You've been here before, Maddie?"

"With Dev. He's really very skilled at communicating with tortured souls. And the difference between them and us is really a very fragile line."

"He's too brave by 'alf, Countess." Nora looked as though she would open the door and bolt if given the chance.

"But didn't he say that sometimes people are here in this hospital that shouldn't be here? Just like your experience at Ashcroft Asylum. What does he do then?"

The carriage pulled to a halt outside the walls of dark rock. "He tries to change things."

Witt awaited them and helped each out of the carriage. "Countess. Lady Victoria. I see you have brought Nora with you. Good afternoon, Nora."

"Yer lordship." She curtsied along with the others.

"What are you doing here, Lord Witt?" Victoria asked.

Madeline said, "I sent word to Devlin to meet us, and if he could not, to see if Lord Witt was available."

"This place is huge," Witt said. "Not the kind of place ladies should go, chaperoned by a man or not, in my opinion."

"Then I'm glad the decision wasn't up to you." Victoria's earlier bout with melancholy was quickly changing to irritation. Why did men feel like they could run everything, do everything, without the input of women? She thanked God for her brother, who cared so deeply about others. Enough to take the brunt of cruelty the ton lavished on those they loved to hate. But that was changing, a little. Or was it? Sometimes she wondered.

"I beg your forgiveness, Lady Victoria. But curiosity can be dangerous when it's not tempered with caution."

Nora looked up at the windows and grabbed Victoria's arm. "Bars," she said. "Just like prison."

"But it's not a prison, Nora," Madeline said. "It's a hospital, and much needed. Lord Witt, will you lead the way and get us past the guards, please?"

Witt faltered for a moment. "Are you certain you want to do this, Countess? It's dangerous. I'm not sure you understand—"

"I understand far more than you realize, Lord Witt. Now let's get to our duty."

Victoria raised her chin at Madeline's words, feeling bolder herself. "Nora, do you have the basket of food?"

"Yes. But I don't think we'll be having much of a picnic in there." She pointed past the bars to where a guard stood and turned his attention to them.

"Nora. Really. You must not joke at such a time. It's rude."

"I wasn't making fun. I was makin' a point. There's others that picnic as an amusement here at Bedlam."

Victoria had to be quick to keep her mouth from falling open. "Nora, how would you know that?"

"My cousin works for a wealthy man 'ere in the city, and she says it happens all the time. 'Tis how some of the rich folk entertain themselves."

The guard looked at them and offered a halfhearted bow. "What will you be wantin', yer lordship, ladyships?"

"We've come to minister to Lord Ravensmoore's patients in the east wing," Madeline said. "The women and girls he's been treating for problems of both the mind and body."

The guard shook his head. "Them there women he's treatin' be demon possessed." He fumbled with several keys. "Peculiar, it is. But if you wants to see 'em, yer welcome, Countess. I remember when you came here with Lord Ravensmoore. Yer a right kind lady." He unlocked and swung open the gate. "Alma will show you the way. She's up ahead through that archway, just follows it till ye see her."

Victoria heard them before she saw them. So much moaning, crying, and even cursing. "Words you shouldn't be exposed to, ladies," Witt said, visibly embarrassed.

A woman large in girth and height awaited them at the next set of gates. She wore a black dress and gray apron. She also carried keys, but not so many as the guard, and she wore hers about her neck.

She curtsied and almost toppled from her bulk. "Me name is Alma. I'm gettin' too old for this 'ere work, but 'tis hard to git folks to work with the lunatics. Where are you wantin' to go?"

"The east wing," Witt said.

"Follow me."

Victoria noticed the bare and splintering walls. No pictures. Cobwebs hung from the ceiling as though the place hadn't been occupied in years. As she passed by a barred window, she looked outside. She couldn't imagine the horror of living in a place like this. All those years she'd been sick, she'd been taken care of by her family. These patients looked out through barred windows. She wondered what they saw, what they thought.

They maintained silence as they made their way to the east wing of Bedlam. And then a large oak door stood before them. Alma, their guide, sighed and pushed the key into the lock and turned.

Screams exploded through the door before it opened. Taking a step back, Victoria bumped into Lord Witt and thought she could feel his heart pounding through to her own. She couldn't force herself to move forward. Fear chased through her soul and settled into her mind, a parasite that nibbled away at what she'd thought the world was all about.

Nora screamed, dropped the picnic basket, and turned a dangerous shade of green.

Victoria followed Madeline into the huge room sparsely furnished with dilapidated tables and a few worn benches. At least twenty pairs of eyes widened in shock, dismay, and possibly curiosity. Victoria tried to keep some semblance of a smile on her face while her gaze darted around the room. Her courage was bolstered by Witt's presence.

Nora picked up the basket, set it on a long table, and pulled out sandwiches, apples, pie, and a cake.

"Let us eat cake," cried one of the women, and together with some others they danced in a circle holding hands while others clapped and cried.

"Yes, you will eat cake and whatever else you like," Madeline declared.

Victoria was amazed at the women, old and young alike.

"Victoria?" Madeline asked. "Are you all right?"

"I'm fine. I was just thinking."

"I think I know what you may have been thinking. But we'll talk more later. Would you like to pass out sandwiches?"

"Yes." She joined Nora.

"Make sure everyone gets something," Madeline directed. "Lord Witt, I have a special task for you, if you are willing to do it."

"And what would that be, Countess?"

Madeline whispered in his ear, and Victoria watched as first doubt and then a glimmer of sadness passed over his features.

"I'm willing to try." He slid onto a bench. Madeline pulled a book from the basket.

One of the ladies gasped. "It's a Bible."

"Victoria?" Madeline asked. "Would you share the reading of Psalms with Lord Witt? I believe it's one of your favorites."

Witt looked panicked for a moment and leaned close to Victoria. "I've never read the Bible."

She looked into his solemn gray eyes. "Consider it an adventure." She smiled.

He arched a brow. "Indeed."

"I'd love to." Victoria nearly burst into tears as she watched all the women gather with the food they'd brought. They sat in groups on the floor and on the benches.

"I would like to say grace." Victoria bowed her head and prayed for the women they'd come to minister to, and then she started the reading of Psalm twenty-seven that had brought her peace through the trials of her illness.

"The Lord is my light and my salvation; whom shall I fear? the Lord is the strength of my life; of whom shall I be afraid? When the wicked, even mine enemies and my foes, came upon me to eat up my flesh, they stumbled and fell. Though an host should encamp against me, my heart shall not fear: though war should rise against me, in this will I be confident. One thing have I desired of the Lord, that will I seek after; that I may dwell in the house of the Lord all the days of my life, to behold the beauty of the Lord, and to enquire in his temple. For in the time of trouble he shall hide me in his pavilion: in the secret of his tabernacle shall he hide me; he shall set me up upon a rock."

A different kind of attention fell over the room when Victoria passed the Bible to Witt. He read in a deep, soft voice, "And now shall mine head be lifted up above mine enemies round about me: therefore will I offer in his tabernacle sacrifices of joy; I will sing, yea, I will sing praises unto the Lord."

Victoria watched peace fall upon the women as a light snow upon the branches.

"... Wait on the Lord: be of good courage, and he shall strengthen thine heart: wait, I say, on the Lord."

Witt closed the Bible. Victoria looked into the faces and into the eyes of the women, who were calm and peaceful now, completely different than when they'd entered the room an hour ago. Surely the presence of God lived here among them now.

When it came time to leave, the youngest of the women, not older than sixteen, came up to her and placed her hand on Victoria's cheek. She didn't say anything. She didn't have to. Victoria looked into her wide blue eyes and saw peace where terror had been upon their arrival.

❦

Later that afternoon Lord Witt did indeed keep his previous evening's promise of a surprise. He took her to the stables in St. James Park, along with one of Ravensmoore's stable boys.

"What's your name, young man?" Victoria asked.

"Nicholas, yer ladyship."

"And how old are you, Nicholas?"

"Ten years old, yer ladyship."

"Ten? And you ride well?"

"Of course, my lady."

She swallowed her annoyance that a mere ten-year-old could ride and she could not. She must remedy this situation and looked at both of them from her perch upon the horse.

"This is not as easy as it appears from the ground," Victoria said, pretending that she wasn't as scared as she felt. "How intelligent do you think a horse really is? I wonder if I can outsmart him if necessary?"

Witt laughed out loud. "That's all true. But for as big as a horse's head may be, it is unlikely, in my opinion anyway, that the brain is huge. If they were very intelligent, they could easily kill us with their hooves, or when the opportunity arose they could simply run away."

"That, sir, does not increase my courage."

He checked the length of her stirrups and the girth.

"Why do you have to check the girth again? You've already done so." Victoria shifted in the saddle, trying to get comfortable.

"Because horses don't like wearing clothes."

Now Victoria laughed. "Clothes? I'd hardly call a bridle and saddle clothes."

"I'll explain as we walk about, if you're ready."

"I'm ready. Just don't go too fast."

"We are just going to walk about the paddock." Witt led her out into the paddock from the stable near Hyde Park.

Victoria looked down at the ground, which felt very far away. "What do I hang on to? You have the reins?"

"See this rope? Hang on to it." Witt had tied a rope around the horse's neck, and when she grabbed hold of it, she did feel a bit more secure, but not much.

"Now I know why I never learned to ride," Victoria said as she tried to get comfortable on the sidesaddle. "These beasties have control, they're huge, and they can dump you on your backside if they have a mind to."

He walked her around the large paddock. He had the reins and control of the horse, but Victoria wondered if this was something she really wanted to learn to do now. *Courage. Courage.*

"How do women stay in this saddle?" Victoria asked. "It's not normal. I know this is how women ride, but it's ridiculous. I think I would feel more secure to ride astride, Lord Witt."

"It's not done, Lady Victoria."

He continued to lead her like a small child. She bit back a dozen things she would like to say in protest, none of them ladylike. "I'm serious."

He stopped and rubbed the horse's forelock. "I've got a better idea if you really want to get the feel of a horse. How would you like to ride around the paddock bareback? That's how most children learn to ride. It's awkward, though. Be warned."

"It couldn't be more awkward than this. Let's try, if you have the patience."

"I'm all yours."

Victoria smiled at the sound of his words. *All yours.* It had a nice ring.

They returned to the stables. Witt called to one of the stable boys, who came running.

"Yer lordship?"

"Remove the saddle and wipe this horse down. Lady Victoria is going to learn how to ride bareback."

The young boy's eyes opened wide. "The lady?" He looked at Victoria and then said, "Are you sure you want to do that, yer ladyship?"

"It can't be worse than riding on this contraption."

"Aye." He loosened the girth and removed the saddle. Then he took a cloth and wiped the horse's back down. "Romeo is ready for you, yer ladyship, yer lordship."

"Tell me, Nicholas. When did you learn how to ride?"

"I've been ridin' all me life." He grinned and looked very proud.

She turned to Witt, and determination settled into her being. "Now, how do I get back on the horse with no stirrup?"

"I'm going to give you a leg up. I interlock my fingers like this, and you put your boot in my hands. Then I'll lift you onto the horse."

"What am I going to do with these skirts?"

She saw Nicholas grin. "My sister wears breeches when she comes to the stables to help."

"I'll have to remember that, Nicholas, but what do I do now?"

"If I can be bold in a suggestion, Lady Victoria?"

"I'm listening." Victoria blushed.

"Simply pull your skirts, uh, around your legs, turning them into breeches, as I give you a leg up. I think you can manage."

She did just that as she was given a leg up onto Romeo. It felt amazingly free to sit astride, and though her feet dangled, she felt more secure.

This time as Witt walked Victoria around the paddock, Nicholas and several of the stable boys watched in fascination.

Victoria could feel her legs naturally cling to the sides of the horse, and with the rope in hand she already felt more comfortable. As soon as she allowed herself to relax, she enjoyed herself immensely.

"I will practice riding every day until I am an expert. And if you cannot teach me, I will get Nicholas to teach me."

"Understand," Witt said, "that you do not come to the stables without a chaperone, and Nicholas does not yet meet the requirements for the position."

"In that case—"

"Look at that!" Nicholas pointed to the sky while he clung to the paddock fence with his other hand.

"What?" Victoria asked. She halted her horse before she shaded her eyes to look in the direction of Nicholas's finger. A sharp intake of breath could not be prevented when she saw a set of birds soaring and seemingly dancing in the air with one another just west of the park.

"Are those vultures?" Victoria asked. A shiver, much like those she'd experienced when ill, overtook her for a moment. Her horse, sensing fear, shivered as well and grew restless.

Witt drew near and held out his arms. "I think it best to dismount."

She easily slipped from the horse and into the safety of Lord Witt's arms until she steadied herself. "Then what are they?"

"Hawks. Red kites. The biggest I've ever seen."

# CHAPTER 9

Where there is mystery, it is generally suspected
there must also be evil.

—LORD BYRON

IMON EXPLORED THE various pubs and eating establish-
ments throughout London, especially those located near
Parliament. It was late evening when he walked into the Rose and
Thorn and found a seat at the bar.

"Hello there, Detector Simon," the bartender said. "What is it I
can get for you?"

"I'd like one of your fine beers and a pigeon pie, Sully, and some
information on the side, if you please."

"What is it you need this time?" The barman set a foaming glass
of beer in front of Simon, and he took a long, healthy gulp.

"Now, that's a fine beverage, Sully. I'm on the case of the killings
at Bedlam and the attack on a person of interest."

The man grinned, revealing a missing front tooth through an
unkempt beard. "Ha, person of interest. Ye mean Lord Stone. All of
London knows about that, Simon."

"That doesn't surprise me, but I'd hoped . . ." Simon rubbed his
chin and frowned, "I'd hoped that it wasn't so. Not yet. Can only
cause trouble. I want to make double sure that neither you or any of
your patrons noticed any untoward disturbances or any unusual or
suspicious persons on the evenings in question."

"I've already talked to a runner from Bow Street, Simon. I don't know what else I can tell ye that I haven't already."

"Well, sometimes important little facts are missed, because at the time we don't know they are important. And 'cause the Bow Street runners are so busy and trust me to follow up on any leads, I likes to be accommodating." Simon wiped the foam off his mouth with the sleeve of his arm.

Sully simply said, "Aye."

"Well? Have you remembered anything of importance on the nights investigated?"

"And what nights would those be, Simon Cox? You know that I'm too busy a man to keep up with everyone who comes and goes from this tavern. The Rose and Thorn is a busy establishment, and my guess would be that anyone with evil intentions on his mind could come and go and I'd never be the wiser."

Simon took another gulp and nearly drained his glass. "Did anyone offer you money for information about the comings and goings of any of the lords of Parliament?"

"Now, Simon. Don't ye think that's something that I would've reported posthaste? Really, man, do you think me to be so dense as to ignore something as important as that?"

"No, Sully, I think your pockets are deep and whoever wants to fill them can count on you to keep your mouth shut. After all, you are the proprietor of this fine place and wouldn't want any rumors floating about that would tarnish the fine name of the Rose and Thorn." Simon grinned.

Sully frowned. "Now you know anything I tell you stays between you and me, an' you won't be telling Sir Nathaniel nor any of the runners what you heard and who you heard it from. Does we have an understanding?" Sully set another beer in front of Simon. "This one will be on the house.

"I saw a young man slip in here the evening before those two patients got killed at Bedlam. I thought nothing of it. Not until after the runner talked to me." He rubbed his hand over his full beard. "It's just that—"

"Hey, Sully! We're getting thirsty down here." A burly man pounded his fist on the far end of the bar.

"I'm comin', so halt yer moanin' or I'll be takin' my time."

"You were sayn'?"

"How's a man suppose to remember what he was sayn' with the likes of drunkards all about? It's just that, I don't know, not exactly. It's just that I don't remember seeing him before. I've got to see to the others. I'll be back."

"And that's supposed to be helpful?" Simon muttered to himself. He twisted about to study the night's patrons.

He watched the men in the bar and the fine ladies that served them. Usual folks. He turned back to the bar to find Sully in his face. "Blazes, man, you almost scared me out off the stool."

"Sorry there, Simon. But as I was trying to tell you. The fellow didn't eat or drink. I can't think of anyone else that comes to the Rose and Thorn and don't eat or drink somethin'. *Most unusual*, as yer fond of saying, Simon."

"I'd say you're right about that, Sully." Simon drummed his stubby fingers on the bar. "How long did he stay? What'd he do while he was 'ere?"

"That's just it. Nothin'. He just sat in the back and watched. Didn't eat, drink, or try to flirt with any of the gals."

"Most unusual. Would you recognize the fellow again if he came in?"

"Maybe, maybe not," Sully said, slapping a beer down next to the gent who sat down next to Simon.

Simon mulled over some thoughts as the bar got busier and so did Sully. He turned to the man next to him. "You come 'ere often, sir?"

"What's it to ye?" The man slanted him a look through cold blue eyes.

"Do you often see any lords in 'ere?"

"Nay."

"Sir, do you ever see any of the lords in 'ere when you come by?"

"For such a short person, ye have a lot of words in ye. And yea, I seen a lord or two in 'ere on occasion."

"Do ye remember who?"

"Yer worse than my wife!" He lifted his glass and emptied the rest. "And that's why I come here. To get away from 'er."

That drew a laugh from those nearby.

A slim man that smelled of the grave leaned his back against the bar near Simon. "Don't anyone in 'ere want to help the small but mighty detector?"

Simon frowned and looked the bloke over suspiciously. "You got somethin' to say?"

The man lowered his voice. "Meet me out back, and I'll tell ye what's suspicious."

Simon nodded. He wondered what the man had in mind to tell him. He finished his drink and hopped down on his previously planted chair and then jumped to the floor. He left wishing Sully a good night and exited through the front doors so as not to cause question.

He looked to be certain that no one followed, and then he walked quickly to the rear of the building. The fellow was waiting, and Simon hoped above all hope again that he had accurately diagnosed the man as harmless.

"So, what is it you wanted to tell me? And who are you?"

"Me name's Thomas. I'm a gravedigger."

"If yer goin' to waste my time on grave-robbin' stories, I've got work to do. You can take those stories to Bow Street."

"Bow Street don't cares about the graves. And besides, this isn't any ordinary grave-robbin'."

"Even if it's not—"

"You said you wanted to know somethin' unusual. For the past few months I've been burying the dead more than once. Made a 'nuf coin to visit the Rose and Thorn as much as I like."

Simon shifted from one leg to the other and rubbed his backside to get the blood moving again. "So what's this got to do with—"

"If you'd let me finish, I'd tell ye."

Thomas looked over his shoulder to be certain no one was around. "Bodies go missin'. Right frightening."

Simon nodded in the dimness, his curiosity piqued, but still not knowing what to think about this information.

"I knows somethin' else unusual. I walked past the man that Sully was talkin' about. Didn't pay no mind until I'd gone about a dozen feet toward the bar. When I turned around he was gone, but the smell remained, it did. Almost missed it."

Simon placed both hands on his hips. "For the love of tomatoes, would you tell me what yer sayin' that I should be carin' about?"

"I'm say'n the man smelled o' the grave, he did. Just like me, but of a higher class he seemed to be."

Simon whistled low and long. "Are you sayin' what I think yer sayin'?"

"I think it could be that Lord Talon fella."

"No proof o' that. Could be anyone." Yet Simon mulled over what he'd learned. Now he wanted to make sense of it before he talked to Ravensmoore.

If Thomas's nose was up to snuff and he'd smelled the grave on the man in the Rose and Thorn, and if that man had something to do with the attacks on Lord Stone and the patients, he might be on to something important. And if all these details related to the grave smells, the grave robbers, and the missing corpses, probably to allow his raptors target practice, then he knew they were closing in on Lord Talon. But this was still too many ifs and not enough evidence.

He sighed. None of it pointed to a specific person yet. It's just a bunch of unrelated happenings. But he was doing what he did best. He was gathering evidence. Sir Nate would be proud. He knew he should tell Bow Street everything, but he didn't want to do that just yet. He wanted to figure this out on his own. Perhaps he'd talk to Lord Witt. He wanted to prove that he was worthy, that he wasn't afraid to go up against evil and those who do evil things, but he would need help.

❧

Witt and Simon sheltered themselves behind a tree in the cemetery. Grave robbers had become an increasing problem. Thomas had told Simon the thieves usually looked for special items of value that may have been buried with the deceased. However, the robbers now looked for bodies that could be used for dissection in the hospitals to train new doctors. This was unlawful, but many of those who accepted the bodies for the medical profession did not stop and ask where the body came from. That was the problem of the one providing the cadaver.

The night turned chilly. "It looks to be a waste of time this evening," Witt said. "It's almost three."

"Now's the time, Lord Witt," Simon whispered, "that we have to burrow in, for that's exactly what the foul things are thinking. There's probably two or three of them hiding somewhere on the other side of the cemetery or even nearby. And they are thinking no one else in his right mind would be here at three in the morning. Be still."

And almost before the words were out of Simon's mouth, Witt

saw one shadow, and then two. He jabbed Simon in the ribs with an elbow.

Simon grunted. "Are ye trying to kill me afore we catch 'em?"

Witt wanted to move out of hiding but knew they had to catch the robbers in the act of defiling a grave in order to press charges, so he waited.

The two figures, with shovels in hand, moved to a fresh grave and began to shovel away the newly buried resident of Angels Gate Cemetery.

One threw some type of covering on the ground. It took them more than an hour to uncover the grave.

"I want to wait till they actually take the body out of the grave," Simon said.

Witt took a frustrated breath.

When the men finally lifted a form from the casket, Simon elbowed Witt, not quite in the ribs.

Witt choked back a cough and cocked his pistol. The sound reverberated through the dead. The robbers dropped their shovels and ran with Simon and Witt on their heels.

"Stop, thieves!" Simon yelled. "Stop before I bury ye on the spot."

Witt fired his pistol overhead, and that brought them to a halt.

"We ain't done nothin' wrong. We're just doin' what we was hired to do."

"On the ground," Witt said, "before I grow impatient."

Both men, one young and one older, fell to the ground.

"I told ye, we ain't done nothin'."

Simon walked around the two prone men. "Looks like you been doin' a lot this evening, gentleman. Mind telling us who you were digging up and why?"

Silence.

"I grow weary of their silence, Simon." Witt's words were heavy with warning. "Let's shoot them and sell their bodies for a profit."

"If we tell ye, will ye let us go?"

Simon put his boot on the back of the man who had spoken. "Not likely."

Then the other said, "I'll tell ye, I'll tell ye everythin'."

"Shut up, ya fool," the older man said to the younger.

"We're just tryin' to feed our families. The one who pays us, we've never seen."

A breeze rustled through the trees, and a far-off streak of lightning lit the sky. A light drizzle spattered across Witt's face.

"You will take us to where you planned to deliver this body."

"But it's goin' to storm," the younger of the pair said.

"And so it is. I don't suppose you have horses for this journey?"

"The buyer pays for them. We get them from the public stable."

"On your feet, then," Witt growled. "I don't like the rain."

When they reached the drop-off spot for the body, the storm peaked. Thunder rattled Witt's bones. Even the grave robbers complained bitterly.

When they entered the clearing, the storm raged. Lightning raced across the sky and hit a nearby tree, splitting it in half.

Simon nearly fell out of his saddle. "The last time I was in a storm like this 'un, I was with Ravensmoore. Lost my pony and almost got hit by a falling tree limb."

"I told ye it was goin' ta storm. Now we'll git killed for sure," said the younger.

"Where are they?" Witt steadied his horse and his nerves.

"Might not come in the storm." The older man's face wrinkled in fear. The body draped across the back of his horse.

"Let's get this over with," Witt said. "Drop the body where you have in the past, and then we'll see if Talon and his friend show themselves."

The two grave robbers rode to the other end of the clearing. Rain slapped Witt and Simon like an angry woman, and the thunder that rumbled through the field made the horses skittish.

The older of the pair dropped the body at the designated spot, and then the two rode like the devil chased them until they were out of sight.

Witt and Simon waited and watched. They couldn't show themselves, or Talon may never take the body.

"He's not coming," Simon finally said. "My nerves can't take this no more, Witt. Let's collect the body and leave. At least we can return the corpse to its resting place."

A huge streak of lightning made the sky glow, and Witt saw a shadow of movement.

"Simon. Now. I see them."

"And if you see them, they may see us and shoot us on sight," he yelled.

"So be it." Witt tore across the expanse of field like a madman.

A shot joined the thunder, and Witt saw the flash of powder through the trees where the body lay. He kept riding toward the spot where the body lay.

"No!" He yelled when he and Simon arrived at the spot. The body was gone. "No!"

"Are you mad?" Simon asked. "I lived in an asylum, you know, and I know who's mad and who ain't. And I'm beginning to think you are on the edge. 'Tis a dangerous place to remain for long."

"You don't have to tell me that, Simon. I'm about ready for Bedlam. We're not going to catch Talon, the grave robbers, or reclaim a body this sodden night. Let's go home."

"Now you've returned to sanity."

# CHAPTER 10

Animals are such agreeable friends—they ask no
questions, they pass no criticisms.

—GEORGE ELIOT

VICTORIA AND DEVLIN arrived at Bethlem at seven thirty
in the morning. Devlin had agreed after much coaxing to
allow Lazarus to accompany them. Her dog had been such a friend
to her when she was sick, she wondered if perhaps he would bring
calm to chaotic minds.

As they made their way through the bare hallways to the east
wing, Victoria said, "I don't know if I'm more excited about this
or that Mercy is arriving from Scotland today. She's been gone too
long. I can't wait to see her."

Devlin laughed. "And now I'll have both my sisters to watch over.
I believe I will need reinforcements, and Madeline will do nothing
but spoil you both more than I already have."

"That's what big brothers are for."

She could hear the women talking and crying and screaming just
as she had the last time she was here, and although she wasn't as
frightened, her muscles still tensed. They approached the door of
the room where Devlin's patients would be waiting. He took out a
key. "Wait here until I tell them what to expect."

Victoria nodded, and she and Lazarus stood out of sight until
he entered. The moment he entered the room, a hush fell over the

place. Victoria was amazed at the reaction. She could hear her brother talking to them and one voice say, "No, no. I'm scared. I'm so scared."

Devlin came to the door a few moments later. "They are a bit prepared, but as you probably heard, there is some anxiety. I think all will be well. Are you certain you want to do this?"

Victoria smiled and nodded. "If you're here, I'll be fine." Devlin led her and Lazarus into the room. She saw a young girl huddled near a window as far away from them as she could get.

"Who is that girl in the corner?" she whispered.

"Her name is Chloe."

Victoria led Lazarus in only a few feet. "Hello. This is my dog Lazarus. He's very big, and he slobbers a great deal, but he will not harm you. He likes women. Men, not so much."

Devlin addressed the patients. "While I meet with you, my sister, Lady Victoria, will visit with whoever wants to talk to her and Lazarus. You are all safe. No need to worry."

A few of the older women stepped forward.

"He's very handsome," said one woman who held both hands across her chest as if she were cold or perhaps scared.

Victoria reveled in the joy the women took getting to know Lazarus. "It's amazing," she said to Devlin when he came to get another of the patients, "how calm they are around an animal. I don't believe I've ever seen a dog have such a powerful effect on people."

"He's always had a powerful effect on you."

Victoria nodded. "I remember when you brought him home. All I wanted to do was comfort him, and he was the one that ended up comforting me far longer and unto this day."

"A dog doesn't judge or belittle. They just want to be loved."

"It's more, though. There's no fear. These women aren't all

wrapped up in their thoughts. They have another object to focus on besides themselves."

Devlin grinned. "Now you sound like a member of the mad-doctoring trade. You may take after me in your curiosity of the mind."

"A detector of the mind. Just as the Bow Street runners and Simon pursue leads, you can pursue leads related to people's thoughts. That's similar to how I used to watch and listen to the talk and movements of visitors that came to Ravensmoore. Sometimes listening is more important than talking."

"I believe you may have discovered the future of mad-doctoring, Victoria."

As they spoke, another young woman shyly approached them. "I like you."

She touched Victoria's hand, and Victoria instinctively wrapped her hand around Chloe's.

"I like you too, Chloe. Would you like to spend some time with Lazarus?"

"I'm afraid. He's big."

"Why don't you introduce Lazarus to Chloe, and then I'll talk to her. Is that well with you, Chloe?" Devlin asked.

Chloe nodded, looking at the floor.

Victoria led Chloe to Lazarus and stopped about two feet away. Three women sat on the floor, and they all stroked Lazarus and talked to one another while doing so. One of the women looked up and said, "Chloe, come meet our new friend."

"I'd like that. He doesn't look so scary when he's lying down."

Victoria let go of Chloe's hand. "He won't hurt you."

Chloe took timid steps forward, and the woman who'd spoken moved to allow Chloe more room. "You can sit here where I was."

Chloe first patted the dog on the head, and when he licked her hand with his big tongue, she shivered with laughter. "He's a gentleman and most amusing."

Then she sat down next to Lazarus and resumed stroking him as she saw the others doing.

Victoria looked around the room in awe. Such a huge difference in the room, and all because of a dog. *Lord, You do work in mysterious ways.*

Just as Chloe was settling in with Lazarus, one of the keepers came through the door with a straitjacket. Immediately the room exploded into chaos.

The fear-filled souls ranted and rocked themselves, and Lazarus barked at the keeper, knowing who had brought the terror.

Ravensmoore stepped in front of the male keeper. "Why would you walk into this area with a straitjacket? Can't you see what you've done?"

The man with dead brown eyes stared at Devlin. "I'm here to do my job."

"And what would that be?"

"I've been ordered to take Chloe for her treatment."

Devlin turned and looked at Chloe, who had scooted into a corner of the room, her eyes wide and misty with tears spilling down her cheeks.

"What treatment? Who ordered it? I'm her physician here."

"You've heard of Dr. Monroe, haven't you, my lord? He has power 'ere, and he says Chloe get the jacket because she's been seein' things again and that yer doctoring ain't workin'," he said.

Victoria knew that Devlin could not allow Chloe to be restrained. He'd worked against the use of restraints, calling them barbaric.

"What treatment?"

"Leeching."

"No. It's of no value." Victoria had let the words leave her mouth before her brother could speak.

The keeper moved toward Chloe, but Devlin put his hand on the man's shoulder. "You heard my sister."

"Yer sister ain't a doctor now, is she, my lordship?"

"Leave now or your impertinence will get you more than discharged from your position. I'm her doctor, and I say she does not need restraints or leeching."

"You'll have to take that up with Dr. Monroe, yer lordship. I've got me orders." And he held the jacket out toward Chloe with a gruesome expression and rotten teeth.

Chloe screamed

Lazarus ran between Chloe and the keeper and growled as Victoria had never heard. A deep guttural threat.

"Get that dog out of here. There's to be no animals on the wards."

Lazarus stood on his hind legs and pinned the keeper to the wall by both shoulders

"He's going to kill me! Git 'em off of me now!" The keeper turned alternating shades of green and gasped for breath.

"Lazarus," Victoria called. "Good dog. Down now."

Lazarus didn't move but stood where he was and looked at Victoria as if to be certain he'd heard the instructions correctly.

"Down, Lazarus. It's all right."

Lazarus looked at her as if he knew it wasn't all right but grudgingly withdrew his hold on the keeper and padded over to where Victoria waited.

Devlin took the keeper by the arm and escorted him to the door. "You may assure Dr. Monroe that I will speak with him, but until I do, I don't want to see you back in this ward. Understood?"

He shrugged away from Devlin and growled, "Ye ain't seen the last of me."

"You'd better pray it is."

Victoria waited at the door with Lazarus. "Are you all right?"

"I'm fine. It's the others I must be concerned with now. You're unharmed, Snoop?" he whispered.

She'd been frightened for Chloe and afraid that Lazarus just might rip out the keeper's throat for a moment, but she remained amazingly calm. "I'm fine."

When they turned back to the patients, it was as if a wave of dark despair had washed through the room and taken the souls of the women with it.

Victoria and Devlin both looked for Chloe. She'd balled herself up in a corner near the barred windows. Victoria knelt next to her. "Chloe? You will be all right."

Chloe looked straight through her. Not a movement did she make of face or body. It was as if she'd frozen into a hard ball of ice and no personality. No soul remained.

Lazarus licked Chloe's hand, but she did not stir. Her emotions were dead.

Devlin took his sister's hand and raised her up. "There is nothing more you can do today. I must seek out Dr. Monroe and put a stop to these atrocities. These women are under my protection, and now I've failed them."

"It wasn't you, Devlin. There are only so many things you can control. You cannot be everywhere at once, as much as you might like to be."

Victoria touched her brother's cheek.

"I'll put you and Lazarus in the carriage," he said. "I'll come home later."

The carriage arrived at the house, and the footman handed her out and then stood aside as Lazarus bounded out of the vehicle, shaking it from side to side and irritating the horses.

"John, would you kindly take Lazarus for a walk? He's so wound up that I'm afraid he might break something in the house."

The footman glanced from her to Lazarus with a skeptical look. "Yes, Lady Victoria, but can he get back in the coach so I can take care of the horses first?"

"Why, John, you aren't afraid of Lazarus, are you? He'd never hurt you."

"I'm just afraid of who will be walking who, my lady. He's a mind of his own, he does, when you're not around. I think he likes to play games."

"Play games?" Victoria asked.

"Hide and seek. He likes to run and hide, and then he barks till we find him."

The door to the townhouse opened, and Victoria turned.

"You're back earlier than expected. Madeline said you'd be gone all morning."

"Mercy! Great heavens." Victoria stared in amazement. "How can you be here? We thought you wouldn't return from Scotland for another month."

Mercy ran down the steps, and Victoria hugged her youngest sister fast.

Like their brother, Mercy favored their mother with dark hair and intense green eyes, whereas Victoria had the fair complexion of their rogue father who died at sea with their oldest brother, Edward.

"It would appear that London has been good for you. You're as strong as an ox."

"And you are gorgeous as ever." She brushed a stray dark wisp of hair away from her sister's eye. "What's happened? Nothing's wrong, is it?"

"No. My plans changed. When I got your message about coming to London, I just had to join you. And then I got word from Madeline that she was coming too, and I wanted to be with all of you. I thought it was time we were all together again. I've missed you all."

"I'm so glad you're here. Wait till Devlin sees you. You'll be good medicine for him."

"Why didn't he come home with you?"

"I'll tell you later. Some problems at Bedlam. Heavens, I've forgotten Lazarus." Victoria turned her attention back to the driver and dog. "Back in the carriage, my Lazarus." They laughed as Lazarus barked and loped forward to welcome Mercy.

Mercy bent down and rubbed the dog's head. "Have you missed me? I've missed you, old friend."

Victoria slanted him a look, and Lazarus immediately turned about and jumped in the carriage, much to the footman's surprise.

He nodded. "Thank you, Lady Victoria. We'll be off now." The driver grabbed up the reins and headed off to the stable.

"Mercy, doesn't he look a bit like the regent going off on a trip? All he needs is a crown and scepter."

"He certainly does. Now, come in and tell me what's happened. I wanted to join you at Bethlem, but Madeline and I got overly absorbed in conversation."

Victoria followed Mercy into the parlor. "Everything didn't go as planned, but Devlin says that's not unusual with the women on the ward. Perhaps you can visit on another day."

"Of course."

They settled into comfortable chairs. "Tell me what happened, Snoop." Mercy looked at her with concerned eyes while she studied her. Very much like the eyes that evaluated her well-being when she lay in her sick bed. She quietly thanked God that she wasn't lying in that bed now and explained what had happened.

"I wonder how Devlin will manage to change Dr. Monroe's mind about treatment on the ward. He fights constantly to change the way the asylums function in England. That's one of the reasons he's in Parliament. But it seems everywhere he turns, there is opposition."

"Victoria, it is never easy to make a difference. Some people fight all their lives for change and never see the outcome of their efforts, the labors of their love. All he or we can do is our best, and ask for wisdom along the way. If we pray on these things and do our part, then we have hope that God will do His part and show us the way to accomplish His will."

"Mercy, I don't need a sermon. I need more freedom to help Devlin in his efforts. I want to help. I've been looking for something worth doing all my life, and now I'm finally able to do something and society says, 'No, no. You're a woman. You cannot do that.'"

Mercy smiled. "You have no idea how much alike we are, sister."

"What do you mean?"

"Let's just say that I'm a little bit of a snoop like you, but I'm more interested in the human body like Devlin," she continued without giving Victoria a chance to respond. "Do you think for one moment if I wanted to become a doctor that society would allow it? When the sun quits shining, perhaps."

"Mercy, are you trying to tell me you want to be a doctor?" Victoria sat on the edge of her seat.

"I'm just making an example of Devlin's situation within Parliament and how hard it is to get what you want even if you are a man. Look at Wilberforce, for the love of sanity. He practically killed himself to bar the slave trade, and it still happens. Illegally, but still. For all his efforts, it persists."

"I think it's time you told me what you were really up to in Scotland. Something tells me it was more than visiting our home in Edinburgh for a change of scenery."

Talon pulled on his boots with a plan to do harm. He was sick of the tortures continuing at Bedlam in the name of medicine. Why couldn't Monroe and Ravensmoore and the Parliament lords keep patients safe? Now his plans had to change again. Anyone who had power over other lives at Bedlam better beware. Someone had to avenge them and make certain that the right thing is done.

"You are too rash, Talon."

"Archer. What do you want? I don't want you here. I don't want your opinion."

Archer lounged in the doorway, dressed in black from head to toe and wearing that cocky grin on his face.

"You need someone who can help you plan your next move. I am not as deeply involved as you are. Let me help."

"Archer, I have Celeste's help. I don't need yours."

"You, my friend, need all the help you can get. I have some thoughts."

"If you have such great thoughts, why didn't you show up earlier? Now you want to come in and save the day and take all the credit. I know how you think."

"Talon, listen to me. You have doubts. I don't. I know exactly what to do. What I was trained to do. I can take on Monroe, Ravensmoore, Parliament, even Lord Witt by myself. I don't need either you or Celeste. You can sit back and watch me create what I was born to create. Complete havoc."

"And what about the other one?"

"The girl?"

"No problem. I'll have her eating out of my hand before long."

"We don't have long. Time is growing short. If I don't act soon…"

Archer sighed. "You are too soft."

Talon looked away. "I need more time, Archer. You promised you would let me handle this. So, let me do what I know I'm capable of. I'll let you know if I need help. In the event that I do, you can tell me what to do if all else fails."

"You know what that is, don't you?"

"Yes, I know."

Talon knew that Archer wanted to take over. That he didn't think Talon and Celeste could do it without him. And although Archer might be an excellent strategist, he wasn't necessarily smarter than Talon.

"I'm flying the hawks again tonight, Archer. Do you want to come, or are you still afraid of the raptors?"

"You can take Celeste, if she's willing to come out."

"Celeste is perfecting the poison. It didn't kill Stone, so it must not be strong enough."

Archer cracked his knuckles. "She doesn't have much time left to perfect her concoction, either. This must all come off as smooth as good brandy."

"I know, Archer. You don't have to lecture."

"It could be your neck in the noose if I don't lecture."

Talon grimaced. "You mean *our* necks."

Victoria entered her brother's townhouse with a gust of wind at her back and was about to stick her head in the library to tell Devlin they were back from their grand shopping expedition when she heard him discussing Lord Talon's attacks with Lord Witt.

She pushed open the library doors just as Madeline and Mercy joined her in the hallway.

The men immediately stood.

Devlin said. "You must have been successful in your purchases to burst in with such exuberance."

Madeline stopped short. "I'm sorry. We've only just come in and—"

"It's my fault. I was about to knock when I heard you talking about Lord Talon."

Mercy frowned. "How did you eavesdrop so quickly, Snoop?"

"I didn't. I only heard them discussing what's on everyone's mind. You must let me help you. I'm sure I could shed some light on this if you would only allow me to join your conversation. Please?"

Devlin looked her in the eye. "No. Absolutely not. I'm not dragging you into this mess."

"But I want to be dragged into this mess. It's very interesting." Victoria pleaded. "Lord Witt. Surely you understand—"

Devlin shook his head. "And don't drag Witt into this. He's not family. And you've forgotten your manners. Lady Mercy has not yet been introduced to Lord Witt. My youngest sister, Lady Mercy."

"A pleasure, Lady Mercy." He bowed.

Mercy curtsied in return and smiled. "I see you are not a stranger to the uncharacteristic ideas that run amuck in our family, sir."

"I assure you that your brother and sister have broadened my thinking in many ways."

Victoria huffed and turned to Madeline. "They won't allow me to help solve the mystery of who Lord Talon could be. Maddie, you know how good I am at puzzles. And Mercy, you'd think they considered women less knowledgeable than themselves."

"Rubbish," Madeline and Mercy said in unison. Madeline folded her arms. "Perhaps you gentleman need all three of us to help you solve this matter. I'm certain that five heads are better than two and that a female perspective can only add a depth of objectivity that will enhance the outcome you now search for.

"And," Victoria added, "you will not waste valuable time and will be far less likely to make fools of yourselves at Parliament."

"I think it would be a commonsense approach," Mercy agreed.

Witt arched a brow. "It looks as though we may be in for some trouble."

"Trouble is not the word, I assure you." Ravensmoore dropped into his chair and leaned back in thoughtful contemplation.

Victoria took a step forward. "I knew you'd come to a reasonable—"

"No."

"But—"

"No, Victoria. No."

"Husband," Madeline said and walked to his desk where he lounged, a stubborn set to his jaw. "We are not talking about searching out Talon by ourselves. We just want to help you examine all the angles. You know how important this is to Victoria."

Devlin looked at Witt. "If we send them away, they will go talk about us in another room and possibly send malicious gossip through the town that will only impede any progress we hope to make."

Witt caught Ravensmoore's nod. "I understand. But should we invite them in and they do contribute, in some small way, of course, then as they say, our time will be well spent and we shall not make fools of ourselves at Parliament."

Devlin stood again. "I see no way we can refuse. But—"

"Wonderful." Victoria clapped her hands together.

Devlin stood. "But we must set some ground rules first."

"Of course," Maddie said. "There must be rules."

Mercy grinned. "After all, men do have their pride."

"Please come in and close the door behind you. If you don't, we may have Henry and Cook in here with us next."

A whimper came from the other side of the door.

"It's Lazarus. We must allow him to enter. He's of no danger related to gossip and broken promises," Victoria assured them.

Witt frowned. "I don't think he likes me."

"Nonsense. He harbors no ill feelings against you. He just knows you are not a dog lover, and so he is more cautious."

Lazarus nudged the door open with his big nose. Then he lumbered over to Victoria and lay down on the floor with a heavy sigh.

Victoria patted his head. "Now, what were you saying about a hunting club?"

"Not a club, Snoop, but a group of men who are using hawks to hunt. They prefer to preserve the old ways and find it more challenging than shooting." Devlin took a large swallow of coffee. "They may know something they aren't even aware of that makes sense."

Witt explained. "Lords Winston, Ramsay, Templar, and Davenport are all members of this hunting group. You can understand that none of them wanted to draw attention to themselves and their sport under the circumstances."

"I should think not," Madeline said. "They would most likely be sitting ducks for the speculators."

Victoria's mind whirled with possibilities of capturing Lord Talon. "This is your best lead, though, the one that makes the most sense. What are the chances that Lord Talon is completely estranged from any of these lords' estates? What do we do now?"

"*We* don't do anything. I can see your wheels spinning, Victoria. You will not be doing any snooping."

Victoria straightened her back and lifted her chin. "I never snoop. I investigate, just as the Bow Street runners investigate."

"But you, dear sister, are not a Bow Street runner."

"And," Witt added, "It is too dangerous for you to even consider such a thing. Your brother really does have to watch out for your well-being."

"Hear me out. All of you. I'm not without discretion. I suggest that we use the upcoming masquerade at Thistledown Hall. Lady Phoebe invited me, and I will be sure that we are all invited. She's very kind."

Devlin stood up and started pacing. "That is out of the question. Promise me right now that you will not get involved with this investigation, Snoop, outside of this house."

Victoria sighed and flashed her sister-in-law a meaningful look.

"Devlin," Madeline said. "I really don't think it would do any harm for all of us to attend the masquerade. We will be very alert to conversations and actions, but none of us will take unnecessary risks. Lord Ramsay is involved with three men who like to hunt with hawks. That does not mean he or any of them are Lord Talon."

Witt cleared his throat. "If I may suggest, Ravensmoore, that the ladies have made a very good point. We will all be together—"

"We?" Victoria asked.

"I'm also invited to the moonlight masquerade." His gray eyes glinted with humor. "I can help your brother keep an eye on each of you for safety's sake."

Witt was helping her. Devlin wouldn't like that. "Thank you, Lord Witt. That's very thoughtful of you."

Witt nodded. Devlin glowered.

"Thoughtful or not, this is no game, and it shouldn't be treated as such. Whoever Talon is, he's got vengeance on his mind, and if any of us get in his way, I'd hate to see the outcome after the carnage he's already wrought."

# CHAPTER 11

Society is a masked ball, where everyone hides his
real character and reveals it by hiding.
　　　　　　　　　　—RALPH WALDO EMERSON

*T*HISTLEDOWN HALL

"It's beautiful." Victoria breathed in awe as she peered through the carriage window. The manor house sat upon a terraced hillside bright with torch light. The stonework was exquisite, and from a distance Thistledown Hall resembled a castle from a fairy tale with four turrets of differing heights on the far left of the magnificent structure. They passed through the gates that led to Lord Ramsay's home, where Phoebe lived with her brother.

The atmosphere induced a sense of adventure that she'd longed for her entire life. When the carriage pulled up to the entrance, two footmen were immediately available to assist them. She and Nora were handed out of the coach, and she entered a world of make-believe.

The full moon masquerade ball! It had been more than two months since Victoria had arrived in London. She'd looked forward to this ball more than she'd realized.

"Nora, I want to watch the guests arrive. I want to enjoy this evening to the fullest. So please, please, try not to scold me for my curious nature."

"And what would that 'curious nature' mean in this regard?" Nora asked.

Victoria leaned near and whispered. "Just a bit of snooping. This place utterly calls me to explore its mysteries and indulge in a bit of spying along the way. Combined with the masquerade, this event is intriguing beyond my wildest expectations."

"If Lord Ravensmoore had not arrived home late, I think he'd have something to say about your snooping. I'm certain that he and the countess want you to have a wonderful time, but both of them will be checking up on you the moment they arrive, so I suggest you not get into trouble."

They climbed the steps, and Nora stepped back into the shadows as Victoria was greeted by Lord Ramsay dressed as the Greek god Zeus and carrying his famous lightning bolt.

"Welcome to Thistledown Hall, Lady Victoria." Lord Ramsay bowed low.

Victoria smiled and curtsied deeply in return. "Thank you, my Lord Zeus."

"Lady Victoria! You look wonderful!"

Victoria looked up to see Phoebe dressed magnificently in a gown of colors and a set of plush white wings on her back that seemed to shimmer and appeared almost as real as her brother's lightning bolt.

"And you are a goddess."

Phoebe laughed. "I am! I'm Iris, the goddess of the rainbow. Don't you just love my wings?"

"They look so real. You could be a rainbow angel."

Phoebe pulled her from the reception line and leaned near. "Madam Tunney is a wonderful seamstress. She fashioned both my wings and my brother's thunderbolt. And aren't you a beautiful Queen of Hearts? The men will be enamored of your beauty and desire your constant attention tonight."

Victoria's heart swelled with Phoebe's kind words. "I wouldn't underrate your appeal to the gentlemen in attendance, Phoebe. You will be turning heads yourself."

Phoebe turned to Nora. "And where is your costume, Nora?"

"Beg pardon, Lady Phoebe," Nora curtsied, "but I'm not one for dressing up."

"I tried to convince her," Victoria said, "but she still refused."

Phoebe nodded. "I must return to the receiving line and continue to greet our guests, but I've got the perfect place for you to conceal yourself and watch everyone arrive." She grabbed Victoria's hand and led her and Nora up a long flight of stairs to an alcove with a brilliant view of the arriving masqueraders.

Victoria squeezed her hand in gratitude. "It's perfect for spying." She let go of her friend's hand and snuggled into the alcove, arranging the skirts of her costume with her maid's help. She was fascinated by each and every couple currently disembarking from phaetons, carriages, and coaches.

"I thought you'd like this vantage point. I'll find you later."

Victoria watched her friend descend the stairs and then quickly returned her attention to those arriving. Everywhere were lords and ladies dressed from the peculiar to the spectacular.

"I will leave you to enjoy your snooping, but I'll be nearby. The gallery of portraits will entertain me. You'll be all right?"

"I'll be fine. Lord Witt should be along soon. And, I hope, Devlin and Madeline. Mercy has called off, but I'm hoping she'll change her mind. I'll watch for them." She turned from Nora to enjoy the parade of costumes.

She smiled as a couple came toward her dressed as a needle and thread. The spool of thread, a dark crimson with the top of the spool actually the hat and the bottom of the spool the decorative vanilla of the mid-calf skirt. Scandalous to be sure. Her partner, the gold needle, well suited her, being tall and thin. His hat spiraled to a point and his trousers were skin tight to more perfectly expose his skinny legs.

The next coach stopped and a gentleman dressed as a high-wayman, completely in black, departed the coach and turned to hand out his mate, a female highwayman also dressed in black, the only differences being the woman wore a black cape and her mask covered only the eyes, and her partner wore no cape and a mask that covered only the right half of his face. They looked dangerous indeed.

"Enjoying the view?"

Victoria jumped and nearly tumbled from the window seat. "You must refrain from sneaking up on me, Lord Witt. It's very disconcerting."

"And how did you know it was me?" He bowed, the bells on his hat and slippers jingling. He was dressed in black and white, the court jester, complete with black and white paint on his face. His mouth turned up in a smile.

"You jingle when you walk."

"Yet you did not hear me approach."

"I was distracted by the costumes. And I'd recognize your voice anywhere."

"Excellent. I will simply change the octave a few degrees higher then," he said and demonstrated.

Victoria covered her ears. "I don't believe that will suit."

"Very well. How is this?" He lowered his voice a couple of octaves.

"Amazing. Quite captivating really. I'd never know it was you. But I prefer your own voice."

"Ah. A woman with excellent taste. Not only in men, but in cos-tume as well." He reached out his hand to her.

Victoria rose from her window seat and curtsied. "I see you approve of the Queen of Hearts." Dressed in a long silk gown of red, white, and black and a black choker of pearls about her neck with a gold tiara topping off her magnificent black wig, she felt every inch the Queen of Hearts. A high white collar fluffed out behind her neck, and a trio of hearts decorated the front of the silk gown.

"Approve is not the word, Lady Victoria. You are radiant and sure to outshine every woman here this evening." He bestowed her black gloved hand with a kiss. "Had I known you were coming as the Queen of Hearts, I would have come as the King of Hearts, but alas, I am not."

Victoria's heart fluttered. She wasn't sure if it was Witt, the excitement of her first costume ball, or simply that she was doing the kind of thing she'd only dreamed of during her years of sickness. "Thank you for your compliments, Lord Witt. I am blessed by your noble gesture."

"Did you call me a jester?" He feigned a hurt look.

"You know I didn't, and you know you are." She smiled, and then activity outside the window captured the attention of them both.

The crest upon each coach represented the estate of each lord. A gentleman dressed as a pirate emerged from the next coach, and one of the footman handed out his matching female pirate, which caused a stir among the crowd. She wore the identical costume of her escort with the exception that the neckline was cut far too low to be proper.

She heard Witt swallow. "Well, that will cause much talk among the gossips tonight and most likely for the remainder of the month."

"Oh, not that long," Victoria said. "Only until the next outrageous activity occurs this evening."

"Beautiful and also wise. May I escort you to the ballroom, before your brother sends not only Nora after us but Lazarus as well?" Witt offered his arm, and she accepted, looking forward to the evening ahead of them.

"No need to worry. Lazarus is being well looked after by Henry at home, and he's not happy about it either. The dear one isn't used to being away from me, and the city has been far more confining for him than I had originally thought. And my brother has not yet arrived."

"Then why don't we try to enjoy ourselves? After all, this is your first masquerade ball, and I believe dancing and talking and eating and drinking the punch is yet to be experienced."

"And don't forget our crucial purpose."

"That is understood."

She looked down a long picture gallery. "Nora said she would be close by, but she's nowhere in sight."

"I sent Nora to sample the table of food and drink and promised that I would behave myself. She made me swear to it."

"She's an excellent chaperone. Did you meet Lady Phoebe when you came in?"

"Ramsay's sister? She wasn't with her brother when I arrived."

"You'll love her costume. She simply glows."

"I've not had the pleasure. But the night is young. I'm certainly grateful that Ramsay's lightning bolt is not real. I think he considered throwing it my way," Witt said, his voice thick with sarcasm.

When they entered the ballroom, Victoria thought she might need her first vinaigrette, that vinegar-soaked sponge hidden in a silver case in the event she swooned, but the feeling of light-headedness soon passed and she simply drank in the beauty that once she only dreamed of from her sickbed. She pinched herself to be sure this wasn't a dream or vision. Beeswax candles glowed from the chandeliers, casting a shimmering light on the guests' costumes as they entered the magnificent room and filled the dance floor. The strings from the orchestra drenched the room in music.

Victoria stood still, watching, listening, almost afraid to breathe. The dancing, the music, the lights . . .

When Witt spoke, it took her a moment to realize that he was asking her to dance. When she didn't answer, he said, "Don't tell me your dance card is filled already. I won't allow anyone to cut in front of me. They will have to wait their turn."

"Lord Witt. I believe we should get some punch first. I have a confession to make on the way." She took his arm and gently guided him in the direction of a punchbowl.

"And what has happened?" He glanced around, frowning, his worry evident.

"I can't dance," she finally said. "I've never set foot on a ballroom floor, never taken even a step of the quadrille, let alone the waltz. I only pretended to dance at home in my room when I was certain no one watched but Lazarus. Once my brother tried to teach me, but I was so weak I collapsed and couldn't get out of bed for a week."

"Then we shall simply have to change that right now."

"I can't." They reached the long row of tables that crossed the ballroom.

Witt picked up two cups of punch. "Now, fortify yourself, Lady Victoria, for tonight you will dance."

He handed her a cup filled with a refreshing concoction she'd never tasted. It smelled of raspberries, and she drank deeply. She lowered her voice so that none of the nearby guests could hear. "I told you that I cannot dance. Please don't allow me to make a fool out of myself. Not at my first masquerade." She looked up at him and noticed a mischievous grin on his face.

"Come with me."

He cupped her elbow and steered her toward the gardens and terraces that graced the outside of the manor house. A cool breeze fluttered through the filmy sleeves of her costume, and Witt's touch sent a shiver sliding over her skin.

"My lord, where are we going? Nora will be looking for me, and if she cannot find me, she will alert my brother."

"Then when she finds us, she will have nothing to complain about."

Witt grabbed her hand, and the sensation of her hand enclosed in his comforted and encouraged. During her illness she spent hours reading the character of those around her, and now, having observed Witt for even the short time she'd known him, she felt she knew him well. The more time she spent with him, the more comfortable and trusting she grew.

They circled around a hedge, and Witt drew her to him and placed his hand on the small of her back and with the other entwined her fingers with his. "Now, I will teach you how to dance."

"What? No. I can't dance, Lord Witt. I will surely step on your toes." She tried to pull away but he held her in position.

"You can dance. You've just never had the opportunity to do so. It's time you learned. It's not very different from learning to ride a horse, and you're almost an expert at that now."

"Wait." She took a breath. "What if—"

"No what ifs. Listen to the music. That is a Viennese waltz. Not so very hard to follow if one has a good teacher." He pressed his hand more firmly against her back and squeezed her fingers, and somehow she moved with him. Her feet didn't quite follow the way they were supposed to, but he didn't stop or correct her. He just kept moving, she kept following, and soon she forgot about trying to learn and just allowed him to fully guide her in the waltz. Heaven. Simply heaven.

She closed her eyes. The music, the night, the dance, and Witt. Everything was perfect.

"Ahem."

They both jumped. Jumped like small children caught doing something forbidden.

It was Robin Hood, and he studied the two of them in a familiar way.

"Excuse me."

"Devlin?" She laughed in relief and surprise. It wasn't like Devlin to come garbed for a masquerade. "Would I be correct in guessing that Lady Marian is somewhere nearby?"

"Nora was worried."

Victoria blushed. "Lord Witt was teaching me to dance."

"So I noticed. Witt, I suggest you keep my sister closer to the house. I wouldn't want the gossips to target her, nor do I want my sister's reputation tarnished. That is not acceptable."

"I wouldn't allow any harm to come to your sister."

"I'd feel better about that statement if you weren't dressed as a jester."

Witt bowed deeply. "*Touché.*"

Devlin arched a brow. "I'll see you both inside, and then I'll find Nora." He disappeared around the hedge.

"I'm sorry," Victoria said. "But I did enjoy the dance lesson."

"We can practice more tonight." Witt grasped her hand in his again, and they returned to the ballroom.

Victoria reveled in the excitement of the evening. She watched the costumed couples move across the ballroom floor and smiled when Madeline and Devlin whirled past her, but she caught site of his assessing glance before he disappeared into the crush. The air filled with the aroma of food, excitement, and a heady mix of perfumes.

"If you will excuse me," Witt said, "I need to talk to Lord Ramsay. I will leave you in Nora's capable hands. I see her and your friend, Lady Phoebe." He nodded in their direction. "I suggest you have something to eat, for when I return we *will* dance."

"In that case, I will have to make certain I have energy for the rest of the evening's festivities." She smiled, left him, and arrived at the buffet just as Phoebe and Nora caught up with her.

"You just missed my brother. He's dressed as Robin Hood."

"Now, that I want to see," Nora said. "I'm so thirsty. I'll get some punch and return for a plate."

"I was hoping you would introduce me to your brother. Perhaps later we will find him." Phoebe stood back and smiled. "I can see your costume better in this light. Enchanting."

"As is your own. I imagine your brother will have to fight off all the men who hope to dance with an angel."

"I'm pleasing my brother this evening. He can't wait to marry me off and says I can't avoid my destiny forever. Still, I'm in no rush. There's no one who interests me. Sometimes I think I'd be perfectly happy as a spinster." She picked up a spoon and helped herself to the same potatoes that Victoria had chosen and a mix of green vegetables. "I see you enjoy a good plate of food too. I like that. It's a good sign to have a healthy appetite."

Victoria closed her eyes and inhaled the varying aromas. "Isn't it marvelous?" She opened her eyes. "There was a time when I couldn't eat because of an illness, and my family teases me now that I eat far more than my brother does." She moved further along the buffet, enjoying the conversation. "Those oysters are absolutely too wonderful to be ignored." She scooped two onto her plate.

Phoebe agreed, her eyes twinkling in the light from the chandeliers. "Would you like to join me in my private library? We can eat there and not be disturbed."

Victoria's eyes widened. "You have your own library? How wonderful."

"My brother is generous, and because I love to read, he gave me my own personal library when I turned twenty. He said he'd hoped I'd be married off by then, but I want to marry for love. My brother insists I'm too particular."

"I would love to see your library. I must tell my chaperone, lest she worry."

"I understand. I have already told mine that she can find me there."

Victoria found Nora helping herself to a plate of ham and told her that she would be with Lady Phoebe. As Nora heaped more ham on her plate, Victoria asked, "You wouldn't be getting an extra piece for Lazarus, would you?" She laughed softly, knowing she loved the dog almost as much as Victoria.

"Perhaps." Nora smiled.

"Lady Phoebe has asked me to join her in her private library."

"And this would be located where?"

"I didn't ask. I'm sure you can find out from one of the footmen. I won't be too long. She's waiting. And please tell Lord Witt and my brother. I don't want to worry them."

"That is much easier said than done. The pair of them fairly dote on you. I do believe that Lord Witt has taken a shine to you, if not entirely to Lazarus."

The library sparkled with feminine tapestries and lovely pastels that would prevent any man from making himself at home in this delicious and cozy oasis. Victoria marveled at a tapestry of Pegasus, the winged horse, that appeared so real she thought he might materialize in the room at any moment. "He's incredible. Where did you get this?"

"My brother brought Pegasus back after a trip to Greece. Do sit down. We can relax in here. I don't feel all that comfortable in crowds. Ellis, that's my brother's Christian name, disapproves when I sneak away from festivities such as tonight. He says that because he has no wife, I should try harder to be a hostess, but I find I'm not very good at it. I'd rather escape into a good book."

"And you have many at your disposal." Victoria touched several leather-bound volumes of Wordsworth, Coleridge, Shelley, and others. "Impressive. But do you ever read, dare I say, anything more romantic?"

"You mean Austen's books?"

"Yes. I just love her stories."

"Of course!" She reached under her chair and pulled a copy of

*Emma* from its hiding place. "I have to hide her novels. Ellis threatened to burn them if he found them. Said they aren't good reading for women. Give us too many ideas of romance." She wrinkled her nose. "As if he would know."

Victoria sat in a chair so comfortable that she could have easily fallen asleep if she weren't so excited. "I see why you love this place. It's magical. But I think you do yourself a disservice when you say you're not a good hostess. You have been an extraordinary hostess to me."

Phoebe laughed. "I think you understand what I mean. It's more than one person I am to entertain and make small talk with throughout the evening. I'm enjoying the ball and the costumes tonight. But most of all I'm enjoying spending time with you."

It seemed like they'd only been talking mere minutes when one of the house servants knocked on the door. "Excuse the interruption, Lady Victoria, Lady Phoebe. I've brought the Countess Ravensmoore."

"Madeline! Or rather, Maid Marian." Victoria wiped tears of delight away with the back of her hand. "Lady Phoebe has been sharing some delightful stories with me."

"Countess." Phoebe stood and curtsied. "I do hope you are enjoying yourself."

"It's a wonderful masquerade. I'm so glad you and Victoria get on so well."

"Lady Phoebe is a storyteller of the highest ilk. I've encouraged her to write them down, for it would be a shame if they were lost."

"A grand idea," Madeline said and then looked at Victoria. "Lord Witt asked that I retrieve you. Apparently you promised him a dance, and he is most anxious that you follow through with that promise. He said to tell you this exactly. 'Lady Snoop. You must pull yourself away from your friend and delight me with the dance steps you learned earlier this evening. I refuse to believe that you are in hiding.' And that's my current obligation."

Phoebe placed her hand on top of Victoria's hand. "Wait, must you go so soon? I really must find out why Lord Witt calls you Lady Snoop. I believe you have kept some of your own amusing stories from me."

"Come with me, Lady Phoebe. We will dance together! Even though I have no idea what I'm doing." She grasped her friend's hand and pulled her from the chair.

Phoebe smiled. "You go ahead. I admit I'm not the social butterfly you are, and I must gather my courage before I commit myself to the dance floor. I promise that I will join you within half an hour."

Victoria gave her a quick hug and left the library in a flutter of skirts, pulled her short mask into place, and followed Madeline through the halls. Cigar smoke greeted them as they neared the ballroom.

She stopped short when she heard her brother's and Ramsay's voices raised in anger coming from a nearby room.

Devlin was arguing about something with Lord Ramsay. Neither man looked up when they passed by, and a footman hurriedly closed the door. Madeline nudged her forward so as not to eavesdrop, and she recovered quickly and moved on, even though her thoughts whirled with questions.

# CHAPTER 12

To be fond of dancing was a certain step towards falling in love.

—JANE AUSTEN

HERE YOU ARE," Witt said as she entered the ballroom. He held out his hands to her. "It's time for another lesson."

"Lord Witt. If you insist, you will most likely have very sore toes tomorrow."

"Why do you think I wore my boots?" He laughed and turned to Madeline. "I promise to be on my best behavior, Countess. You can watch for yourself."

"I'll be doing the watching, to be sure." Nora bustled forward. "There you are, Lady Victoria. I thought you were still in the library." She frowned and crossed her arms.

"I'm sorry, Nora," Madeline said and placed a gentle hand on the maid's arm. "I went looking for your charge at Lord Witt's request. He was just suggesting that I watch to assure his best behavior. But since you are here, Nora, I am going out by the entrance to get some fresh air. The cigar smoke has given me a headache."

"Of course, Countess." Nora cocked a narrow brow in Lord Witt's direction. "And I intend to watch you very closely, yer lordship. I don't take me responsibilities lightly."

Witt saluted her in all seriousness and then turned his smile and his attention to Victoria. "Are you ready?"

"Are you?" She beamed with excitement, not caring whether she could dance or not. She was going to enjoy herself.

Witt whirled and twirled her around the ballroom as if she were the best of dancers. She thought she'd drop from exhaustion after he taught her the intricate steps of the quadrille. Definitely not a dance for the inexperienced. Yet she couldn't have enjoyed herself more, she imagined, than if she'd been at Almack's. Maybe she'd conquer that famed place next. She smiled to herself, but it must have shown.

"What are you thinking, Lady Victoria? Your smile begs the question."

"I don't mind telling you that this has been the most exhilarating evening of my life." She kissed him on the cheek before realizing her fatal *faux pas*. "I'm so sorry." She pulled back, flushing several shades of pink.

"I'm not sorry in the least." Witt bowed.

Devlin materialized behind Lord Witt. "Well, you should be. Victoria, I think it's time we go. It's been a festive evening, and I'm glad you have enjoyed yourself, but I don't want you getting overly tired."

"I don't think that could happen this evening, my brother. But I understand your concern. I promise I will control myself if you allow me to remain. I simply responded to the thrill of the moment."

"That's exactly what I fear." He cleared his throat. "Victoria, it is late, and I know there are other ladies present who would like to dance with Lord Witt. Let's give them opportunity."

Victoria looked about her. "There are? I don't see anyone."

Devlin put his arm through hers. "Yes, my dear, there are. Excuse us. Witt, but since my sister has shown that she's a quick study on the ballroom floor, I would like to dance with her myself. You don't mind, do you?"

Witt grimaced. "If I cannot dance with her, then I can think of no one else I'd prefer she dance with tonight. She is by far and away the most enjoyable partner one could hope for."

At that, Devlin whirled her away. "You wear your feelings on your sleeve, Snoop. You must be more cautious. You are unfamiliar with the ways of men. And I believe Lord Witt is smitten."

"You are mistaken, Devlin. He is a kind man, and I think he's lonely."

"Be that as it may, he's a man, and I know how men think."

Victoria decided to change the subject rather than argue. "What were you arguing about with Lord Ramsay? Will it shed light on Lord Talon?"

"More about the reforms needed in the asylums that he vehemently opposes. Now think on it no more. Have you seen Madeline?"

"She said she was going outside because the cigar smoke was giving her a headache. Let's join her."

Devlin nodded. "Agreed." He led Victoria outside into the crisp night air.

"There you are, my Robin Hood," Madeline said. "And I see you've brought the Queen of Hearts with you."

Devlin wrapped his arm around his wife's waist. "You take my breath away, Maid Marian. What an enchantress you are."

Another coach arrived. A footman opened the door, and someone dressed as a gypsy alighted from the coach.

"I can still tell what you're thinking," the gypsy said and smiled beneath her half mask.

"Mercy! I thought you weren't coming." Victoria rushed to her little sister.

Mercy dressed in bright colors that drew the eye to her dark beauty.

Victoria laughed. "And you are dressed as a gypsy from the stories you used to make up to entertain me. How creative!"

Mercy swirled in a circle, and her colorful skirts swished around her ankles to reveal slippers the color of jade and an ankle bracelet. "You remembered."

"Mercy!"

Victoria watched her brother scoop their sister into his arms. Tears came to her eyes. Her heart nearly overflowed when they were all together.

"I haven't seen enough of you since you arrived. I'm glad you decided to come this evening."

"I got lonely for all of you after you left the house. I think a wee bit of the melancholy has been eating at me, so I knew I better join my family."

Devlin lowered her back to her feet.

Mercy laughed, a deep, rich, feminine laugh. "You are once again surrounded by women, my brother."

Victoria said, "Let's go in, and we can all take turns around the ballroom together. I was just getting good at dancing."

Mercy looped her arm through Victoria's and said, "Dancing. I can't think of anything else that chases melancholy away faster."

Madeline turned to Devlin. "You are coming, aren't you?"

"Of course. I wouldn't dare unleash the three of you without a male to beat off the onslaught of admirers that will surely persist through the rest of the evening."

Upon entering the ballroom, Victoria immediately noticed that Lord Witt was talking to Lord Ramsay. She glanced quickly at Devlin, who had an uncharacteristically deep scowl on his face. She whispered to Madeline. "Something is amiss between your husband, Lord Witt, and Lord Ramsay. And I would very much like to dance with Lord Witt again. Would you help me?"

Madeline and Victoria quickly informed Mercy of what was

going on, explaining that if there was any hope of dancing with an eligible bachelor, certain strategies would have to be taken, and quickly.

"Mercy, I'll introduce you to Lord Ramsay. He and Lord Witt seem far too deep in serious conversation for a masquerade ball. A jester speaking to Zeus and holding a lightning bolt, albeit an imaginary lightning bolt, is somewhat unnerving."

Madeline put her arm through Mercy's and gestured to Devlin and Victoria so they would follow. Upon approaching both Lord Ramsay and Lord Witt, the men's intense conversation halted abruptly.

"Excuse me, Lord Ramsay, Lord Witt," Victoria said and curtsied. "But I must introduce my youngest sister, Lady Mercy. She only arrived in London this week."

"Forgive my late arrival, Lord Ramsay," Mercy said. "I didn't think I would be able to attend this evening, but I'm so glad to join the festivities now. Your home is beautiful."

"Thank you, Lady Mercy. I hope you enjoy yourself this evening."

"Lord Ramsay," Victoria said. "I enjoyed spending time with your sister once again. Lady Phoebe is a wonderful storyteller. I think we are becoming very good friends."

"Indeed." A look of what Victoria could only interpret as annoyance passed over Lord Ramsay's features, but he quickly recovered himself. "I'm afraid my sister has taken ill and will not be joining us for the rest of the evening. However, I encourage you to visit at any time. I'm most certain that Phoebe would be pleased. She is sometimes shy and doesn't get invited to many parties."

"Should I go to her?" Victoria asked. "I can keep her company for a while."

"That's very kind of you, but she said she wants to sleep. She'll be fine. She suffers from severe headaches and prefers a dark room away from the lights. Her maid is with her."

"Would you like my brother to attend her?"

"That is unnecessary," Ramsay said. "This happens occasionally. She will be fine in the morning."

"Mercy," Victoria said, "I know you want to go shopping again, and I believe we should invite Lady Phoebe to go with us this time. If that is all right with you, Lord Ramsay? We would like Lady Phoebe to visit some of the shops with us in the very near future. Women can never have enough hats or slippers. And it takes forever to get a good pair of slippers made."

Lord Ramsay nodded. "I'm sure she would be delighted to receive an invitation. If you'll excuse me." He bowed and left them.

Witt moved closer to her side, and Victoria blushed.

Mercy smiled and quirked a dark brow.

Victoria tried to ignore her sister's knowing look.

"Lady Mercy," Witt said and bowed. "You are looking very mischievous this evening."

Mercy twirled in her costume and laughed. "Forgive me, Jester Witt, but I've given up formalities this evening. When was the last time you saw a gypsy curtsy?"

"You have a point."

Devlin and Madeline joined them.

"Are you enjoying yourselves?" Devlin asked.

Victoria smiled. "Immensely. And we discussed taking Lady Phoebe to the milliners and perhaps even placing an order for new slippers."

"I may join you for that excursion," Madeline said. "I would love to visit the *modiste* while in London and be fitted for a new riding habit."

Devlin grinned. "I know what comes of that. Several gowns as well."

They all laughed.

Witt said, "I was just thinking how much alike you and Lady Mercy look."

"Thank you, Lord Witt," Mercy said. "That is most kind of you to notice, for I do look more like my brother than my sister, but if one peers closely you can see we are sisters indeed."

Witt stared into Victoria's eyes until she felt a blush creeping into her cheeks.

"I see it now. There's a hint of similarity about the nose and shape of the eyes."

"Well, now that all the introductions are made and all the ladies plans are settled," Devlin said, "should we stroll about the gardens together?"

"I was hoping that the Lady Victoria would honor me with another dance." Witt kept his eyes on Victoria as he spoke, and goosebumps spread up her arms.

Victoria noticed that Devlin was about to intercede when his wife elbowed him gently, and he refrained from interfering.

"I would love to further test my dancing skills this evening, Lord Witt." And she placed her hand in his, and once again they indulged in a waltz that left her breathless.

Witt wondered how he'd allowed Victoria to talk him into this wild scheme. How would they ever be able to discover the killer at a masquerade ball? For heaven's sake, those in attendance could even come dressed as the killer for what the ton would term *amusement.* Much like some of them visit the poor souls at Bedlam for the purpose of amusement. If they could be the ones behind the bars for several hours, that would change their thinking. By heavens, he was beginning to sound like Ravensmoore.

"And what are you thinking at this moment?" she asked. "I must say I am enjoying my dance lessons, Lord Witt, and never dreamed it would be so enjoyable."

Victoria dazzled him as the Queen of Hearts. She simply mesmerized him, and that could make his job more difficult than it already was. If she found out that he was investigating her brother at the regent's request, she would never forgive him, but if the regent suspected that he'd allowed his heart to rule his head, he could lose his estate and title at Prinny's whim. He found himself in a quandary. Maybe Prinny wouldn't be so hard on him, but what if?

"It's taken far too long for you to answer, so I must assume that you are keeping secrets. I must warn you against such deeds because I have a talent for worming the truth out of people, and I will not allow you to be an exception. That would show weakness."

"I prefer to dance." He placed a hand on her waist and clasped her other hand in his. And for several minutes all he did was gaze into her eyes. He turned her around the dance floor until she could barely stand and he could no longer think of anything but her.

Before the dance had ended, though, Victoria said, "Don't you think we should once again try to decipher who it might be that is attacking the lords of Parliament before the night is at an end?"

"My dear Lady Snoop. Don't you remember what happened earlier when we disappeared into the garden? What if your brother comes looking for you? He or Nora or the countess is sure to do so if we are gone too long."

"Then we will not be gone too long, and we will stay within sight of others so no one may complain. I know what we can do." She grabbed his hand and pulled him out the French doors at the far end of the ballroom. On this side of the house, a dozen small tables had been scattered about so that guests could rest and spend time outside near the gardens but not be suspected of impropriety.

"Let's go over there." Victoria gestured toward a table another couple was leaving to stroll in the gardens.

This table was far enough away from the others that they would not be overheard if they kept their voices low, yet they were still in public and could not be suspect of any wrongful behavior.

Witt smiled. "Your chaperone just peeked through the window curtains to see what we are about." He pulled a chair out for her and let her settle in before he sat down across from her. "Now, what do you propose?"

"Let's start with things we may have thought suspicious this evening."

"If you mean lords and ladies dressed up in wild and unusual garb, that might be one possibility we could term suspicious."

"Lord Witt, would you please try to be serious?" Victoria accepted a glass of lemonade from one of the servants who were keeping watch of guests' needs. Witt picked up something a bit stronger.

"I saw both you and my brother speaking to Lord Ramsay tonight. What's amiss?"

"I wouldn't say anything is amiss. It's only that some things that men talk about are not fit for women's ears. Outside of that, I'd say he's more than angry about changing any of the asylum laws that are currently in place. Thinks it will cost him and others too much, and he doesn't want to part with his beloved coin."

Victoria thoughtfully considered this. "If Devlin can change Lord Ramsay's mind, then perhaps the others against the changes will follow. Is that what the problem is?"

"Possibly," Witt said.

"And was your conversation one of those conversations? Or is it that you want to keep useful information to yourself? I wish I had a ink and paper to write these thoughts down."

"That is a useful idea, Lady Victoria, but this is not the place. Perhaps when you are home you can write them down."

"A worthy notion. I will, and I think you should as well. Tomorrow we can compare notes."

"I will write my thoughts, but I don't know if I can share them with you tomorrow. Business of the estate and other duties call. My man of affairs is coming up from the country, and I've much to do."

"More important than catching Lord Talon? Your priorities are sorely in confusion."

"You, Lady Victoria, have never run an estate, have you?"

"No. But my brother has, and I can assure you that he is not thinking about business when there is a murderer on the loose. I would think you'd be more concerned about your own well-being."

"I don't want to argue with you, so let's discuss our ideas. I think Templar may be a candidate for further examination. Not that he personally could do this, but he is a lover of falcons and hunting. He probably owns more birds of prey than anyone in the area."

"So, you do believe that someone may be using raptors to maim and disfigure the lords of Parliament?"

"The injuries I've seen don't look to be the kind of thing made from a weapon."

"It's hard to imagine anyone being able to manipulate a bird to do such a thing. To what end?"

"That's easy, in my opinion. It's safer. It's the bird doing the attacking. The falconer is safely at a distance and more likely to escape. And maybe it's a way of distancing themselves from the attack. Perhaps the person responsible doesn't think of the attack as something they committed personally."

"I hadn't considered that, but it makes perfect sense that someone could indeed distort these attacks in that way. Unnerving, to say the least. But we still don't have any idea why this person has chosen to attack the lords. It must have something to do with the laws."

"Or perhaps it's a commoner who is angry with those who have money. It wouldn't be the first time someone committed a crime because they were jealous or greedy."

Laughter and applause spilled onto the terrace, interrupting their conversation. "Curiosity wins," Victoria said. She stood and rushed through the French doors. Her attention turned to the other end of the ballroom where a costumed guest entered on stilts to the enthusiastic applause of the audience.

"I think this may be the first time I've seen such an entrance. The man is to be congratulated," Witt said. "But I'm not pleased that he interrupted our conversation."

"He is very brave. I'd be scared to attempt such a trick. I think he is the only one dressed as a clown this evening."

The stilts continued across the ballroom for all to see, and the one trying to control them appeared to be growing tired as he swayed first from one side and then the other.

Witt said, "I do believe this guest may be a little bit out of control."

"Lord Witt, you must help him. If he falls, he could be seriously injured."

The clown weaved violently and came crashing toward them. "Help!"

The clown fell into Witt's arms, and both crashed to the floor.

"Lord Witt, are you injured?" Victoria asked.

"I don't think so. But that's more than I can say for our acrobat here. He looks to be out. You might want to get your brother," Witt said.

But when Victoria stood, Devlin was already making his way toward them. He knelt beside the clown as Madeline and Victoria stood over them.

"What took you so long?" the clown whispered.

"Simon?"

Victoria watched Devlin's features change and the tick in his cheek pulse as he clenched his teeth. Victoria bent over both Simon and Devlin. "I urge you not to lose your temper, my brother. I realize that you and Simon have some, what should I say, history? But don't foget to turn the other cheek. There are many people here.

And Simon, you better think of a way to save yourself, as I don't think my brother has a mind to aid you at this moment."

"And, Victoria, I am only human. Saving is not what I had in mind. Carving may be closer to the truth."

Simon's eyes widened, and he coughed and waved his arms. "I'm fine. Really. I just had the wind knocked out of me, but thanks to the Lord Doctor I am revived."

Devlin looked at Lord Ramsay, who seemed most amused. "Perhaps your footman can help this man out of his costume and into a chair where he may rest for a moment."

"Of course, Ravensmoore. Or Lord Doctor. Or Robin Hood." Ramsay smirked. "Whoever you are."

Devlin ignored him.

"Breathe deeply, brother." Victoria put her arm though her brother's arm as he rose from Simon's side. "You'll feel better as soon as you take your wife for a waltz. Really, it works wonders."

"I've more the impulse to throttle to find relief, though I cannot argue that breathing is of the utmost importance."

Witt laughed. "You must admit that the clown added to the excitement of the evening. And those stilts! I don't recall ever seeing such a thing at a ball."

'Nor I, Lord Witt. Simon has a history of practical joking."

Madeline comforted Simon as the footman directed him to a chair. He became quite attentive when she placed a platter of food in front of him. Victoria smiled. "This would be excellent timing for that waltz I recommended to Devlin. Go now. All is well."

He nodded, and Victoria watched as he led Madeline away from Simon to the ballroom's polished floor. "Nora," she whispered into her maid's ear as she turned away from Devlin.

"Yes, my lady."

"I need some fresh air. Would you join Lord Witt and I in the gardens? But a little distance would be appreciated."

Nora cleared her throat. "I'll do my best, but don't expect too much freedom. You are still an innocent in many ways."

Victoria thought about how much she loved this woman. Then she smiled. It would be nice to leave everyone behind for just a few moments.

She turned to Lord Witt. "Where were we, milord? Ah, yes. Trying to decide who in attendance might be the mysterious and deadly Lord Talon. I have a theory."

"And that would be?"

"Come walk with me in the gardens again."

Together they walked toward the French doors leading out onto the terrace. Nora followed.

"Each lord of Parliament will be meeting with your brother and me," Witt explained. "We want to find out if there is anything that would lead Talon to attack us, and it's too difficult to gain that knowledge at Parliament. Each man's pride is huge and not to be tampered with in public."

"But how can you do that, since you are a peer? Who will interview you?"

"The regent already has, and he's the one that's ordered me to carry out this plan. He takes it very seriously, but he feels it's a personal slight against him."

"Will you be the one to interview my brother, as well?"

"Yes."

She squashed the first thought that entered her mind. He couldn't possibly believe Devlin guilty of these heinous attacks. "My brother is a physician, Lord Witt. He tries to save the sick, not kill them."

"I don't believe your brother guilty, but I do have to interview him for information, just as I must interview the others."

They continued their walk through a maze of tall hedges.

"You think one of the lords guilty, though, don't you?"

"I'm not sure, and I don't want to debate this with you anymore. It was a bad idea."

"I think it's time I returned to the ballroom. My brother's right. I've overdone it again and grow tired. Forgive me."

"There's nothing to forgive. I imagine Nora is on the other side of this hedge."

"Of that you would be correct, yer lordship," Nora said from the other side. Victoria could hear the smile in her maid's voice.

"Can you see through this hedge?"

"No."

"Good." He bent his head to hers. The space between them evaporated, and his lips met hers in warm, fascinating wonder. She melted into his embrace. The pressure from his lips, molded so perfectly to her own, fueled her heart with an elixir more healing than any medicine had ever offered. One hand slipped behind the back of her neck, and she pressed closer to him. He gently broke the spell and kissed her forehead.

"I hope you sleep well, my Lady Snoop," he whispered against her ear and brushed a final kiss across her cheek.

# CHAPTER 13

There's method in his madness.
—WILLIAM SHAKESPEARE

ALON STROKED THE falcon's neck. "That's a good hawk. Good bird. Wellington. You surpass all my expectations. I knew you would. Perhaps we can scare them off this time for good. Let's hope so."

Talon waited until the time was perfect. He'd been watching Lord Davenport for weeks now. Studying his habits of going to his club after Parliament was done for the day, just as many of the others did. But Lord Stone did something routinely that the others didn't; he visited a friend every Wednesday evening precisely at eleven o'clock. A woman whose company he enjoyed more than his wife's, it appeared.

It had been very difficult to train Wellington, but he showed more skill than Goliath or even Pandora. Talon crooned to his favorite hawk. "No worries, Wellington. You are my chosen one and have a stronger body and a larger wingspread than all the others. That will only serve to help you. Take heart."

Talon's heart beat faster. "There he is, Wellington." He took the hood off the hawk's head, and Wellington looked about for his prey. The hawk's pupils dilated. He blinked until the gold cornea all but disappeared. Talon reached into his pocket and withdrew a piece of meat. "A special nugget for you, sweetest, and you know there will be more when you return." Talon fed the bird a piece of meat. He'd discovered the hawk preferred this morsel, and it made training him to attack a target easier.

Talon held the bird aloft and released the tether. A beautiful sight. Wellington soared high into the moonlit sky and circled the turret of a nearby building. And then he began his descent, circling his prey.

It had been important, Talon discovered, to look for places where few others were walking, for the bird could not decipher one target from another. So Talon hoped the hawk would know what to do. It would be his second attack at flesh and blood, and Talon could only hope that all the practice had been enough. The hawk wasn't used to flying in town, and this was far different than the open road where Lord Stone had been attacked. A greater level of difficulty for Wellington.

Lord Davenport approached the bridge crossing the Thames. Talon had learned that the water was an effective trigger for the bird and had spent hours training the hawk during the nighttime hours both at home and over the Thames to be certain of an efficient attack.

"Fly, Wellington, fly. That's it, that's it. Now!"

The coaches and carriages departed the moonlight masquerade ball one by one. Victoria enjoyed spending time with Mercy as they talked and caught up on their lives and dreams for the future. They climbed into Witt's coach along with Nora. Madeline and Devlin had decided to return to town in a separate coach so as not to crowd. "I believe tonight the most memorable night of my life," Victoria said. She sat next to Lord Witt and directly across from her sister.

"The ball was a delight." Mercy reached over and clasped Victoria's hand. "I loved watching you dance tonight. There was a time—"

Victoria watched her sister's eyes grow moist. "I know, Mercy. It's wonderful, isn't it?"

She thought about all the conversations she'd had with God while lying in bed, crying herself to sleep, wondering why she had to suffer so much. And then she said, "It's my miracle."

They chatted away the rest of the ride home. Victoria thought Witt only pretended to sleep, though she wasn't certain. His breathing was even, but she sensed he was awake and didn't want to intrude on their sister time.

Eventually Mercy succumbed to the swaying of the coach and slept. Nora smiled at Victoria and then turned her gaze outside on the opposite side of the coach.

Victoria admired the view of glistening water as she looked out over the calm expanse prior to crossing the bridge, the same bridge she'd traveled the same day she'd arrived in London. Her thoughts drifted into memories of that morning. The dense fog. The lurching of the coach. Following Lazarus into the mist. The injured man. Finding herself in Lord Witt's arms.

"Lord Witt," she whispered.

"Are you dreaming, Lady Victoria? I do hope it's of me."

She looked at him in alarm. "Did I say something?"

His warm gaze nearly melted her thoughts into a puddle of gibberish.

"You said my name."

Before she could answer, Nora gasped and pointed to the window.

Victoria's heart leapt. "What is it, Nora?" She followed her maid's gaze. There was nothing to be seen. "Nora—" The sight froze her ability to continue for a moment. "Lord Witt, do you see it? A hawk. There's a hawk soaring over the water."

Witt called up to the driver. "Stop! Stop the coach." He jumped out the door while the coach still moved. "Stay here. Stay inside the coach," he yelled over his shoulder, and disappeared.

Victoria looked at Mercy and both looked at Nora.

"Don't even think it," Nora said to them.

As if with one movement, they exited the coach and hurried onto the bridge.

Witt yelled, "Davenport, get back! It's Talon!"

Wellington soared on the light winds over the water, searching for his target. *Whoosh. Whoosh.*

There was no one else on the bridge, and that's exactly what Talon had hoped for at this late hour. "Now, now, now," Talon whispered and pretended he was the hawk with arms out at his sides, pretending to soar.

Wellington attacked head-on, his talons digging deep. Davenport screamed in agony and ran blindly across the bridge. "Help! Help!" The hawk returned in moments, and this time Davenport saw the raptor as it approached, and he threw his arms across his face. Wellington attached himself to the frightened man's scalp, and the hawk raked through the layers of skin like a razor through a man's beard.

Davenport leaped from the bridge into the water.

Witt dove into the frigid river after him. Victoria watched, her hand to her mouth, as Lord Witt grabbed Davenport's coat and pulled him to safety.

Witt called up to the bridge where a crowd of merrymakers from the ball had now gathered. "He's alive."

"No!" Talon cursed and raised his arm for the hawk. Wellington returned, and Talon fed him again. "I had not anticipated that he would jump into the water, my friend. It is my fault, not yours."

He'd recognized Lord Witt immediately. Lord Davenport would unfortunately survive. Talon hooded Wellington and turned his back on the view of the bridge and his failure. "The least he could have done was drown."

Talon returned Wellington to the mews. But knew he would be unable to sleep. He then decided to return to Bedlam to see the girl. To make certain she was safe and not being abused. The night he'd killed the two men, he'd been afraid that was going to hurt her. He'd acted with unexpected force.

He'd been relieved when he'd received word through a bribed guard that she was now under the care of the women in the east wing, the women whom Ravensmoore guided in a direction similar to what the Quaker, Tuke, was doing in York. Celeste would think it funny. He had them planting flowers and such on the asylum grounds. The best thing about this was that Talon might be able to talk to her in the light of day.

They weren't identical twins, far from it. But there was a resemblance. Talon had a plan, a plan so he could take care of his sister at home.

She needed care, for she was troubled and made poor decisions. He guessed he would have to admit that she wasn't the brightest of women, but she certainly didn't need to be locked up. His brother had locked her up so that he didn't have to be reminded of their mother. His sister looked very much like his mother, and that was something his brother could not abide. There were other reasons too. But his sister was a reminder, and Talon? Well, Talon was a mere inconvenience. His brother simply used Talon because Talon trained the best hawks. Little did his brother know that Talon owned the best of the hawks and trained his special hawks to a higher degree than probably any falconer believed possible.

✦

The next morning Witt stood on a street corner and read the *Times* headline: "Lord Talon Strikes Again. Lord Davenport Recovering."

"Pardon yer lordship," a street urchin interrupted his reading. "Would ye be Lord Witt?" Witt looked at the boy hiding his face under the rim of a hat. "I am he."

The urchin pressed the message into Witt's hand and disappeared into the throng.

Witt unfolded the piece of paper and read: *Lord Ravensmoore is next.*

"The devil raises his ugly head again," he whispered. He folded the slip of paper and placed it inside his coat pocket, looking into the crowd. He'd never find the boy, and it was a waste of time to seek him.

Witt looked for his carriage, and when he found it, he instructed the driver, "Take me to number three Grosvenor Square." He sat back against the seat and watched sightlessly out the carriage window.

*Talon is playing with me,* he thought. *He knows I'll go straight to Ravensmoore, but then what does he expect will happen? And what purpose would it serve to tell me? Why not deliver the message to Ravensmoore?*

"Driver," Witt yelled.

The driver lifted the hatch and asked, "My lord?"

"Take me to Carlton House instead."

Witt was told that his majesty would see him momentarily. He was finishing his bath. Prinny tended to preen, and Witt knew it would take far too long for the regent to dress. He boldly asked an audience while the regent attended to his long dressing affair.

He entered the elaborate dressing area. "Your Royal Highness," Witt said and bowed low, hiding a grin. The regent did not appear very majestic in his underclothing.

"Lord Witt, what is so urgent that you could not wait?" Prinny placed both his arms around the shoulders of two valets while the third managed to pull his majesty's pants over each leg without appearing to struggle

"Another threat, sir." Witt pulled the slip of paper from his pocket and held it up.

"Against who?"

"Ravensmoore."

"The devil! Have you told him yet?"

"No. That's why I'm here."

The regent shrugged off his valets. "Let me see that note." He grabbed the missive from Witt's outstretched hand and scanned it. "What do you propose?"

"I want to arrest Ravensmoore."

"You want to arrest him? Have you completely lost your mind?"

"Not yet, sir."

"Sit. Explain yourself." He turned to the valets. "Get out of here. I will call for you later." The valets scrambled out the door, but all threw Witt a look of annoyance as they departed.

Witt had a seat in an overstuffed chair after Prinny had seated himself. The room boasted dark cherry furniture and ostentatious gold silk bed liners and drapes that adorned a gigantic four-poster. A heavy scent of woody soap hung in the air.

"Now what is this about arresting Ravensmoore? I admit that I had doubts about the man working as a physician when there is no need for a nobleman to engage in such an activity so far beneath his station. But I'm finding his trade an asset for now."

Witt carefully chose his words. "Ravensmoore is no coward. If I show him that note, he will take precautions, but we don't yet know or understand what we are up against or who we are dealing with. As you say, sir, he is proving valuable, and he is a nobleman. If anything were to happen to him, it could very well impede our progress and strike further fear into the hearts and minds of those less sturdy. If he's in jail, he cannot be harmed with the guards we will provide."

"That makes sense. But how can you succeed?"

"You must order me to arrest him, sir. We will say some accusation has been made against him and that he will be released when the accusation is proved false."

"And since you seem to have worked this all out, Lord Witt, just what am I to accuse the man of that will make sense? You haven't shown anyone else this note?" The regent rubbed his thumb over the missive and frowned.

"No one but you."

"Then we will say someone has accused him of being Lord Talon."

Witt's immediate sense of doom must have showed on his face.

"You can think of something else that is plausible?" the regent asked.

"His family will never forgive you."

"No. His family and Ravensmoore will never forgive *you*. But it will all be cleared up eventually. Is that a problem, Witt? They will think that you have placed him under arrest, and they are only to know that you will do everything in your power to discover who has made this accusation."

"And how long will this charade need to be kept up, sir?"

"As long as is necessary."

"Then I will not have him arrested as long as I can keep an eye on his movements. I'll stay close, but when the time is right, you will hear of it and understand that danger is nearer than ever."

# CHAPTER 14

Doth the hawk fly by thy wisdom, and stretch her
wings toward the south?

—JOB 39:26

WITT FOLLOWED DEVLIN into the dregs of the city. He
wanted to learn more about this man. They passed a
crippled beggar who sat on the steps of a crumbling building. The
man looked to Witt like what he imagined a prophet from the Bible
would like. Long hair, but crawling with vermin, tattered clothes,
and feet almost bare but for the ragged shoes that provided little
protection.

To Witt's amazement he called the man by name.

"Hello, Mr. Morgan."

And to his further amazement, he stopped to speak to the man.
Witt slipped into an alleyway after being careful no robbers awaited
him. Then he watched Ravensmoore.

"How are you feeling today? Better, I hope."

"A bit better, me Lord Doctor. I'm not puking today."

"Do you mind if I look at your eyes, Tom?"

The man nodded. "You can look all you want."

Witt watched Ravensmoore pull down the man's bottom eyelids
and examine them. Then he pulled a pouch out of his bag, handed
it to the beggar, and wished him a good day.

As Devlin made his way down the filth-filled street, he noticed women stopping to curtsy and men stopping to bow. He never imagined these wretches would adhere to any of the social graces.

Witt followed at a discreet distance, but he noticed people staring at him. They'd obviously caught on to the fact that he was spying on the Lord Doctor.

When a group of three made their presence known behind him, an uneasy dread quickened his stride.

Devlin appeared out of a tumbled shack and grabbed his arm. "What do you think you are doing?" He turned to the men. "Thank you. He's a friend." He gave each of the men a coin.

"Now, why don't you tell me what you're up to, Witt? It's taken me months to build a level of trust here, and I don't need you ruining that trust."

"I wanted to see what you do during the times you aren't at Parliament."

"And why is that of interest to you?"

"Because it's of interest to the regent."

Devlin stopped. "What do you mean, it's of interest to the regent?"

"I wouldn't be telling you this if it weren't for Lady Victoria. I care about her, and I don't want to do anything to hurt her. If I hurt you by doing what the regent wants, then she will never forgive me."

"First, I will not allow you to hurt my sister, ever. Second, what is it that causes the regent so much concern about me?"

"You are not typical. The regent likes to know what to expect from his lords. He thinks he should forbid you to practice medicine. It's a trade, after all."

They continued walking through Southwark.

"And what do you think, Witt?" Devlin slanted him a dark look.

"I think your sister is right. You have a gift. At least, that's what she calls it. I wouldn't call it a gift but a skill. A gift is endowed by God, from what Lady Victoria says, and I'm not sure I believe in God."

A young woman about fifteen years of age ran screaming toward them with a bundle in her arms. "You are the Lord Doctor?" she asked. Fear filled her brown eyes, and tears streaked her face.

Devlin nodded. "What's wrong?"

"My babe's not breathn'." She handed the baby to Devlin. "Please make him breathe. I had to leave 'em for a while, and now he's not breathn'. Please, save 'im."

Witt took one look at the baby wrapped in nothing but rags and knew it was too late.

Devlin put his ear to the baby's chest and put a finger between its lips to search for anything that may have lodged in his throat. Then he looked at the girl. "I'm so sorry. There's nothing I can do. He's dead."

"No! Please make him live. Please. I can't lose 'im. He's all I 'ave," she wailed.

Witt looked at the girl's crumbling face, and something in him broke for her. He wanted to help her too. He wanted to do something.

She grabbed the dead baby from Devlin's hands and fled across the street.

"What happened to that baby?" Witt asked, still staring at where the girl had disappeared into what was most likely her home.

"Sometimes babies just die in their sleep and no one knows why. That baby died of starvation. Probably while the mother entertained men off the street to keep a roof over their heads."

Witt couldn't believe that a baby would be allowed to die of starvation. Horrific...and preventable. "Why doesn't someone do something? What about the church? Isn't the church supposed to do something?"

"The church is made up of people, and people are the only ones who can make a difference. Just as Parliament argues about what is to be done and what laws to make, they also have to take into consideration the needs of the poor."

"So, why don't we take better care of our poor?"

"Not enough people care to be the hands of God. It's as simple as that."

"I care. I want to help. Tell me how."

"I'd start out by praying if I were you, Lord Witt."

"I'm not even sure I believe in God, so why would I need to pray?"

"You can still help, but great wisdom comes through Jesus Christ. You may want to read Proverbs at some time. You may find it fascinating."

"What if I don't want to believe?"

"I'd ask you why."

"Because of the horrible things that happen in the world, and God or Jesus does nothing about it. That baby, for instance. God could have saved that baby, but He chose not to, if you believe. What sense does that make?"

"We may never understand the ways of God, Witt. But I believe that we live in an imperfect world with unrealistic expectations of God."

"What do you mean, unrealistic expectations? Is it too much to hope for compassion?"

"We should never lose sight of hope, never. Sometimes it's all we have when God doesn't answer our prayers or doesn't answer them fast enough."

"I don't know what to believe."

"Let me ask you why you have a fondness for my sister."

"She's different."

"In what way?"

"She's courageous. She's been through a lot with her illness, and she's not given up hope, and she's enjoying life."

"And where do you think that strength has come from?"

"I thought it probably came from the strength of her family."

"And where does our strength come from?"

"You are going to say from God." He smiled.

"Now you have the answer to your question."

Talon concealed himself among the branches of a tree and watched and listened at the open window outside Lord Winston's townhome in Grosvenor Square. He could hear Ravensmoore, Davenport (who unfortunately still lived), Witt, and Ramsay talking about lawmaking and the ongoing need for asylum laws that would protect patients. It made Talon rage inside, but he knew he could not let himself be caught. It would serve no purpose, and Talon very definitely had a purpose. He would change the changers so they could see what had been wrought.

Lord Davenport said, "We've done all that can be done. The asylums are far better now with the laws currently in place so that each asylum is monitored. We would know if abuses continued as before."

Talon watched Davenport gulp down his brandy and undo the last few buttons on his waistcoat so he could breathe more easily. The fat old slug. What did he know? And then as if reading his thoughts, Lord Ravensmoore slapped the table with his hand. "You have no idea of what you speak."

Davenport turned purple with anger. "How dare you!"

"How dare *you*, sir!" Devlin rose and walked around the elegantly laid table. "When is the last time that you visited Bedlam? Or you?" he said and pointed to Lord Ramsay.

"Don't preach at us, Ravensmoore." Davenport tossed back the black hair from the left side of his face. "Whoever trained that raptor to attack me should hang! He deserves no pity or lodging at Bedlam, and you expect me to feel sorry for him? Not bloody well likely. If I find out who did this to me, I won't wait for the judges to throw him into Bedlam. I'll kill him myself!"

"Lord Davenport." Witt sat back in his chair. "You were told not to walk about alone at night, and still you did not listen. I'm sorry for your attack and the scars it's left, more sorry than you know, but you risked your very life by walking over that bridge alone. Perhaps *you* should be thrown into Bedlam."

"You go too far, Lord Witt!" Winston stood and threw his napkin on the table as if inviting a duel. "I must ask you to leave. You do no good here."

"I've done all I can here. You close your minds, along with your ears." Witt stood and went to the door leading to the hallway. He turned and looked at each of them. "I don't know what will happen next, but you can be certain that this kind of chatter will not resolve a thing." He turned and couldn't help slamming the door on his way out.

"Witt!" Devlin caught up with him halfway down the street. "You overreacted. How are we to catch this monster if we don't work together?"

Witt scowled. "Why don't you ask Davenport that question? His stupidity almost got him killed."

"And what's your excuse? Too much pride?"

Witt's mind stormed with a hundred different replies, but he kept them at bay.

"I was just walking off my anger, if you must know. Nothing is going to happen here in Grosvenor Square. This is probably the safest place to be by oneself."

"I wouldn't care to risk my neck to find out, and my sister would not let me rest if she discovered that I did not try to stop you."

"I am not a child to be protected, Ravensmoore. You of all people should know that. I am not your sister's concern."

"Well, she thinks you are. The devil can dance on my grave if you think I'm going to sit around and see you break her heart!"

"No worries there. She wouldn't have me if—"

"If what?"

"Nothing. Nothing worth discussing. It can't be changed."

"You give her no credit for the incredible woman she has become, Witt. She fancies herself in love with you, and your pride stands in the way. As I said, I will not let you break her heart. Go on if you're too stubborn to use the brains the good Lord gave you."

"Wait." Witt knew he couldn't leave Ravensmoore alone, and if he was going to hunt tonight, then he had to have Ravensmoore out of harm's way.

Something stirred in the shrubbery. "Who's there?" He tried to see and knocked the leaves and branches back. "Who's there? Come out!"

A rabbit scurried out of the shrubs and across the cobblestone street. Witt laughed and took a deep breath. "Ravensmoore. Don't ask me to explain, but we must go to Bow Street immediately."

"Why now?"

"Because I think I know who Talon is. I'll explain on the way."

As they walked down the street, both men looked at one another and then skyward when they heard flapping wings overhead.

Victoria paced her room, sat down on her bed, rubbed Lazarus between the ears, and then got up and paced some more. "I'm troubled, my friend."

She stood by her window and stared out onto the mist-filled street. Lazarus put his paws on the window ledge and growled. A shadow at the edge of the street moved. She was certain of it. She held her breath, though she didn't know why. Perhaps because so many had been cautioned not to be out alone at night. Then Lazarus barked.

"Simon Cox!" She'd recognize that little person anywhere. She'd come to know Simon when he visited Ravensmoore. What was he up to?

Fear wrapped its ugly arms around her when she saw what followed Simon in the misty shadowed evening. A cloaked figure with a falcon tethered to his wrist. It couldn't be! Not right out in the open. And then she saw the figure slip behind a tree across the street. She had to do something, but what?

She raced from her bedchamber to her brother's. "Devlin! Madeline! Wake up, wake up, now!"

The door opened almost immediately. "Victoria, are you ill?" Madeline tied her wrapper and secured it about her waist.

"No. It's Talon. The man and his hawk were walking down the street and disappeared behind a tree. And Simon was ahead of him. Simon didn't know he was being followed, Madeline. What are we going to do?"

"Devlin's not here. I'll call for the footman and send one to Bow Street."

"We've got to do something, now. Lazarus!"

"No!" Madeline shouted. "You will not do this, Snoop. I forbid it!"

"But Madeline. It's Simon out there." She heard the urgency and fear in her own voice.

Madeline looked at Lazarus.

"Let him out, Snoop. But you do not leave."

Victoria raced down the stairs to the front entrance and opened the door. "Find him, Lazarus. Find Simon." She released Lazarus.

The dog bounded across the street, seeming to follow some invisible trail, and disappeared into the night.

"Oh, dear Lord, please don't let Simon or Lazarus get hurt. Protect them, Jesus."

Nora rushed down the stairs in her nightgown and cap. "What's happened? Are you all right?"

Victoria quickly filled her in while the footman raced to investigate and alert the authorities.

While Nora and Madeline were in deep discussion, Victoria ran for the stables, wishing she'd had the presence of mind to have pulled her boots on, as her slippers were a poor substitute. She knew she shouldn't go. It was dangerous and dark.

"Saddle a horse for me," she ordered.

"'Tis not safe to go out alone, yer ladyship."

"Then saddle a horse and come with me."

Within minutes Victoria and a groom were on their way.

*Forgive me, but I must do this. Protect us, Lord.* She took a deep breath as she maneuvered her mount out on the street. She kept her mount at a trot, praying all the way that she wouldn't hear the flapping of wings. With Talon in the area, anything could happen.

She called Simon's name. Surely even Simon would wonder at this madness and stop to see what the commotion was all about. She prayed he would. Her heart continued to thump along with the hoof beats. Sweat trickled down her neck and back. "Simon, where are you?"

She rode out of Grosvenor Square with the groom close at her side. The late hour had cleared the streets of all but the bravest souls, or those most dangerous. A harsh tug of her skirt made her gasp in fear.

"Eh, dearie. Got time for a gentleman of the street? Yer mighty fine, and I'm likin' the looks of yer horse too." He grabbed the bridle.

"Get away from me!" Victoria kicked at him, but her slippered feet were useless.

He caught her foot easily.

"Let go!"

The groom lashed out at the man with his whip. "Get away from the lady now."

But the stubborn fool held tight to her ankle.

Wings suddenly beat against her cheek. She pulled back in terror. Talons ripped at the man's face in front of her. She backed away, breathing hard. The screams of the man fighting the hawk echoed in the empty streets.

*Talon had rescued her.* Drawing in a shuddering breath, she scarce could take it in. Had it been intentional? Or had the hawk missed its target and attacked the man instead of her?

"Get out of here, Lady Victoria," the groom yelled.

She pushed her horse into a canter across the edge of the park until she heard someone call her name. She drew her mount to a walk and listened, hoping she would hear it again. "Victoria! Where the blazes are you?" It was Witt's voice calling from somewhere in front of her.

After a moment she saw him approach on horseback. Her eyes filled, and she blinked back her tears.

"Over here!" she called in a hoarse whisper. "I'm here." Her voice sounded foreign to her own ears.

"Victoria. What in the name of Bedlam do you think you're doing? Countess Ravensmoore sent word to Bow Street and—"

"It's Talon. He's here."

Witt dismounted, whisked her off her horse, and wrapped her in his arms. "It's all right. You will be all right. I sent the groom home. He said the man who attacked you ran off."

She shivered, and he held her closer until she caught her breath. "I was trying to warn Simon. I sent Lazarus after him." She stepped back from Witt and looked into his eyes. "It was Talon. He was stalking Simon."

"We'll find him."

"And where is my Lazarus? I haven't seen him at all. What if he's hurt? What if they've both been—"

"Don't think it. I'll find them as soon as I get you home." He hugged her close and kissed the top of her head.

She closed her eyes and melted into him.

Moments later Lazarus barked.

Victoria's eyes flew open. "It's him! It's Lazarus. Here I am, Lazarus. Come boy," she called. "Come here, Lazarus."

A shadow of movement burst through the bushes. "We're here, Lady Victoria." A funnier sight she'd never seen. Simon riding on Lazarus.

"I heard the wings." Simon jumped off the dog. "The hawk took off with my hat, the bloomin' buzzard."

Lazarus trotted to Victoria and nuzzled up against her legs.

"You, my little friend," Witt said to Simon, "are the luckiest of men this night. You could have been killed."

"Simon! I'm so grateful you are safe." She hugged him.

"I'm sorry to have frightened you and caused such chaos, yer ladyship. Forgive me."

"As long as you are without injury, you are forgiven."

Lazarus licked her hand, seemingly jealous of her attention to Simon.

"Oh, Lazarus. I thought I'd lost you." She knelt and hugged him, rubbing her hands over his neck. "Aren't you my brave dog." A sudden warmth dampened her hand. "Lazarus? You've been hurt. Witt. He's bleeding. We must get him back home where I can see what kind of damage he's suffered."

Witt gave Victoria a leg up. "Simon, you can ride with me."

"No. I'll walk with Lazarus. He helped me, and now I will help him."

Witt mounted his horse and the three of them and Lazarus hurried back to Grosvenor Square by going north on St. Audley Street.

When they arrived, Madeline ran to her. "Victoria! Are you all right?" She embraced her and then stepped back to make her own evaluation. "Don't you ever do that again."

Mercy ran out of the stables. "You scared us nearly to death."

Victoria quickly dismounted and hugged her sister.

"Do not under any circumstances risk yourself like that again."

"Lazarus has been hurt. He's bleeding. I must attend him. Mercy, will you help?"

"Of course. Bring him into the house."

Victoria started toward the house, then turned back to Witt. "Please come in, Lord Witt. I owe you a debt. The least I can do is to offer you something to drink."

Witt shook his head. "I must track Talon. I hope we discover where he was going."

"I'm coming with you," Simon said.

"You need to alert Sir Nate first, Simon. You've had a close call with Talon this evening. Take a footman and tell Sir Nate I'm heading out the western road. Then meet me there."

"Lord Witt," Victoria said. "Don't go. Please. It's far too dangerous."

"I must try. Nate will come or send a runner with Simon." Witt turned his horse and headed the direction of the western road.

"Fool. The man's a fool. And he worries of the risks I take." Victoria looked heavenward as she prayed for his safety. "Men!"

"My sentiments exactly," Madeline said and put her arm around Victoria's shoulders. "I have no idea what is keeping Devlin so long at Lord Winston's. Wasn't Lord Witt there with him this evening?"

As they walked toward the house, Victoria stopped. "Something's wrong. Lord Witt said he'd been at Bow Street, but he and Devlin had been together at Lord Winston's."

# CHAPTER 15

The LORD is nigh unto them that are of a broken
heart; and saveth such as be of a contrite spirit.
—PSALM 34:18

WITT LEARNED HOW to track when he was in the military. It was an important tool as a spy, and although he hadn't used it for a while, it was much like riding a horse. Once you learned, you never forgot how. He had to locate Talon. He couldn't face Victoria or the Countess Ravensmoore if he didn't. When they found out that Ravensmoore was in jail, Witt's life would look very bleak, very bleak indeed, perhaps even more so than when he'd first returned from the war.

Talon had been running east. Did he continue on in that direction? Witt didn't think so. He could have easily doubled back, and unless luck was on his side, Witt didn't have much chance of following at night with only the moon to guide him. Something kept niggling at him, though. Stone had been discovered in St. James Park. Not too far from the western road. Could Stone have been on the road that night? His wife hadn't thought so, and after a month Stone still hadn't regained his senses. When he did wake up, little could be made of his gibberish.

He tried to think like Talon. He imagined that Talon would do anything, try anything to outsmart anyone in pursuit. Witt decided to follow his gut instinct and continue west simply because Talon could more easily get to a main road and away from London more quickly if he did so. And Witt had told Simon to send Nate or a runner and didn't want to change his mind at the last minute and cause further confusion.

Still, there was the risk that Talon could have gone anywhere else, but he had the raptor with him. He'd been following Simon, which had been interesting. Simon wasn't a peer. But he did help Bow Street and he was a friend of Ravensmoore. Had Simon learned something that had put Talon on the defensive? If so, he needed to speak to Simon when he returned.

An hour later, he'd still found no sign of Talon.

*Whoosh. Whoosh.*

A hawk whisked past with a maddening flap of wings. Fear and anger burst through him. "Show yourself, Talon, whoever you are," he yelled. "Face me like a man, and don't use your hawk. But you can't do that, can you? You're a coward, and the only thing cowards can do is run and attack in hiding."

This time he heard something that confounded him. Awareness flared. Two raptors! But how was that possible? When seen, he only had one. What could…the horse! They were attacking his horse! The animal bolted.

He reached for his pistol.

And then he heard the sound he'd hoped never to hear again. Even worse than the hawks. Hounds!

"God, if You're up there, this would be a good time to let me know."

Witt scrambled to his feet and ran. He didn't think it was humanly possible to run faster. Still, the hounds closed in. His mind flashed to the terror of another evening five years earlier. He tamped it down, fighting the fear. He'd only have one shot and no time to reload. That wouldn't hold off a pack of hounds.

They had his scent now. The barking told him that much. The

four-legged devils pursued him across the field. He prayed again. For protection, for speed...that Victoria was right and God truly did exist. A God who would protect him. Even as he ran, he searched the area for a means of escape. The anticipation of fangs and teeth ripping through his flesh again sent another spike of fear through him.

Witt tried to scale a tree, knowing that he would be caught but at least spared from the beasts' fangs. His boots slipped on the bark and he fell to the ground. He glanced back. They raced across the field in the moonlight. Devil dogs. Too close.

He ran for the dense part of the forest, hoping it would slow the dogs' progress. "God, help me find a way." The prayer came easier now. He dove through the thickest part of the trees and brush. Branches slashed at his face and hands, a foretaste of the pain to come if he didn't escape the hounds.

He ran until he thought his lungs would burst, ran until he came again to a clearing, and then he heard a different sound. Not dogs but horses. Perhaps Nate or a runner, or Simon. But it could be a trap as well. He figured he could subdue one rider if it came to that, but not one rider with hounds to help him. Closer came the hoof beats and the hounds.

"Witt! Hurry!"

"Victoria?"

He swung up behind her and took control of the reins, not stopping to think about this fearless act by a woman he'd been teaching to ride. The hounds tore at his boots.

Then one of the hounds leaped onto the rear of the horse and tore into his coat as the others surrounded them. Witt pushed him away. The horse reared in terror. "Hang on!"

He squeezed his legs against the horse's sides to bring him under control. Another dog leaped when the horse's front legs came down. Witt used all his leg strength to stay on the horse and protect

Victoria. He urged the horse out of the fray of snarling teeth, but as soon as they avoided one, another took its place.

"Victoria! Don't let go! I'm going to fire my pistol and hope the dogs will back off enough for us to get away."

"They're trying to bring the horse down. Fire now!"

Witt nearly dropped the pistol as he struggled to keep the horse under control. He gripped it now and sent a shot into the air.

The hounds scattered, and they broke free and into a full gallop. Within minutes they had outrun the dogs. After he was sure they were safe, he reined the horse into an expanse of trees well off the side of the road. "We must rest your horse." The heat from her body mingled with the scent of her hair, an exotic mandarin and musk. "I don't want to see him go lame because of me." He leaned into her and couldn't resist kissing her neck.

"Lord Witt." She turned to him, and he captured her lips in a kiss that seared his soul.

"Forgive me, but you overpower me tonight." He thanked the invisible God that had sent Victoria to rescue him. And the danger of what she'd done overwhelmed him. "You must be mad to have put yourself in such danger."

He dismounted and pulled her down to face him, trying to control his passions. He could barely make out the shape of her face in the darkness, but he ran his thumbs over her face, sketching her features. His voice hardened. "Don't ever do such a foolish thing again. That's twice in one night that you've risked too much. You could have been killed!"

"And you *would* have been killed you, you idiot," she whispered back at him in the darkness. "Who else would have helped you if not for me? I don't see any of your Bow Street friends here to help. You—"

His mouth closed over hers. He'd never experienced a kiss so filled with desire. But was it his own or hers? He pulled her close

and marveled at the way their bodies molded to each other in perfection. He loved it that she kissed him back, yet with the abandon
of one unskilled in the art of kissing. He indulged himself for a
moment more before his gentlemanly senses kicked in and he
forced himself to pull back. "No. I will not take advantage of you,
Victoria."

"Then I must take advantage of you." She molded her lips to his.

He couldn't help but smile against the kiss.

"You really get yourself into the most difficult predicaments,
Lady Snoop. We shouldn't be out here alone. Your brother would
shoot me and I couldn't blame him."

"Are you a man or a mouse, Lord Witt?" Victoria asked. "I could
have sworn that a moment ago you were a man, but I see you've
turned into a mouse at the thought of being confronted by my
brother."

He kissed her again for that and fell right into her trap. "You,
Lady Snoop, are a tease."

"I am not a tease," she insisted. "I am most intent on kissing you
some more."

Victoria leaned in to him, and he wanted to kiss her again but
knew he could not. Heaven only knew what would happen when
she discovered the regent had asked him to investigate her brother,
and worse, that her brother was currently sitting in jail. All because
of him. He pulled her arms from around his neck. "Victoria.
Victoria?"

"Yes?"

"We need to leave. If your family finds you missing again there
will be h—"

She kissed him.

". . . to pay." He smiled.

"Witt, you really must quit swearing."

"I don't mean to offend you. It's simply a bad habit formed many years ago and quite frequent among the more masculine gender. We must leave." He put his hands around her waist and lifted her back on the big bay gelding before she could protest.

"But Witt, I do think we've lost those who were hunting you."

He swung up behind her. "That is not the point. You put your-self in danger. You are out with me and have no chaperone. And somehow we must get you back into your room unnoticed. If I were you, I would be very, very scared." And then he stilled.

"What's wrong?"

"Where did you leave Lazarus?"

"He's in the stable. I asked one of the boys to look after him when Mercy was finished treating him. His wound from Talon was not serious, thank God."

"And just how do you think we are going to keep this a secret now?"

"I bribed him."

"The boy or the dog?" Witt smiled. He always seemed to catch himself smiling when he was with her.

"Both, of course."

"Good girl."

Witt and Victoria arrived at the Ravensmoore stables at three in the morning.

"What have *you* done?" Madeline asked before they reached the stables

"Countess," Witt said. "I assure you that nothing untoward has happened to your sister-in-law. In fact, she saved my life."

"And that wouldn't have been necessary if you'd stayed here and not gone out alone as warned, Lord Witt."

"You're right of course, Countess. But I had to try and track Talon."

"Madeline. I'm sorry." Victoria said. "I just couldn't not take this risk. His life was at stake."

"Does he mean so much to you that you would risk your reputation and your neck? Did he not tell you what he's done?"

"What do you mean? He hasn't done anything except try to find Lord Talon."

"He's already had his suspect arrested, my dear."

"What are you talking about, Madeline? You make no sense."

"Lord Witt, would you care to tell Lady Victoria why you went riding off into the night when you already had put your suspect in jail?"

"I–I can explain."

"Sir Nathaniel sent a messenger to me." She turned to Victoria. "And you have much to learn of men, sister."

"Madeline? What's happened?"

"Devlin sits in jail while you and the man who put him there are out gallivanting across the countryside."

Victoria gasped. "What are you saying?" She turned to face Witt. "You didn't. How could you?"

"I had suspicions. I made a mistake. I'm sorry, I—"

"All these weeks I've been boasting concerning my ability to understand others. Confident in my knowledge from all those years I spent ill at Ravensmoore that I knew human behavior well." Victoria wiped angry tears from her cheeks. "How naïve you must think I am. You played me well, Lord Witt. Did you pay attention to me to hurt my brother? Did you believe he was not a man of integrity after getting to know him? I don't know you. I allowed myself to think I meant something to you. What folly." Her hand shook with rage, and she considered slapping him. Instead she turned away and dashed toward the house.

"I suggest you explain to the magistrate your error in judgment and have my husband released immediately."

"Of course, Countess. I—"

"Immediately, Lord Witt. I expect my husband home before dawn." She turned and followed Victoria into the house.

⚜

Talon fell to his knees on the western road.

"How could you lead him so close to us, Talon? It was not wise."

Talon railed. "Do you really think I tried to lead him here? I'm not stupid!"

Celeste tried to comfort him. "It's all right. They have gone, but the hawks could have been injured. And you loosed the hounds. How will you manage that?"

Talon put his hands to his temples and screamed, "Why do I have to do everything? Why do I have to manage everything? Can't you do more?" He pressed on his temples till he felt numb. "That's what I want to be this night. Numb. I don't want to feel tonight, Celeste. Use the needle."

"Do you think—"

"That's just it, Celeste. I don't want to think. I'm tired of thinking. We must get back to our homes. When we reach your lab, you will give me the needle, won't you?"

"Of course, Talon. I love you."

Later that evening Celeste did indeed administer the needle. Talon then went to his library and lay down on the settee so he would no longer have to think. He could dream. He would dream of a life without difficulty, a life where people you loved didn't hurt you and family was a place of safety, not a place like an asylum where all was chaos and pain. He wiped the tears from the corners of his eyes and drifted off to a place he considered heaven. Not that he believed in a real heaven, the kind after death, but a place of peace, where no one inflicted pain.

The rattle of keys alerted Devlin. The heavy door to the cells of the jail opened and swung wide.

A guard nodded. "Ye have a guest."

The heavyset man stood aside, and Simon Cox strutted past him, a basket in hand. The difference between the two reminded him of David and Goliath.

"Simon." Devlin raised an eyebrow and then sat on the floor to be at eye level with his old friend who grabbed onto the bars but remained standing. "What brings you here?"

"Not the aroma, I'll tell you that. Whew! This is worse than Bedlam. I'm here because of you, of course. The countess would never forgive me if I didn't follow her strict orders. I think she may have been tempted to throw her teacup at me earlier, but you'd be proud that she restrained herself. That was only because I promised to come and be certain you were not injured."

He set down the basket he carried. "I convinced the guard that I wasn't going to give you a weapon and let him search the goods. I had to give him a meat pie, but Cook and the countess knew that would likely happen so they packed up enough to feed three of you. And that includes me."

Devlin smiled in spite of his circumstances. "I must admit that I'm glad to see you, and I hope you can help clear up the mystery that has led to my incarceration. Has Lord Witt lost his mind?"

"That's for you to decide. All I can say is that he's collected an interesting amount of evidence against you."

"Blast it! Don't they know how ridiculous this is? I most certainly do not go around attacking my peers, though I've been tempted to wring some of their necks at Parliament."

"Shhh." Simon raised a finger to his lips. "This is no place to make such comments. The walls have ears. The evidence is false, of course."

"What do you mean? How would you know if it is false or not?"

"I haven't been able to piece it all together yet, mind you, but the regent supports you being behind bars."

"But why would Prinny allow this preposterous arrest?"

Simon shrugged. "Some of the so-called evidence has to do with Countess Stone."

"What's Countess Stone done?" Devlin raked his hand through his hair. His shirt clung to his back, and sweat rippled down the sides of his face.

"She's brewed a story about you being Lord Talon so you can draw attention to yourself and your usefulness as a doctor."

"That's a story beyond belief. I know everyone is desperate to put an end to these attacks, and Countess Stone has good reason to be angry at the person who nearly killed her husband. But I'm not Lord Talon."

"You don't have to convince me of that." Simon handed him a meat pie.

The whiff of onions and the taste of real food almost made him drool like Lazarus. "Heaven. Tell Cook I'm increasing her wages. Is Madeline well?"

"She's worried sick about you. She and Lady Victoria are plotting on how to break you out of this pigsty."

When Devlin nearly choked, Simon said, "Not to worry. I've got Bow Street runners investigating on your behalf."

"Simon. You know what will happen. Talon will attack again. And though it will clear me of all suspicion, it will result in more agony and possibly worse. Don't let that happen."

"You think I wouldn't prevent it if I could? I want this madman found as much as anyone."

"I know you do, Simon. It's just so frustrating not being able to do anything." He slammed his hand against the bars. "What does God think I can do from in here?"

"The same as Paul did while in prison. Pray."

"I do pray! That doesn't help me feel any less useless. I know the power of prayer. I want to do something to help solve these attacks."

Simon brightened as he gnawed through his favorite sandwich of cheese and ham. "That's it! You can help solve these attacks. You have no other way to help at the moment."

Devlin looked at Simon with what felt like fire flaming from his eyes. "Do you want to explain that before I'm tempted to—"

"Hold on, hold on. What do the Scriptures say? Be still. Be still and know that I am God."

"Sometimes you can be so irritating when speaking truth."

Simon grinned. "I know." He pulled a jar of lemonade from the basket of food. "The countess said you might enjoy this and that she sends her love and every mushy kind of sentiment you can think of that I can't bring myself to repeat so I had her write it down." Simon handed him the lemonade and then the missive.

"I will be your hands and feet for now. What do you want me to do?"

"Above all, keep my women safe. Madeline will help you with Lady Victoria. She's the one most likely to get herself into difficulty. She's naïve to the evil in the world, Simon. She thinks she's not, but you and I know better. Lazarus should remain by her side at all times."

Simon looked at the floor and cleared his throat. "I will make certain they are protected. Now, what about the attacks?"

"Simon?" Devlin narrowed his eyes along with his thoughts. "What's happened? What aren't you telling me?"

"Lady Victoria tried to warn me tonight that Talon was stalking me. After releasing Lazarus to search me out, she took a horse and followed when she saw Talon stalking me. She's fine. But a ruffian tried to attack her, and a hawk attacked him."

"What? The hawk attacked the man and not Victoria?"

"That's right. And Witt came looking for her. Unfortunately, when Lazarus found me, he'd been injured. I didn't even know it. Lady Victoria found blood on his neck. It looks like Talon, but he will heal according Lady Mercy."

Devlin took a deep breath and tried to calm himself. "I must get out of here. There is too much at risk. Victoria could have been killed, and you as well. Be careful, Simon. Talon is not to be taken lightly. He's not stupid, and if I'm not wrong, he has something very valuable at stake. He's delusional, possibly worse. Probably because of some evil that was visited upon him at an early age, but that can't be helped now. Talon must be stopped, and it won't be easy."

"But where to start?"

"Start with Lord Witt. He's the one who had me locked up. If he thinks I'm guilty, we must find out why. There must be more to this than Lady Stone's accusations."

"And if he refuses to help?"

"Lean close, Simon. Have him followed," Devlin whispered. "This is what else I want you to do."

# CHAPTER 16

For I know the thoughts that I think toward you,
saith the LORD, thoughts of peace, and not of evil, to
give you an expected end.

—JEREMIAH 29:11

*W*ITT SAT IN the library in his favorite chair he'd had the servants bring from the country. The thinking chair, the chair where he discovered things he was too busy to see earlier in the day or the week. This chair had belonged to his father and was quite comfortable. He'd worn his worry marks into its burgundy-colored arms over the years. It was a comforting routine, a ritual of sorts, which made him ponder other rituals. Rituals of celebrating birthdays, Christmas, and he wondered about Sundays, the Sabbath days. All those Sundays when good people went to church. Wasn't that a sort of ritual in itself? Wasn't getting out of bed? He wondered and rubbed his thumb against the material, the familiar, comforting material that allowed him to think about God and Victoria.

Who was he kidding? He didn't want to think about God. He wanted to think about Victoria. Problem was that Victoria thought about God. She believed in God, worshiped God, and prayed to God. The last time he'd prayed, it had nearly got him killed. But maybe it had saved him. After all, he was sitting here. Praying wasn't safe. Maybe because he wasn't good enough. Didn't you have to be good enough before God would pay attention to you? Victoria didn't think so, but then she'd been sick all her life and probably didn't have anything better to do than to pray to her invisible God.

And here he sat thinking about God and thinking about talking to Him. Maybe he was ready to join the poor souls at Bedlam. Poor souls. Where did those souls go when they were done with Bedlam? Why did they have to suffer? Why did anyone have to suffer? He supposed it was just the way it was, and thinking about it or some all-powerful Being that ran the whole mess might just get one admitted to Bedlam. But there was the ritual on Sundays, so maybe he wouldn't end up in Bedlam. Maybe he would go to church. Church with Victoria. He rubbed both thumbs against the material, and then he heard the door knocker and knew, just knew, it was Victoria. Blazes and brimstone.

Myron appeared at the door. "Lady Victoria Grayson wishes to speak with you."

A loud bark announced her chaperone, or at least one of them.

"And the monster."

Myron laughed and said, "Which one? The dog or the maid that accompanies her?"

"Both! I will see all three. Show them in."

"I believe they already are in." He moved out of the doorway where the trio stood waiting to be admitted.

"Myron, will you bring a pot of tea and some muffins, and whatever leftover soup bone may keep the dog occupied for a while."

"I'm so sorry, Lord Witt," Victoria said as she held Lazarus on his leash, "but I must talk to you and it couldn't wait. I hope you don't mind."

Witt stood and nodded. He wanted to tell her everything would be all right. That he wasn't the fool she thought him to be. "Sit down, Lady Victoria. Nora. I know what's brought you here, and I cannot help you."

"Why not? When Devlin didn't come home, I couldn't believe it. But then the more I thought about it, the more it didn't make sense. What aren't you telling me?"

He took his seat and tried to find the words. His mouth went dry. "Your brother must remain in jail for now."

Nora quietly took a seat in a corner. Victoria sat heavily on the settee across from him. "I don't understand. Why won't you help him? I've decided to not allow my pride to rule my heart."

He wanted to slither out the door like the snake she was sure to think him to be. She couldn't understand that he was only trying to protect her brother. If he told her about the threat, the note from Talon, she might even agree with him. But then she would tell Countess Ravensmoore and her brother would be told, and Prinny would have to have him released. He's like to lay the blame at the feet of Countess Stone, who had filed a formal complaint, though it didn't really make any difference because she had no proof of anything. He would just have to weather this storm. He'd come this far, and it would be too dangerous for Lady Victoria's brother if he were to share the real reasons behind Ravensmoore's imprisonment. He wasn't about to turn back now. But what price would he ultimately pay for this deception? "I cannot help him."

Lazarus pulled at his leash, and Victoria dropped it. He walked over and lay at Witt's feet.

"No. You wouldn't be so cruel. I don't believe you. You couldn't. Why?"

"I have my reasons, but I cannot disclose them." He rubbed his index fingers and both thumbs against the chair. He adopted a façade of calm. His heart raced with the misery he was causing, and sweat trickled down his neck. Had he gone too far?

Myron entered the room and set down a tray laden with tea and biscuits. Then he reached in his pocket and pulled out a thick beef bone. Lazarus sat up and drooled. Myron placed the bone on the floor by the dog, and Lazarus gratefully accepted the treat. He held the bone between both giant paws and began to gnaw at the gristle.

Witt felt like a traitor. And indeed, perhaps he was. A traitor to Victoria and her family and to possibly his own heart. *Fool!* All because he'd tried to protect a man he thought in serious danger. Prinny was not happy with the state of Ravensmoore's position in society, and perhaps that was partially the reason he'd agreed to Witt's plan. But Witt suspected that was not true. He thought Prinny genuinely concerned.

Tears formed in Victoria's brilliant blue eyes, and he thought he would crumble into a million pieces if she so much as touched him. But she didn't.

She stood. "Nora. Please bring Lazarus along. We've imposed on Lord Witt long enough. We must leave." She looked at him in such a way that he felt like a very small child who had broken the most important rule of the house.

"As I've told you before, I thought I was a good judge of character, but I was a fool. A naïve little fool. You knew just how to manipulate me and my family. I will not make that mistake again. I wish I'd never come to London. This is an adventure I could have easily done without."

She turned and rushed out of the room, Nora and Lazarus following close behind,

Witt hit the arm of the chair. Now what was he going to do? His mission seemed as though it'd been quite successful, and yet everything felt wrong. Hidden scars ached along with his heart.

Talon approached Bedlam with fierce determination after losing the opportunity to be rid of the dwarf. He was too much trouble. Talon had thought he'd be successful in his quest, but Lady Victoria had intervened and set that dog of hers loose on him. They'd never think him so bold as to take another risk so soon after the attack on Davenport. A different guard at the same door waited with the same greed. "Here are the keys. I've had her put in a cell by herself."

Talon's rage flared. "I should kill you for that," he hissed in the guards ear. Talon wrapped his specially made gloves around the man's throat and squeezed until tiny rivulets of blood trickled down his neck.

The guard winced in terror. "I won't do it again."

"The keys." Talon removed the gloves, carefully sliding them into his pockets along with the inlaid hawk talons, then held out his bare hand until the guard dropped the keys in Talon's palm. "I will see you later. Don't make me regret paying you."

The guard sucked in a deep breath and nodded.

Talon easily made his way to the east wing of Bedlam. When he arrived at the isolation cells, he whispered, "Chloe, I'm here."

"Talon?"

A thin arm snaked between the bars of the cell, if it could be called a cell. It was a hole in the ground, covered by bars, where they placed the "disruptives."

"It's me, Talon." He gripped her hand gently. "Let me get you out."

Talon unlocked the grate and grasped his sister's hand, pulling her into his arms for a quick hug.

"I have to get out of here, Talon. The Lord Doctor has been very kind to all of us, but if he remains in jail, I don't know what I'll do, nor the others."

Talon brushed back a stray lock of hair from Chloe's forehead. "The guard said this was the only way we could see each other without the others knowing. I'll make sure you return to the cells and not that hell hole."

"Talon." She wrapped her arms around him. "I don't want to stay here anymore. Can't you take me with you tonight? Can't we leave together?"

"No, Chloe. It's far too dangerous. You know the risks. We have to wait until my plan plays out, and then we will be safe. I'll get the Lord Doctor out of jail. I'll come back to you as soon as I can."

"But how?" Tears glistened on her cheeks.

"I have a plan."

Talon pulled a bit of bread and meat from a coat pocket. "Eat. If you were in the hole, you haven't eaten today, have you? Poor thing. Poor Chloe." He stroked her hair while she devoured the food.

When Chloe finished eating, she looked at Talon with big brown eyes. "Am I mad, Talon? Do you really think I should be here? I don't have the visions any longer."

"You are no more mad than I am, dear one. Now I must go. The guard comes." Talon pulled his special gloves on again.

"I'll take my blunt now." The guard held out his hand, and Talon dropped a bag of coin in his palm. "Take good care of her, and you will continue to make a better living."

He hugged Chloe close and kissed her cheek. "I'll come back. Do not worry."

Talon watched as the guard led Chloe away. She looked back at him in her tattered clothes and shoes.

"Don't leave me."

Talon's heart broke for his sister. He wiped away a tear and then retraced his steps. The other guard waited and made no attempt to speak to Talon.

The guard unlocked the door, and Talon paid him as he left, as he always did, for there was no other way he could be certain to help his sister. It was time he discerned more about the plans that Ramsay and the others discussed. He would need to be more prepared as time drew closer to his ultimate goal.

Unable to sleep after Victoria's visit, Witt decided to continue his search, no matter the cost. His guilt drove him to take the risk. He had to set things right, and the only way to do that was to capture Talon.

Witt pondered his dilemma as he rode west in hopes of finding some sign of Talon. If he told Victoria the truth, she would hate him. If he continued this deception, she would know or would find out, and then she would still hate him.

Flapping wings alerted him.

He looked up just as two terrifying, shadowy figures dove out of the dark sky. He threw himself from his horse.

But he was too late. The talons of both raptors sliced through his coat, ripping open his skin.

He muffled an oath. He didn't want Talon to know he'd been injured. Better to let him think he was still able to defend himself.

"You must give yourself over to the law, Lord Talon. It will do you no good to keep on running. Show yourself." He squeezed his eyes tight against the searing pain.

"'Tis unnecessary for me to show myself. You'll be dead soon enough and never know the truth." Talon's voice, throaty, raw, and unsophisticated, made Witt's mind race with dread. Was Talon going to finish him off? He was wounded, but not at risk for death.

"I'm not going to die, and you are not going to escape."

He collapsed against the earth, unable to lift his head. Still, he tried to keep up the charade. He kept the fear and pain out of his voice.

"Guess again."

The earth against his cheek trembled. Riders were coming. And fast.

And then he heard two people arguing. Someone was with Talon. The other... a woman?

"Another day," Talon said.

Hoof beats grew closer. "Witt, where are you?" It was Simon Cox.

"Over here," Witt yelled. "But beware. Talon is near." He heard hoof beats pounding as the riders drew nearer.

Suddenly two riders broke into the clearing. Simon's mount reared, coming close to trampling Witt in the dark. The second rider, seeming more tentative, slowed before barreling toward him.

"Lord Witt." Victoria's voice shook with emotion. She dismounted and came to his side. "Are you injured?"

"The raptors sliced though my coat. Be on your guard."

Simon called from his horse. "Don't tell me you let him get away? What direction did he take? I must pursue him."

Witt rose to his knees. "I wouldn't recommend that, Simon. He's not alone."

"Do you mean to tell me that there's two of 'em workin' together?"

"I think it's possible. I heard them conversing."

Witt reached out for Victoria's hand.

She steadied him, then quickly withdrew it. "We found your horse on the road." She would not meet his gaze.

Simon rode over and handed him the reins. "Can you mount?"

"I think so," Witt said, his voice shaky.

"You will need a doctor, and the best one is sitting in jail where you put him." Victoria's voice was thick with anger. "Maybe now you will see to it that he is released."

By the time they reached Witt's home, he was in agony. Even more troubling was Victoria's anger toward him. "Victoria, forgive me." Witt needed to tell her now. "I did it to protect him." He ached in his body and mind. Something didn't make sense. He shouldn't feel this weak. So weak he couldn't hold up his head. Everything around him began to spin. "I received a note," he said, his voice little more than a whisper. "Ask the regent." He felt himself began to slip from the saddle. Simon was beside him before he hit the ground.

All was beginning to fade to black when he looked up to see Victoria bending over him.

"Witt! What's wrong?" she breathed. "You are seriously hurt. Why didn't you say so? Oh God, forgive me for being thick-headed."

He groaned. "Not y–your fault."

❧

Devlin awoke in his cell to the jangle of keys. "Ravensmoore. You are needed at once at Lord Witt's home."

Devlin squinted into the bleakness to see who'd spoken. "Sir Nathaniel? Is that you?"

"Yes, but there is little time to explain. Simon came to me."

"What's happened? Are the women all right?"

Devlin sat up and stretched. "Why in the name of medicine would I want to go to Witt's home instead of my own?"

"Lord Witt has been attacked by Talon. It's in the name of medicine that you must go. Witt was attacked by two raptors. That is why you are released. You cannot be Lord Talon, but then, we knew that all along."

"My medical bag is at home."

"Lady Victoria has already sent for it. Come quickly. He is…not himself and grows more agitated by the moment."

When they arrived at Witt's townhome, Devlin heard Witt screaming and thrashing about. Victoria sat in the parlor with her hands together in prayer and Lazarus with his paws crossed on the floor. Victoria looked up. "Devlin."

"Sir Nathaniel Conant, this is my sister, Lady Victoria."

"I wish I was meeting you under different circumstances, sir." She curtsied.

"I am at your disposal, Lady Victoria. If you should need me, send a messenger to Bow Street." He tipped his hat and left them.

"Mercy is upstairs trying to help. She has your medical bag. Let me help, Devlin. We must save him. It's horrible, just horrible, that he is suffering so."

Devlin embraced her. "Stay here. I may need you later. But wait here for now."

He rushed up the stairs and entered the room where Witt lay in complete torment upon his bed. His valet, who introduced himself as Myron, stood nearby. Mercy bent over Witt and laid a cool cloth on his forehead.

"How long has he been like this?" he asked Mercy.

"The writhing and pain has increased moment by moment. He won't allow me to remove his shirt."

"The lady must leave," Myron said. "Then I can help you understand some things of importance."

"This is more than a raptor attack." Devlin approached the bed. Blood soaked the sheets beneath Witt's shoulders and back. If it were only the skin tears, he wouldn't dare lay on his back. He'd be trying to ward off as much pressure as possible. This was something out of the ordinary.

He turned to the valet. "Do you know of anything that he's taken that would cause him to hallucinate?"

"Hallucinate? No, yer lordship. He was fine earlier this evening. He's never been like this except perhaps once."

"And what happened then?"

Myron simply shook his head.

"We must get him out of his shirt and coat." He turned to his sister. "Mercy, I know you want to help. But please comfort your sister for now. I will send for you later."

She nodded and left the room.

Witt fought them like a madman as Myron removed his cravat and Devlin ripped off the shirt.

"What happened to him?" Angry, red, and raised scars covered his chest. Ravensmoore's soul ached for the man.

Myron said, "Most of the rest of his body is the same."

A knock at the door interrupted. "Wait!" Myron warned.

Devlin opened the door. "Simon."

"I've come to help."

"Not a word, Simon. Not a word leaves your lips about what you are going to see. Do not think about telling Lady Victoria. Do you understand?"

Simon nodded and looked past him to the bed. "He's dying, aren't he?"

"Not if I can help it." Devlin opened his bag and took out a bottle of liquid and a scalpel.

Myron asked, "What is that?"

"Laudanum."

Simon and Myron restrained Witt while Devlin forced the laudanum down his throat.

"Will it work?" Simon lifted a bushy eyebrow.

"We'll know in a few minutes."

It took time, but Devlin watched Lord Witt's body begin to relax. "Depending on the seriousness of the wounds inflicted by the raptors, he may need more laudanum within minutes. Let's turn him over."

Myron gasped. "Birds did that?"

"Not just birds," Simon said. "Hawks, big ones. All raptors are birds of prey. In this case, Lord Witt was the prey."

"But the gashes are so deep and long."

Devlin nodded. "It looks as though someone took a rapier to his back. The old wounds must have been very painful when he was attacked. Dogs?" He looked at Myron.

"Several. They mauled him till he was left for dead. I'm surprised they didn't tear him to pieces. I did not want to say this in front of the lady."

Devlin nodded. "Looks like they came pretty close. Let's strip him out of these clothes."

Myron and Simon went to work, and within moments boots and clothes were thrown into a bloody heap.

Devlin did a quick inspection of Witt's body to check for bruising and abrasions. The dogs had certainly maimed the man's body. No wonder he preferred the country life. Devlin covered him to the waist with a sheet and began probing the multiple talon wounds. Witt moaned but did not regain consciousness.

"What's this?" Devlin noticed a deep brown color running through the insides of the wounds the raptors had left on the back of his neck. "I think he's been poisoned. Talon is raising the stakes. I hope the laudanum together with whatever poison this is doesn't create some kind of reaction that will make him worse." Devlin labored to clean the wounds of their poison, but it had already entered the blood.

Devlin cleaned out four serious wounds and many other shallow lacerations. Witt started coming awake, and he was given another dose of laudanum since the first didn't seem to cause any ill-effect. When his patient was calm again, Devlin decided not to stitch the wounds closed but to leave them open and draining so as not to trap the poison.

"Simon. I think you need some fresh air. You look a bit green. The sun is coming up. I want you and my sisters to take Lazarus and visit the apothecary down the street as soon as it opens. Ask if they know of any poison that would cause such a reaction as Witt's had if a hawk's talons were painted with a poison. Mercy knows something of herbs."

"I'll get them now." Simon hurried from the room.

Devlin looked at Myron. "I want you to stay with him every moment. Don't leave his side. If he awakes, I'm sure I'll hear him. I'm going to rest, and when Simon and my sister return, you will rest. We'll alternate times to watch over him."

❧

Victoria awoke to Simon's pale complexion. "Is he dead?"

"No. But if I were him, I wouldn't want to wake up."

"I've been praying all night and asking God why this happened."

"It happened because he was a horse's rump and went off looking for Talon by himself. God can't make people use their heads."

"And didn't you do just the same thing, Simon Cox? Calling the kettle black."

Mercy intervened. "Stop it! Blame is useless and will solve nothing."

"Well, your guilt doesn't matter at the moment," Simon continued. "Your brother wants us to take Lazarus to go to the apothecary to see what Talon might be using on his birds. He said to use his carriage."

Lazarus jumped in the carriage and nearly knocked Simon out the other side.

"What in all things normal did you do that for?" he asked the dog.

"He likes you, Simon," Victoria said. "He remembers you."

"Then perhaps I'd be better off forgotten."

Simon opened the door to the carriage when they reached the apothecary store. Lazarus bounded outside as Simon wisely stood out of the way, and then he handed out Victoria and Mercy.

"Do you want me to ask?" Mercy looked at Simon.

"I am a detector, now, aren't I, my ladies? I know you want to be, Lady Victoria, but after all, you are a woman."

"Simon Cox! If I ever hear you say that again, I'll ask Lazarus to give you a ride into the Thames."

He scooted ahead of the women into the store. A bell jingled as they entered, and another patron clad in a heavy cloak passed them on the way out. Something about the customer niggled at Victoria's mind, but she couldn't place it. Maybe later something would joggle her memory.

The store was filled with bottles and jars of all sizes and assortments. Powders and liquids of different colors filled every corner and shelf.

A rotund man with a bald head tottered into the room. "May I be of assistance?" he asked. "And I prefer that dog of yours wait outside, my lady, before he destroys my store. I don't think it would take more than a single wag of his tail."

"I assure you, he's well behaved," Victoria said.

"He'd better be, or I'll be handing you the bill for anything he destroys."

"It's me that'll be giving directions." Simon looked from behind a wooden cabinet filled with interesting items. "Lady Mercy, I'll allow you to do the ordering. A man will likely die if you don't hurry."

"And you'll be need'n' what, my lady?" the apothecary asked.

Victoria covered Witt's hand with her own and prayed on her knees next to his bed. And then she whispered, "I love you."

Nora had arrived while they were at the apothecary and now slumbered in a chair on the other side of the room facing the window.

Witt lay on his chest to keep the pressure off his wounds. Again, the blood seeped through the bandages. He needed fresh ones, but she hated to disturb both him and her brother.

"My Lady Snoop."

She jerked her hand back. "Lord Witt, are you awake?"

Silence.

She held her breath, waiting for him to say something.

"Probably just the laudanum speaking," Nora said, standing behind her.

"I do wish you wouldn't sneak up on a body like that, Nora. You frightened me nearly to death."

"Ah, yer a long way from death, thank the good Lord. Many a time I watched yer brother pray over you just like ye was praying over Lord Witt." Nora held out her hand and Victoria gratefully accepted as she stood and didn't let go.

"I remember hearing him sometimes, and it seemed like a dream, for I could not reply, only listen, and it was so comforting."

Nora nodded. "Prayer's a powerful thing."

"But he doesn't believe, Nora. Or at least he's not sure what he believes."

"That never kept anyone from praying for those that needs it. And if ever a man needed prayer, Lord Witt does."

Devlin quietly opened the door, and Mercy followed him into the room. "How's our patient?"

Victoria let go of Nora's hand and went into her brother's arms. "He's bleeding through the bandages."

Devlin hugged her close. "Then we must change them and check for infection." He turned to Myron, who entered the room with two lamps burning bright with flame.

"Victoria and Nora, would you each take a lamp and hold it so I can see what I'm doing? Valet, you and I are going to change these bandages."

"Devlin, allow me to help you. I feel so useless."

"You may be taking after your sister. It was always Mercy who loved to help me when you were sick. If she were a man, she'd make a good doctor."

Victoria watched a glimmer of disappointment cross Mercy's features, but she hid it and focused on the task at hand.

Devlin felt Witt's forehead. "He's grown hot. Mercy, let's get to it." While Nora and Myron held the lamps, Mercy helped Devlin remove the bandages. When they got to the last layer, the beginning of infection was noticeable as oozing pus pulled away on the bandages.

"I'll need willow bark to place on the wounds, Mercy."

"I believe we got everything we'll need," she said with pride.

"Nora, I need warm water and clean strips of linen. Victoria, I want you to help Mercy prepare the herbs, and then you will help me clean these wounds."

A sense of usefulness penetrated Victoria's fears as she studied the ugly red wounds on Witt's back. The fresh ones looked horrible, and with the poison involved she imagined it would take a miracle for him to survive. But he'd obviously survived a previous attack that could have killed him as well. She remembered a scripture from the Bible saying that God has a plan for everyone, not one of disaster, but one of purpose and hope.

When Nora brought the water and strips of cloth, Victoria immediately went to work with Devlin's guidance. Mercy crushed the willow bark, and Victoria and Devlin cleansed the wounds with the powder. Within minutes Witt worsened instead of improving.

"What's wrong? He's in pain." Victoria looked to Devlin for direction.

"Blast! I think he's sensitive to the willow bark."

"What can we do? There's got to be something."

"A poultice to draw out the poison, if that's what's causing this, and then apply another of yellow root and thyme. Then we can only wait and see. We can use more laudanum, but this isn't looking good."

Victoria went to the kitchen with Mercy to make the poultice.

"We used to do this all the time for you, Snoop. Do you remember?"

Victoria wrinkled her nose. "I remember the smell. Wretched stuff."

"Put the dried herbs in the mortar and use the pestle to grind the herbs to a powder. Keep at it. We must make sure it's very fine. Good. Now," she reached into a cabinet and grabbed a bowl, "pour the herbs in here."

"How much water do we add?"

"Enough warm water to make a thick paste, but we have to be certain not to make it too stiff. Add the water in small increments, just until the mixture is thick, but we must be sure not to get it too thick."

Victoria followed Mercy's instructions until the herbs were folded into a paste that was substantial enough to cover Witt's wounds.

# CHAPTER 17

The quality of decision is like the well-timed swoop of a falcon which enables it to strike and destroy its victim.

—THE ART OF WAR (CHINESE)

ALON TOOK METICULOUS care of his hawks. The camouflaged mews held five hawks, but they were all special. Wellington, in particular, seemed almost human, like a beloved dog to its master. But all of them were like his children, and he would not abuse them as his father had abused him.

Talon's father had made no secret that he loved his hawks more than his children. Talon used to think that if he did things just right, his father would love him. That seldom worked. Still, he considered himself lucky that he wasn't female. His father despised females most of all. When his mother had been caught in a scandalous relationship with another man, he'd come close to killing her. So she ran off and left Talon behind. That's when Talon knew there was no God, and he knew there was no escape from his father's wrath. The anger he hadn't been able to vent daily on his deceitful wife, he'd taken out on Talon. The only time his father seemed to tolerate him was when he was with the hawks. So Talon became an expert in the art of falconry, that ancient sport of kings, in order to gain his father's approval, but still, it was never enough.

One day he made a new friend. Celeste. Celeste understood him, accepted him for who he was, and she wasn't the least appalled on the day he broke into tears because his father had beat him, chained him to his bed, and starved him for a week. That's when Talon knew he was going to kill his father, before his father had killed him first.

When his eldest and only brother was away at school, Celeste helped Talon concoct a poison. And that night, when his father entertained one of his women, Talon slipped the poison into his father's ale. When his father's lover awoke screaming the next morning, no one was the wiser. It was said that she'd killed him with her lovemaking, and everyone jested that it must have been the best way a man could die.

Talon's brother returned home from his studies and devoted himself to caring for the hawks. Unlike his father, he didn't torture or belittle his brother. He simply ignored him, and so Talon learned another skill, the skill of being a chameleon, of being unseen in plain sight. Then his brother started drinking, and just like his father, he chose to abuse Talon in that ungodly manner. Now Talon had to take steps to be certain the abuse ended. If they released the girl from Bedlam, she could only return to the house if Talon ended the terror.

Even if the lords weren't killed, they would be destroyed socially, and that was enough. Never again would they fit in, and then they would understand what that was like, how rejection hurt, and how shallow society really was when you needed acceptance.

But the one. *That* one. Would have to be destroyed.

His hawks accepted him, and that would have to be enough. He'd met someone at the masquerade, though. Someone that made him want to fit in again, and that hurt as much as it soothed and excited. She would never understand, and her brother was a lord as well. Her brother was different, though. He didn't fit in either, and Talon liked that: a lord who didn't fit in. However, Ravensmoore was not a chameleon. He stood out because he was different and because he was a lord. His sister was a chameleon, though, and she was desperately trying not to be one.

Lady Victoria was different. He liked her for her kindness and compassion. She was real in a society of fakes, and she had noticed him. She had commented on his costume, but then everyone was commenting on everyone's costumes. Wasn't that the point of these silly masquerades?

He would talk to Celeste. She would know what to do. After all, Celeste was a woman.

Three weeks after his attack and still weak but healing, Witt attended church with Victoria. He couldn't remember the last time he'd been to church. The cathedral was beautiful. The stained glass, the altar, the cross, the voices raised in praise. He wondered what God thought of him. He wasn't comfortable around others worshiping God. But Victoria had seemed to gain strength through her relationship with God, and she thought he could too. But still, it had been a long time.

He picked up the Book of Common Prayer, followed the service, and listened to a sermon about fear and prayer, and he wondered if the vicar had ever known the kind of fear that he'd known. The kind when you're about to die or at least you think you are about to die. He knew fear, and he didn't want it to control his life anymore. He didn't want to hide in the country, he didn't want to constantly relive the nightmare of his attack, he didn't want to always be proving to himself and others that he was brave enough, good enough. He wanted to be accepted as he was with all his faults and scars.

Everyone dressed in their Sunday best, but he couldn't help but wonder what went on in their minds. Hunting Talon had made him wonder about a lot of things. And he couldn't get his mind off the women he'd read to at Bedlam along with Victoria. They needed what Victoria called God's love. Yet the more Witt thought about God's love, the more questions he had. If God loved, then why did so many people suffer? Why the wars, the plagues, the madness, and the hopelessness? He couldn't make sense of it.

"Are you feeling better?" Victoria asked him as they sat across from each other in the carriage. Nora, sitting beside her, had already drifted off and snored softly.

"Physically, yes."

"But?"

"But I'm not going to give up."

"No. You are changing the subject. Deftly, I'll admit, but with the same result."

"But the regent expects results, as does the rest of Parliament, and I can't track Talon down."

"I think perhaps you should spend some time with Simon Cox. You know that Simon spent years in the asylum in Yorkshire. He knows more than you give him credit for, Lord Witt."

She looked beautiful. Her blonde hair curled gently about her face and her eyes, those magnetic blue eyes that saw so much in other people. And always held compassion. She was beautiful from the inside out, and although she seemed to have put her anger aside, he wasn't convinced she had forgiven him for thinking her brother had anything to do with Talon.

A twinge of pain creased his forehead where the wound healed. Only a scab now, but still he had headaches.

"You need rest. Make certain that Myron takes good care of you."

"I'm fine." He smiled at her. "Thank you."

"As I said, you need your rest."

"I'll rest later. For now, I have an appointment."

Witt found Lord Ramsay at White's, the only club Ramsay frequented, and he knew that Ramsay would be on the defensive. Ever since it was discovered that Ravensmoore was not Lord Talon, it had taken the wind out of his sails. He didn't like being wrong or being made to look wrong.

They sat at a corner table near a window. Ramsay's jaw tightened, and his eyes narrowed. He looked as though he might leave at any moment. Only the regent had ordered all the lords of Parliament to cooperate.

"So what do you want from me, Witt? You would have been wiser to remain in the country."

"I don't like this any better than you, Ramsay." Witt's thoughts flashed back to another time with this man now sitting in front of him.

"Do you practice falconry?"

"I do, and you already know that."

Witt looked at him for signs of nervousness. There was none that he could detect. "And how many hawks do you own?"

"None of your business."

"But it *is* my business. Prinny's made it my business. I am going to send someone from Bow Street to inspect your mews."

"Not while I breathe!" He stood and knocked the chair over behind him. "Questions are one thing, but invading my property is quite another."

"Why, Ramsay, do you have something to hide? How many men train your falcons?"

"One. And you, the police, or the runners are not welcome. You'll regret this badgering, Witt."

Witt remained calm and sipped his tea. "I hope you don't regret your decision, Ramsay."

Ramsay turned to leave.

"I wonder what you'll be thinking if Lord Talon and his raptors attack you as they attacked me. It's not pleasant."

He turned back and stared at Witt with hard eyes. "You shouldn't have been on that road by yourself. Isn't that what you've told everyone else?"

"After Simon Cox was stalked by Talon and the ruffian who attacked Lady Victoria was also attacked, I felt I needed to act."

"But you are not a member of Parliament."

"I got too close."

Ramsay leaned back into his chair. "I've heard talk, but how do I know you haven't concocted this entire situation?"

"Ask Ravensmoore. He helped me heal, but the injuries were deep." Witt did not want to share the information about the poisoned talons. He and the others thought it best to keep that information to themselves. In fact, they had not shared the information with anyone except the regent in order not to cause more panic. If it were known that someone outside Parliament had been attacked, there would be no controlling people's fear.

"If Ravensmoore attended you, then he's seen the other scars as well. Did you tell him what happened?"

Witt's thoughts grew dark. "You mean, did I tell him that you left me for dead while the hounds from hell mauled me?"

"There was nothing I could do, Witt. The rain kept my gun from firing. I couldn't have fought them."

"You didn't even try." Witt lowered his voice. "You could have thrown rocks or yelled at them or—"

"Stop. I made a mistake. I thought you were already dead. I didn't think there was any way you could have survived."

"You've never seen my scars, have you, Ramsay?" Witt slipped his fingers through his knotted cravat until the material lay lose around his neck.

Ramsay squirmed and looked about the club. A number of gentleman sat at their tables reading the paper, drinking, talking. "This is not the place."

"I think it is." Witt unbuttoned his silk shirt, and by that time, though his back was to them, others began to look and whisper.

Witt opened his shirt.

Ramsay's eyes widened in horror, and then he looked away. "I'm sorry. I wish—"

"I used to wish too, Ramsay. I used to wish that you would have at least tried. Most of my body is covered with these old scars. They only hurt when it rains or when I move suddenly. Now I have the new scars."

'Don't."

"I'm not about to cause complete panic here in the club. I'd suggest you keep the raptor attack our little secret, or I may have to remind Parliament that you left a fellow officer to die."

Witt raised the golden knocker at the entrance to Ravensmoore Manor. Soon Henry and his all-too-serious countenance opened the door.

"I would like to see the Countess Ravensmoore."

Henry, the butler, said nothing, only quirked a curious brow. He showed Witt into the parlor. "I will inform the countess that you are here."

Witt nodded and studied the room with a fresh eye after Henry's departure.

Three sets of windows were hung with heavy red drapes and pulled back with gold cords. The fireplace didn't burn today since the temperature had become unusually balmy for this time of year.

The walls of the room were cream. A chandelier hung from the middle of the comfortable setting, and two wingback chairs graced the area before the fireplace. A settee of red and gold sat against a far wall.

But what caught his eye was a portrait of Victoria with Lazarus. It had been painted when she obviously was not well, but she glowed with an ethereal beauty despite the dark circles under her eyes. She wore a blue gown that attempted to hide her thin and angular body as she lay upon a couch in a library at what he assumed was the Ravensmoore estate in Yorkshire. Lazarus sat on the floor next to her with his big head resting on her legs.

"She's beautiful, isn't she, Lord Witt?"

"Yes. Yes, she is." He forced his eyes away from the hypnotic portrait and turned to find the countess smiling at him. "I am sorry. There's something special about that portrait."

"You mean besides the fact that Victoria is in it?"

He bowed deeply. "I'm not doing a very good job of disguising my feelings, am I, Countess?"

"It's understandable. You're in love with her, aren't you?"

"Am I that obvious?" He didn't want to talk about love, not yet anyway. Not when he hadn't even talked to Victoria about his feelings. Didn't know that he should.

"Countess, I need your advice."

"You are seeking my advice about Victoria? How intriguing. Come, sit down. Tell me what is on your mind." She led him to the two wingback chairs. "I've asked Mrs. Miller to bring some refreshment while we talk."

Witt sat down and faced the countess. She was a beauty, and compassionate as well. Ravensmoore was fortunate in his choice of a wife.

"I want to give Victoria a special gift for her birthday, but I want your and Ravensmoore's thoughts on this before I proceed."

She leaned forward. "Out with it. I can take the suspense no longer."

"I think you know that I've been teaching Lady Victoria how to ride. I want to give her a horse."

Madeline clapped her hands together. "That's wonderful! She'll be thrilled."

"I want to know if you and your husband think it is overmuch to give such a gift since we are not promised to each other and haven't spoken of such matters."

"Do you plan to speak of such matters?" The countess arched a brow that made avoidance of the subject impossible.

"I don't think a woman such as Lady Victoria could bring herself to marry a man whose body is scarred in such a way that it would be quite repulsive to the gentler sex."

"That answer in itself tells me you do not know Lady Victoria well enough to speak of marriage yet. I suggest you give her the horse if it is truly a gift from the heart. Then I suggest you discuss your future with her, if there is to be any, and then come to my husband."

Mrs. Miller rapped gently on the door with a tray of sandwiches and tea. "Excuse me, Countess. I've brought your refreshment."

"How wonderful. Thank you, Mrs. Miller."

Mrs. Miller placed the tray and tea on the table between them and departed.

Madeline poured the tea. "Please eat. Mrs. Miller would be mortified if it wasn't depleted when you leave."

Witt bit into a heavily laden sandwich of ham and beef. "Your cook should be complimented."

"She reminds me of that daily, Lord Witt."

Witt swallowed and then asked, "So, have you forgiven me yet?"

"For having my husband thrown in jail? I am far more bull-headed than he is, but yes. Typically, it would have taken me longer to come to forgiveness, but since it cleared him from any suspicions, I have forgiven you."

Witt let out a breath. "I'm very glad to hear that."

Witt arrived at 3 Grosvenor Square the next morning. He knocked, and Henry answered, "Good day, Lord Witt." Henry bowed. "Lady Victoria will be down—"

"I am ready, Henry," he heard Victoria say. She hurried past Henry and met Lord Witt before he'd even entered the house.

"I'm very excited for my riding lesson, Lord Witt. Shall we go?"

He smiled. "If I didn't know better, I'd think you were trying to avoid someone. Are you in a hurry?"

She chewed on her lower lip for a moment. "No, not at all. It's just that," she leaned close and whispered, "I won't be able to ride astride if Nora comes."

"It won't matter. You'll have to ride side-saddle today. I'm taking you through Hyde Park. After you rescued me and rode out by yourself and your further practices, I expect you will do quite well."

Victoria's eyes widened. "On horseback? In Hyde Park? With you?"

Witt nodded and his pulse quickened. "If you'd be willing to be seen in public with me?"

"Of course. I'd love to test my skills out in the open."

"I'm not going riding," Nora said, joining them outside. "It's far too warm for me today. That's what I was trying to tell you upstairs, my lady."

"Then what do we do for a chaperone?"

Nora grinned. "I've taken care of that."

Nora had agreed to accompany her in the carriage but remained strangely tight-lipped about who would chaperone once they reached the stables.

"This day has turned out to be beautiful. The skies are cloudless and the bluest of blues for England in the spring."

Nora sneezed. "Must be something stirring in the air, for my eyes are itchy. The lilacs and bluebells paint a pretty picture. Ah, the Hawthorne trees are blooming. Bet that may be my culprit."

When they arrived at the park, a horse was tacked up and ready for Victoria.

"I do believe that's the most beautiful chestnut I've ever seen," she said. "He must be close to six hands."

"You are becoming an expert on horses." Witt said. "He's exactly six hands and a very hospitable gelding."

Victoria left the carriage to examine the animal. She ran her hand over his very healthy coat that glistened under the sun. "He's magnificent. I'm riding him today?"

"You can ride him every day if you'd like."

"What do you mean?"

"If you'll accept him, he's my birthday gift to you."

Victoria gasped. "I couldn't possibly! He's too magnificent."

"He's one of the horses I raised in the country. I'm beginning to think I'm going to raise many more. I rather enjoy it."

She looked at the horse from the front. Kind, gentle eyes looked back at her. "Oh, Witt, I don't know how I can accept him. It's too much  He's too much." She rubbed her gloved hands over the star on his forehead, the only marking she could see on the beautiful beast.

"That is why I got your brother and sister-in-law's approval first."

"You asked permission?"

Witt nodded. "Come. Let's ride, and then you can decide."

Victoria looked toward the coach where Nora was sneezing something fierce into her handkerchief. "But Nora's not staying."

Nora was pointing toward the stables and then waved her handkerchief as the coach moved off to take her back to Grosvenor Square.

"Wait for me," Simon called.

She turned and looked at the stable entrance.

Simon, wearing his scarlet waistcoat of Bow Street under his coat, rode out on a sleek black pony. "I am your chaperone."

Victoria couldn't help but laugh as she settled her foot into Witt's crossed hands and he gave her a leg up.

"There. How does that feel?" he asked.

"A very long way from the ground," she said and gathered her reins.

"You'll get used to him soon, I think."

Witt swung his leg over the saddle of his dark bay, a full hand higher than Victoria's mount.

Lord Witt and she walked their horses through the park. "This side-saddle will be the death of me. I much prefer riding astride, as I did all those days in the paddock."

Simon bobbed up and down on his pony, trying his best to post at a trot just to keep up with the long strides of their horses.

"Don't forget that I'm the chaperone here and there will be no riding so close together. I will remain in the middle."

"Why do you think I had you ride the pony, Simon? It wasn't because you are short. It was so you couldn't keep up with us." Witt grinned and looked down at Simon.

Simon looked up at Witt. "Lord Ravensmoore gave me this crop," he tapped it against Witt's boot, "and told me not to be afraid to use it on you if it became necessary."

"Simon Cox. Rest assured that I do not gallop across Hyde Park molesting women."

Simon harrumphed. "'Tis what you say. Your word is suspect because of your investigation of Ravensmoore." The pony snorted and laid his ears back when Simon used his heels to urge him forward.

"Enough, you two," Victoria said. "Even the pony grows annoyed. Such little boys you men can be. This gives us the perfect opportunity to discuss what must be done next to find Talon."

Simon rolled his eyes heavenward. "I await in eager anticipation of Lord Witt's thoughts on the subject."

"Simon!" Victoria stopped her horse. "That is enough. Just because my brother gave you permission to be, what should I say? Unruly? I expect you to be my chaperone, and that means being kind to Lord Witt."

"I understand, Lady Victoria." Simon sighed. "However, Lord Ravensmoore said—"

"And I'm saying we should set all differences aside." A light breeze kissed her face. The horse she rode put his ears forward and looked at a squirrel skitter across their path, but he didn't spook. She was enjoying this ride.

Witt asked Simon, "Will you share with us what you have learned during your own investigating, Simon?"

"And how do I know that you won't use that information against me?"

"I give you my word that I will not compromise your knowledge in any way. I only wish to help, and if we put our heads together rather than working in the dark about each other's knowledge, then we may actually be able to outsmart Talon."

"What makes you think so?" Simon asked.

"We all have an Achilles' heel."

When they had finished the long ride in the park, it was obvious to Witt that Victoria fancied the horse. "So, what are you going to name him?" Witt asked. "I believe the two of you were meant for each other."

Victoria smiled and looked at Witt and then at Simon. "I think you will both approve. I'm going to call him Sir Henry, for the founder of the Bow Street runners, Sir Henry Fielding. The perfect name for a horse that can be used in my detecting schemes."

Later that evening while reading Jane Austen's book *Emma*, Victoria's thoughts wandered to Witt's statement about an Achilles' heel, and she couldn't help thinking about what her Achilles' heel might be and how God viewed a specific weakness like that which Greek mythology touted.

She got up and went to her brother's library with Lazarus padding behind her. She looked through the volumes until she spotted Homer's ancient Greek poems, the *Iliad* and the *Odyssey*. Achilles was a handsome Greek warrior and paramount in the Trojan War. His weakness: his unprotected heel.

How does God see her weakness, her fear? Her Achilles' heel. She thought that Lord Witt might be her area of greatest vulnerability.

She opened her Bible to Romans 8:26 and read, "The Spirit also helpeth in our infirmities: for we know not what we should pray for as we ought: but the Spirit himself maketh intercession for us."

Victoria imagined that Achilles relied on himself and on no other. Perhaps that was his real weakness.

She closed her eyes. "Give me wisdom, dear Lord."

Victoria dreamed that night. A clash of heavenly angels fighting the army of Achilles. When she awoke in the middle of the night, her bed linens were soaked with sweat, and she felt as though she'd been in battle herself.

⁂

Victoria and Nora went to the park two weeks later. Nora was no longer sneezing, and blooms of pink rhododendron and even some early foxglove had appeared on the landscape with the bluebells and lilacs. The park sparkled a rainbow of color in the sun, and a gentle breeze drifted across the grass, stirring the oak and silver birch leaves. Victoria breathed in the scent of roses. Victoria was on horseback and Nora in the carriage. "The driver and I will follow you. Enjoy yerself, Lady Victoria, and your fine horse."

Victoria proudly rode her horse, Sir Henry. She patted his neck and marveled at the spectacular chestnut color and felt far more comfortable on this huge gelding than the smaller horses she had learned to ride on. It had been more than generous of Lord Witt. She wondered if he knew how much she loved him.

The wind blew gently and tousled Sir Henry's mane. She had fallen deeply in love with Witt while he recuperated from his wounds and discovered that he wasn't perfect, just as she wasn't perfect. And there was nothing like almost losing someone to make you realize how much you care.

Her thoughts focused on Witt and his scars. How had he survived the dog attack? And what did Lord Ramsay have to do with it? She knew there was some animosity between them, but she didn't know how it was related to the attack.

Witt had talked in his sleep in the beginning of his recovery. Devlin told her that it may be due to the laudanum, but she didn't tell Dev everything that Witt talked about. It wasn't like he was having a long conversation. He'd talk as if he were reliving bits and pieces of his past. Ramsay's name. Her name. The terror of the attack of the hounds during the war.

A girl waved to her from a grove of trees. She seemed to be in some distress. "Nora, see that girl by the trees? I think she needs help. I'm going to check on her."

"Lady Victoria, I don't see no girl."

"She was just there. I'll be right back."

"We can't get the carriage over there. You wave to me if all is well, and I won't fret. Then come right back and tell us what is needed. Maybe she's sick."

Victoria shaded her eyes for a moment to get a good look at where the girl had stood and then set out at a trot. She heard Nora yelling to be careful and something about not needing any more injuries to care for.

When she approached the copse of trees, no one was there. "Hello? Is anyone here?"

A young man appeared. "Please help. She's over here. I'm afraid we may need your carriage."

"I'll get the driver. Let me see the girl."

"Right here."

"Where?" Gnawing awareness grew. Something was wrong. She turned her horse, but it was too late, and she was deep enough into the shelter of the trees that Nora and the driver could not see her. And then a sliver of agony sliced through her leg. She could not maintain her balance or call out, and then the ground rushed up to meet her.

# CHAPTER 18

The way to love anything is to realize that it may be lost.

—G. K. CHESTERTON

WHAT DO YOU mean, she's missing?" Witt rose from his chair, and the agony that ripped through him had nothing to do with his injuries.

"Nora, tell me exactly where you were the last time you saw Lady Victoria."

Nora explained all that had happened and where Victoria had last been seen in the copse of trees near the middle of the park where she liked to ride. "I had the driver tie my bonnet on one of the trees so the area could be found. But are you strong enough, Lord Witt?"

Witt caught the look of concern that passed between Nora and Myron.

"Myron, help me get my boots on. I'm going after her."

"But you're too weak for a confrontation, my lord. You mustn't—"

"Now, Myron! If you care to stay employed. And then tell the groom to ready my horse. Listen carefully. You must inform Ravensmoore immediately. Return with Nora and tell him that I am going to the park to see if I can track them. But I have my suspicions that once again I will travel west toward the Ramsay estate. I think Talon has taken Lady Victoria."

Witt knew fear, but he'd never experienced this kind of fear. If he lost Victoria now... *Faith and prayer are the way.* He remembered her words. *Have faith and pray. It is the only way.* "Help me, Jesus. Help me save her. I can't do this by myself."

Witt rode hard, pushing both his horse and himself. He could easily track Sir Henry. His blacksmith used special horseshoes so his horses would always be easily identified. He focused all his concentration on finding Victoria. Where would Talon take her? The obvious versus the unexpected: which would Talon choose?

Nora's bonnet signified the copse of trees that Victoria had ridden into. It didn't take Witt long to find Sir Henry's tracks with the markings of the Witt crest, lion and owl. Trampled grass. No sign of anything else other than the tracks headed west. Ramsay had to be involved in this, but why? Something didn't make sense.

Once again Witt fought off a dreadful fear that settled in his gut. In an effort to keep his senses, he wondered what his Snoop would have done. Victoria loved a mystery and tried to link all clues together to solve them. "How would you think, Victoria? You've left me no clues."

She loved using Scripture to solve her problems: *Seek and you will find, knock and the door will be opened.* That was about seeking God. This was about finding Victoria. Were the two linked?

But Talon wouldn't be seeking God. Talon would be seeking revenge. But for what? He still didn't know. Talon loved his raptors, and raptors loved to fly. Talon might want to fly his raptors in the open to gain a sense of freedom. But what's the purpose of taking Victoria?

He must know something about her if he knew how to draw her to him and what she would be doing. He didn't have the raptors attack her! He wanted to use her. To get to him? Or Ravensmoore? Or for some other purpose? He followed the tracks until he came to the western road, and then he rode like all the demons of hell were chasing him.

Nora and Myron burst into Ravensmoore's home after nearly running over the lords and ladies of Grosvenor Square. "Lord Ravensmoore, Countess. Where are you?"

Lazarus barked to near howling.

Devlin opened his library door. "What's wrong? You nearly scared me out of my skin."

"It's Lady Victoria. She's been taken!" Nora began weeping, and Myron handed her a handkerchief.

Madeline stopped on the stairs, halfway to the landing. "No!"

"Tell me exactly what's happened!" Devlin grabbed his medical bag out of a nearby closet.

Nora quickly explained. "Lord Witt has taken the west road where he was attacked. And something about the Ramsay estate."

"If Witt's tracking from the park and possibly gone west, I wonder if it's better to search elsewhere in case he's wrong. I don't think…dear God, it couldn't be."

Madeline rushed to his side. "What couldn't be? What are you thinking?"

"I must go to Bethlem."

"Bethlem! For what purpose?" Madeline asked.

"Nora and Myron, stay here in case a message is sent. Madeline, we must keep our calm and our senses, for it appears that Lord Talon's behavior has escalated to the point of no return. He's kidnapped Victoria. He thinks he can get away with it, and he's come to the park in the light of day. Until now he hasn't taken any captives. He needs her for something. Perhaps he wants to bargain.

A trade? Ransom? I don't have time to examine this further, but you're coming with me. I might need your help."

"Thank God. I could never sit here and wait."

Victoria's vision was enveloped in darkness, and something covered her head. She listened. Birds. Probably hawks. She'd been duped by Talon.

*I'm a fool. Great detecting. I walked into a trap in the middle of the day. Brilliant!*

She tested the knots that held her hands. To her dismay her feet were also bound. *Lord, grant me wisdom, for I have not been using the mind You gave me, or I would not find myself in this predicament.*

"Hello. Is anyone here?" she called out.

No human responded, but hawks—she assumed they were hawks—flapped their wings.

She could smell the hawks. The molting, the droppings, their feed. She settled her mind and listened for other sounds. Crickets, frogs, an owl, then silence. Nature stilled. Someone was coming.

A door latch, footsteps. "You're awake."

Victoria didn't recognize the voice. It was neither deep nor soft, but settled somewhere in the middle.

"I am awake. Why am I here, Lord Talon? You are Lord Talon, are you not?"

"I am. Would you like something to eat?"

"No. What did you give me? It's made me a bit queasy."

"It's a unique physic that Celeste made for me. She assured me that you would not suffer."

"You lure me away from my chaperone, drug me, and bring me to I know not where, and you think I don't suffer? You are ill-advised."

"I have brought you some food and drink. Celeste will come

out later and feed you since you deny your hunger. For now I must leave."

"Who is Celeste?"

"A friend. I think you'll like her."

Victoria could hear him open one of the mews. And then she realized what he was about. "You're leaving with a hawk."

"Does that surprise you?"

"No. But I've seen what your hawks did to Lord Stone and Lord Witt. You will be caught."

"I know. But not until my work has been completed."

"What work? Why do you need me?"

"You, dear one, are a mere distraction to keep them busy while I attend to my work."

Victoria's mind raced. She wanted to stall him, to keep him from completing his work.

"Do I know you?" She focused in on his voice. Perhaps she could discover who this was, and if she was a mere distraction, perhaps she wasn't in any immediate danger.

"We have met."

Victoria stilled. She hadn't expected that response. "Where?" She pressed for information.

"I must go. I may not see you again. But if I don't, either Celeste or possibly Archer will attend you. Good-bye, Lady Snoop."

*How could he know my family's name for me?* Devlin and Madeline. Were they in danger? Did he plan to attack Witt again? Nothing was making sense. She had to escape. But how?

Witt's fear fought to overpower him, but he ignored the horrible feeling of helplessness. He had to think, and that was almost impossible. Never had he imagined that falling in love would make him feel so vulnerable. And then he saw something on the road glinting in the moonlight. He jumped off his horse and knelt. Victoria's necklace. And next to it, the hoof imprints of Sir Henry.

Witt rode on at a slow pace, listening for a rider or for the hawks. He came upon the clearing where he and Simon and the grave robbers had been the night of the storm.

*What was he missing?* Sometimes, Simon had said, you can't see what is in plain sight. It's right in front of you. Witt turned his horse a quarter in each direction. North, south, east, and west. And again. Nothing. And then he heard a whisper of memory from Victoria's lips. "Be still. Be still and know that I am God."

And so he stilled, and listened, and prayed. "Help me, God. Help me find her."

# CHAPTER 19

Ask, and it shall be given you; seek, and ye shall find; knock, and it shall be opened unto you: For every one that asketh receiveth; and he that seeketh findeth; and to him that knocketh it shall be opened.

—MATTHEW 7:7–8

A BIRD SETTLED ABOVE the trees and disappeared. Not a hawk. Perhaps an owl. He'd had to look higher to see it. And then he realized the truth. The answer lay directly in front of him. *The trees!* Talon had built a hiding place among the trees. A perfect place for his hawks. Why hadn't he seen it earlier?

As he looked for signs of this invisible place, Witt thought it would be difficult for Talon to carry more than his hawks into the trees. Victoria was light, though, and may not present a problem for someone like Talon.

He stood still and studied the design of the trees. He was beginning to doubt his own sanity when he saw what could be a change in the natural design of the trees. Witt looked at all the trees that surrounded him and saw no other such imperfection. Could it be possible?

He rode toward the spot but stayed close to the edge of the clearing to avoid detection. If Talon was up there, he may have already been noticed.

Witt stopped short of the area he wanted to explore. His heart pumped hard. If Victoria was being held captive here—and her captor, Lord Talon, watched over her—he didn't dare take any chances that might prove fatal for Victoria.

Witt dismounted and then scaled a foothold of rope that spiraled around the tree. When he reached the top, he realized this was a hunter's perch. The view was well worth the climb. In the moonlight Talon could target anyone on the road. It also made him suspect Talon wasn't here. If he had been, Witt would never have made it this far.

But was the lunatic hiding someplace else nearby? Watching him, perhaps right now? He shivered, remembering the attack.

He swept his gaze across the wood. The darkness made it almost impossible to see under the canopy of trees, but some moonlight filtered through the leaves. Then he saw the glint of a roof.

He descended rapidly, then scrambled to where the hut sat camouflaged, a nest for Talon. "Victoria! Are you in there? Victoria?" He couldn't see anything but felt the walls and floor of the hut. Bird droppings. Perches. A mews. But Victoria wasn't there. "Victoria!"

He moved inside the shack to have a better look.

Talon hadn't brought her here. A dead end. What was going on?

Victoria found it increasingly hard to breathe with the hood over her head. She caterpillared herself around the cage, trying to dislodge the covering. Groaning in frustration from her unproductive efforts, she stilled and prayed. Why was it that the more she lived in this world of confusion in London, the more challenged her faith became? When she was protected in the cocoon at Ravensmoore, she had relied totally on God and her family. But she was in a position to be taken care of, and now when she'd imagined her faith would bolster her courage, she found herself thinking that her faith was very small. "God, help me not be such a milksop."

She wormed her way around the cell until her head bumped into a protrusion on the wall. She rubbed her head against it, trying to figure out what it was. Nothing came to her. She lightly tapped her shoulder against it, and then her head where her hood fit more loosely.

The object seemed sharp, perhaps a hook, a bolt, or a nail. She couldn't imagine a hook so close to the floor, but perhaps a nail left over from the construction of whatever she was in. Whatever it was might serve as a tool to help her get loose. She pictured how she might use it to dislodge the hood, and her heart took hope.

She tried rubbed her head against it again. This time she felt the fabric on her hood catch.

She pulled back trying to dislodge the head covering. The thing wouldn't budge. And she was stuck in an even more uncomfortable angle.

Sweat trickled down her forehead, stinging her eyes. "This would be a good time to send help, Lord. Human or superhuman, man or angel is fine with me."

She mustered her energy, which was fading, and tried again.

This time the hood slipped from her face.

"Thank You, Lord." She gulped in a deep breath and started to cough. "So much for fresh air."

Her eyes couldn't fix on anything. Darkness engulfed her as much as it had when the hood was in place. She blinked to be certain they were open. Shapes began to form as her eyes became used to the dark. She was in some kind of elaborate cage. The hawks were in their own, separate from her.

She tried to scoot her body over to what appeared to be the door of her cage. She weighed her options, which seemed to be few.

Using the same nail, Victoria rubbed the rope around her hands in a sawing motion. "At last!"

She broke free, and then she quickly untangled the binding

from around her feet and groped for the door of her cage. She was yanked back by the force of her momentum when she hit the cage door. "What's this?" She felt behind her to discover she was tethered like one of his hawks.

"Dear God, this is too much." She followed the tether. It took precious minutes to release.

She sat for a moment, assessing her predicament. It was so dark she could barely see the hand in front of her face. She had no idea how far above ground the cage was. What if she opened the door and walked out into thin air? She shuddered at the thought.

She whispered another prayer. All she knew was that she needed to do something, start somewhere, but where?

She crawled back to the door and pushed. It didn't budge. But then, she hadn't thought it would, only hoped. A deep breath and another whispered prayer, and then she ran her hand up and down the side of the door, feeling for the lock.

She ran her hands outside the wooden bars and was rewarded with a splinter that dug deep into her left palm. "Ouch!" She pulled back and picked out the wood and then sucked on the wound, trying not to think about the bird filth that likely peppered her skin. Then she proceeded more carefully.

After several minutes passed, she put her head in her hands and allowed herself to weep. Anger overtook her inability to escape, and she kicked at the door. Immediately, the bottom gave way, but the top held.

Smiling to herself, she pictured the top, figuring out the locking mechanism before she reached for it. Then she stood on tiptoe and felt the strip of leather loped around the wooden slats. She slipped it up and over the slats and the door swung open.

Sarcasm gripped her. "That was easy."

She wondered if any traps might await her. She slid her hand along the side of another cage-like structure until her fingers found the crease and then followed the next structure to the left and followed it to the next, until her hand scraped against a wire cage.

A sharp peck and squawk shocked her and she drew back. Another hawk.

Her hand trembled and she stepped back to avoid attack, then side-stepped to the left, afraid of making a wrong move.

She bumped into a wall, but when it squeaked, she moved through it, carefully feeling her way, and then she fell into space.

$$\approx \! \! \! \Re \! \! \! \approx$$

Witt heard the screams and raced outside the shack he'd been exploring. "Victoria! Where are you?"

"Witt! Help!"

"I'm coming! Hang on."

A sudden tearing made that impossible, and Victoria slipped through the air and crashed onto Witt below her.

For a moment there was no sound. "Victoria?"

Witt's hand skimmed over her until he found her face. He lifted her head into his lap and stroked her hair. "Victoria. Wake up. You're going to be all right." He prayed that was the truth. "Victoria?" He tapped gently on her face. "Wake up."

"What happened?" She tried to sit up, but he kept an arm across her so she wouldn't move too fast. "Be still. You've fallen out of a tree."

"A tree?"

Witt gently helped her to a sitting position, keeping both hands on her upper arms for support. "Did you see him?"

"No. It's Talon's hiding place, at least for the hawks. He was here, he talked to me."

"What did he say?" Witt held his breath.

"He was leaving. He left with one of his hawks."

"He's going to attack someone again. But who is his target this time?"

"Can you ride?" Witt pulled her to her feet.

"I think he took Sir Henry."

"You'll ride with me."

Witt and Victoria rode in tandem and approached the bridge from the west as Devlin, Madeline, and Lazarus approached from the east. "Look. It's Sir Henry. He's all right." Victoria gasped. "We're too late."

When they got closer, they could see Ramsay's lifeless body, blood pooling around his head and neck.

Witt lowered her to the ground and dismounted.

Devlin and Madeline rushed from the carriage.

Victoria gathered her horse's reins and rubbed his neck. The warmth from his skin comforted her as much as she hoped to soothe him. Turning away from Ramsay's body, she leaned her head against the gentle animal and for a moment took comfort in him. Closing her eyes, she tried to maintain her composure, but what she'd been through had taken its toll.

Devlin was beside her in a moment and wrapped his arms around her. "You're safe now, my little Snoop."

She buried her head into her brother's shoulder.

Witt took the reins from her.

A sob escaped. "I was with Talon when he left the mews with his hawk."

"Did you see him?"

"No. He'd placed a hood over my head. He treated me like one of his hawks."

Devlin sent her into Madeline's embrace. He knelt next to Ramsay's body to check his pulse. "He's dead."

"Victoria. I'm so sorry this happened," Madeline said. "You've been through so much."

"Something even more dreadful is wrong, Maddie. I don't know what it is, but I think it has to do with a relationship involving Talon and Ramsay. I think Talon perfected the poison he used against Lord Witt. I think that's why Ramsay's already dead."

"I think you are probably right about the poison, Victoria," Devlin continued. "We need to go home."

"I'll wait here while you notify Bow Street," Witt said, rubbing his horse's forelock. "You better ride Sir Henry home. He doesn't seem to have any injuries, but it wouldn't hurt for the groom to rub him down and feed him."

Devlin nodded. "I'll go to Bow Street first. We have a puzzle to piece together, Witt. I think it will take all of us to figure out why Talon killed Ramsay."

Witt delivered Victoria safely into the coach, and then he handed Madeline in next to provide comfort and support.

"Witt," Victoria put a hand on his arm. "Who will tell Lady Phoebe?"

# CHAPTER 20

Give sorrow words; the grief that does not speak
whispers the o'er-fraught heart and bids it break.
—WILLIAM SHAKESPEARE

*V*ICTORIA LAY AWAKE for a long time. She no longer understood her own feelings. It seemed like a lifetime ago that she had been confined to her sickbed dreaming of adventures and romance.

She sat up in bed and swung her legs over the side. Lazarus nuzzled her toes, and she patted his back. Then she slid to her knees and, facing the bed, prayed for direction, the direction only God could lead her in. She had fallen in love with Lord Witt, but the future looked anything but bright. What was she going to do? What were they all going to do? Poor Phoebe. She couldn't stop thinking about how devastated she must be. How horrible it would be to lose one's brother.

Lord Ramsay was dead. Nothing made sense, making this mystery even more difficult—and dangerous—to solve. She was certain that it went much deeper than anybody realized, and she also felt certain she was the one who had to solve this puzzle.

She stood from her prayers and wiped away her tears. Moving quickly and quietly, she rummaged through her drawers for the garments she knew she must wear on such a night. Moments later she was dressed in black from head to toe. Lazarus looked at her and cocked his head to the side as if asking, *Where do you think you are going?*

"I believe I will need your services this evening, Lazarus."

It didn't take long to slip from the house. It would be difficult to find her way from the house to Lord Ramsay's estate. She knew her plan was fraught with danger, but these days she seemed to be taking more risks than she had ever imagined. Right now, however, she needed help.

Simon. She smiled as she thought of him. Yes, Simon would accompany her.

The problem was getting a message to him. She knew just where to find him, but she couldn't go there alone. "I'll just have to do what everybody does in this town," she muttered to herself as she headed to the stables. "Bribe someone. And I know just who that someone will be."

Victoria gently shook Nicholas, the stable boy, awake. "Shh."

"My lady!"

"Nicholas, I need your help." She quickly explained to him what she wanted to do, and he shook his head in refusal.

"Please, my lady, your brother will have my head, and then what will I do for a job?"

"If my thinking is right, then you would have no need of a job." Victoria smiled in spite of the dangers. "Understand this, Nicholas. Lazarus will not allow anything to happen to us. I promise you that."

Nicholas looked at her as if she had gone quite mad. He looked at Lazarus, and then he looked back at her. Standing up, he said, "I'm gonna be in a heap of trouble. But I'm gonna do it anyway. I think yer very brave, Lady Victoria, even if yer not very smart."

Victoria laughed. "Well, now, you might be right about that, but still it's something I have to do. Now, get us out of here as quietly as you can."

Nicholas readied a buggy and horse.

Victoria's heart raced as she, Lazarus, and Nicholas quietly pulled away from the house and disappeared into the evening in search of Simon.

Victoria sent Nicholas into the tavern to look for Simon. Moments later Simon met her outside. "Have you lost your mind, Lady Victoria? Do you have any idea how dangerous it is to be roaming the streets of London at night with no more protection than a stable boy and a big dog?"

"Simon, you don't understand. Get in this buggy right now. I need your help."

"I won't be gettin' into any buggy until you tell me exactly what yer about. Besides, that there's barely enough room for the two of you and the dog. Now I suggest you start talking."

"I'm going to find Lord Talon. Are you coming with me or not?"

"Well. Why didn't you say so? Boy, sit up on the horse and make room. Let's go." Nicholas jumped onto the horse's back from the buggy, and Simon hopped in the buggy with Victoria and Lazarus. "The beast takes up more room than two of me. Lucky for him, he saved my life that night Talon was hunting me."

"Listen carefully, Simon. I think I may have figured out who Lord Talon really is. But I don't want to make accusations until I have more proof. The first thing we have to do is travel the western road again. That is where the mews are, but Talon won't be there. He'll have already discovered that I'm gone. The place will no longer be a safe spot for him."

Simon scratched Lazarus under his big drooling chin. "And what exactly do you think we are going to do if we catch Lord Talon, or, heaven forbid, Lord Talon catches us?"

"I haven't thought about that yet. I just know we have to try and we have to try now." Victoria frowned in thought. "I think I might be able to reason with Lord Talon. After all, he didn't hurt me."

"Are you going to share this information with me, or are you going to keep me guessin'?" Simon placed one stubby hand on his hip. "Just who do you think Lord Talon is?"

"I can't tell you yet. It's a bit of a mind mystery. Very confusing."

"You sound more and more like your brother. I'm beginning to wonder if all this talk of the goings on of the mind that you and your family discuss is a healthy thing." Simon quirked a bushy golden eyebrow.

"Of course it's healthy. How else is anyone to discover how the mind works if we don't study it?"

"Perhaps it would be best not to know what goes on in most folks' minds. It could be quite scary and downright embarrassing."

"I'm not talking about reading someone's mind, Simon. I mean learning why people think the way they think. You actually lived in an asylum. My sister-in-law told me all about your adventures, so I know you are not naïve about such things."

"I wish I weren't so smart sometimes. But then I wouldn't be in a position to work with Bow Street. They like that I've been in an asylum. Think I know what it's like to be mad, but I never was mad, Lady Victoria. Just in the wrong place at the wrong time, is all. Anyone can end up in an asylum. Even you."

"I pray not."

"If your brother, a lord and physician, wanted you committed to Bedlam, do you think you would not end up in Bedlam? If you think not, then yer naïve."

"My brother." She stopped and one single thought came to her mind. "Simon. I think you may have solved another piece of the puzzle. Drive faster."

An hour later they arrived at the gatehouse of Thistledown Hall. "Now what are we going to do?" Simon asked looking up at the massive entrance and the darkened windows of the gatekeeper.

"We open the gate. No one is about, and we have to get to the house, which still lays another quarter of a mile away."

Simon shrugged his shoulders and hopped out of the carriage.

Victoria watched as he examined the gated entrance. She breathed a sigh of relief as the gate swung open making very little noise.

Simon stepped back into the carriage. "There was no lock. Nicholas, drive through before we are found out."

The horse walked through the gate, and they continued their late-night excursion to Thistledown Hall. When they arrived at the entrance to the hall, no footman came forward to greet them or hasten them away.

"Now what?" Simon asked. "We can't go in uninvited. I'm beginning to think I should have listened to my own instincts, but then who would have kept you out of trouble?"

"Exactly." Victoria agreed. She frowned, thinking about what could be done and how she could proceed with her not-so-well-thought-out plan. After a moment she said, "Lady Phoebe will be devastated from news of her brother's death. I'll tell the butler or footman that I am concerned about her and did not wish her to be alone. It's the truth, but it may also lead us to an even greater truth."

"I don't see how this is going to help us find out who Lord Talon might be." Simon rubbed the stubble on his jaw. "If you succeed in getting inside, what should Nicholas and I do?"

"Use your detecting skills to investigate the grounds. See if you can find anything that might give us some idea if anyone else is training, keeping, and breeding raptors. If you are caught, you simply say the horse pulled a shoe and you came to seek assistance since you don't know if I'm staying the night or not."

Simon nodded. "Let's see if we can bring anyone to the door."

Victoria and Simon climbed the steps. A black wreath of mourning already adorned the entryway. Simon pounded on the door with his fist, unable to reach the knocker and obviously wanting very much to be in charge of the situation. No one responded. Simon applied his fist to the door again, and just as he neared the third knock, the door opened.

A sleepy-looking footman stood before them. "'Tis late, and the household is aggrieved. What is it that you wish at this late hour?" He adjusted his wig.

"I am Lady Victoria of Ravensmoore. I wish to see Lady Phoebe. I thought it best that she not be left alone at this distressing time. Is she still awake?"

"The Lady Phoebe has asked not to be disturbed. I'm sure you can understand."

"Yes, of course. But we did drive in from London, and although it was probably unwise, I very much want to comfort my friend. Would you be so kind as to ask her if she will receive me? We shall await her answer inside."

Although annoyed at the request, the footman opened the door. "You may sit in the parlor." He pointed to the open doorway where a candle glowed. He must have been asleep in the room when they arrived.

Ten minutes later, the footman returned. "The Lady Phoebe asks that you come to her rooms. She is too distraught to come down to greet you and begs your understanding."

Victoria nodded. "I understand completely. Will you take me to her?"

The footman nodded.

"And my driver and chaperone need a place to stay the night. Can you have someone show them to the stables? Our horse has thrown a shoe and will have to be attended to in the morning. My driver is skilled and will be able to replace the shoe himself, so we will not further inconvenience anyone."

"I will have a boy show them to the stables, yer ladyship."

"Thank you." She then turned to Simon. "Simon, please tell Nicholas to wait with you until someone can take you to the stables. I will call you to the house tomorrow after I see how Lady Phoebe fares the night. And I think Lazarus should stay with you. He won't like it, but I'm not sure I should keep him with me under the circumstances."

Simon nodded. "As you wish, my lady." He winked and turned to the unfriendly footman. "Lazarus and I will wait outside with our driver till you send someone."

The footman accompanied Victoria to Lady Phoebe's rooms on the second floor of the manor home and knocked on the door.

"Come in, Lady Victoria," Phoebe called from the other side of the door.

"Thank you," Victoria said to the footman who had already turned away from her in order to take up his post once again or hopefully to send for help for Simon and Nicholas. Her thoughts turned to Phoebe as she entered the rooms.

"Phoebe?" Victoria looked into the dimly lit room and saw Phoebe lying in bed. "May I come to you?"

"Please do," her voice cracked.

Victoria went to the bed and saw immediately how red Phoebe's eyes were from crying, and Victoria's heart broke for her. "I'm so sorry about your brother. How can I help?"

Phoebe sat up a little straighter in bed. "I'm so glad you came." She dabbed at her tears with a silk handkerchief with the letter *P* on it. "I'm so lonely and distraught. I must talk to someone. I must...unburden myself. Can you hear me out?"

"What do you mean, unburden yourself, Phoebe?"

"Please sit down—" She patted the bedcovers. "—here on the side of the bed with me."

Victoria's heart beat a bit faster, wondering what it was that Phoebe wanted to tell her. She gathered her skirts and sat on the bed, taking Phoebe's hand in her own. "You're very cold. Should I stoke the fire for you?"

"No. Not now. I need you to listen to me. I want to tell you a story, but I warn you now that some of it will be hard to hear. Can you listen?" she asked. Fear or uncertainty entered the Lady Phoebe's eyes.

"Of course I'll listen."

"I'm glad he's dead." Phoebe stared into Victoria's eyes.

"What do you mean, you're glad he's dead?"

"I pray you won't judge me, my friend, but I never had the kind of relationship with my brother that you have with your brother. I hated him."

Victoria's mind raced in astonishment of this revelation. "You hated him? What do you mean? The first time I saw you at the theatre, he'd taken you out for your birthday. He seemed genuinely kind and wanted you to enjoy your evening."

"Yes. He wanted me to enjoy myself. So he wouldn't feel guilty later when he enjoyed me. Do you understand?"

Victoria's hand flew to her mouth. She felt bile rise in her throat. "No. Oh no."

"It's true. And it didn't start with him. My father also abused us. He would take turns using us, and then one day my brother discovered the truth. Instead of saving us, he joined my father in his debauchery."

Victoria suddenly realized what Phoebe had said. *Us.*

"Phoebe. You said your brother and father took turns using *us.* Did you have a sister?"

"Yes. I still have a sister. Her name's Chloe. We're twins. She's a patient at Bedlam."

"Does she look like you? An identical twin?"

"No. We are not alike in many ways."

"I know who she is." Victoria thought of the young woman who overcame her fear of Lazarus. The young woman who Devlin saved from the guard who was going to get an unwanted treatment the day they had visited.

"You met my sister?"

Confusing and frightening thoughts filled Victoria's mind. A thousand questions surfaced, but she wasn't certain where to start. She prayed silently for a moment, asking God for His wisdom and direction.

"Phoebe." She entwined her fingers with that of her friend. "Why is your sister in Bedlam?"

"That is difficult to explain, but I will try." Phoebe squeezed Victoria's hand and took a deep breath, as if preparing for a difficult journey. "When Chloe and I turned sixteen and it was time to enter society, my brother continued to find ways of preventing possible matches. Men were interested, and many made offers. But it soon became clear that no one was good enough for us. That's because my brother wanted us for himself."

Victoria didn't want to listen, as the story filled her heart with such horror and sorrow, but if she didn't, how could she know how to help? "So you both had offers from men who wanted to marry and yet your brother held you captive. Did you ever try to tell anyone what was happening to the two of you?"

Phoebe looked away and pulled her knees up to her chest, letting go of Victoria's hand and clasping her hands around her knees. "Chloe tried. I was too frightened about what my brother would do. I remained silent."

"What happened? What did Chloe do?"

"She committed the worst sin of all in the eyes of my brother. She fell in love." A sob escaped Phoebe's throat. "She fell in love with Lord Stone's eldest son, William. She told him everything. He was repulsed at first, and then he was angry. So angry that he challenged my brother to a duel. He raged against my brother and confronted him."

"Did no one try to stop them?"

"Perhaps even worse than the challenge was the fact that William told his father. Lord Stone forbade William to marry Chloe, telling William that if the accusation was true, my sister was ruined. This sent William over the edge of despair, and I believe that's why William followed through with the duel. No one but Chloe knew why. Even I didn't know why. My brother killed William."

"Phoebe. Look at me."

Phoebe rested her forehead on her knees for a moment and then, without lifting her head, she turned and looked at Victoria. Tears slipped onto her knees.

"What did Lord Stone do?"

"He confronted my brother, but there was little that he was willing to do. Dueling is illegal, and he made certain that my brother paid the consequence. But I believe that Lord Stone's pride was greater than his grief. I don't think he wanted the details to come out. It would cause further scandal, and he had six sons, so the need of an heir was of no consequence. There had been rumors that Lord Stone and William did not like each other. Perhaps he thought William's death a blessing."

Victoria gasped. "How horrible."

"When Chloe learned that William had been killed by our brother, she went mad. She grabbed a knife and tried to kill him. He had her thrown into Bedlam, and that is where she remains. But I plan to bring her home now." Phoebe smiled for the first time since Victoria had entered the room. "She'll have a real home, and I'll be able to help her get better. She wasn't mad in the way others are mad when they are put into an asylum. She was stricken with the darkest depths of grief."

Victoria didn't have the heart to tell Phoebe what she was thinking, that perhaps all these years in Bedlam along with being separated from her twin and the grief compounded by William's death plus the ungodly abuse of Chloe and Phoebe had taken a dark toll.

Victoria pictured Chloe and then decided to hold her tongue and save this discovery to discuss with her brother. He understood the darkest workings of the mind. Even those as dark as Victoria thought might be at the heart of this tragic mystery.

# CHAPTER 21

In the universe, there are things that are known, and things that are unknown, and in between, there are doors.

—WILLIAM BLAKE

*A* SLIVER OF SUNLIGHT cut across Victoria's closed eyes and beckoned her to wake. On that border between sleep and consciousness she dwelled for moments, and then she remembered.

"Phoebe? Are you awake?" She covered her face with her hand and rolled away from the unwelcome light. She squinted through her fingers to see if Phoebe still slept.

No answer came. She sat up and looked around the room as the conversation from the previous night came back to her.

She would never understand the horrendous actions of Phoebe's brother, the evil that had seeped into the sanctity of this wonderfully feminine room fit for a princess. "Phoebe?" she called out again. "Are you in here?"

Victoria roused herself from bed and explored the chamber. She performed the minimum of primping and morning routine and went in search of Phoebe. The house closed in around her in its silence, and her heart broke for her friend. What if Chloe could not be dismissed from Bedlam? How would that affect Phoebe? Victoria desperately needed to discuss this with Devlin and find out what was possible. She wanted to investigate further how Chloe had come to be in Bedlam and what Devlin thought her chances were for functioning outside the hospital.

She descended the large, ornate staircase, but she stopped halfway down. Her breath caught as a thought that had been nipping at her consciousness came back to her again. Full force.

*Could Chloe be Lord Talon?*

She could barely breathe. Surely not. Surely the thought was just the product of an overactive imagination.

Chloe? It couldn't be. Could it?

When Victoria reached the bottom step of the long staircase, a young maid informed her that breakfast awaited her. When she entered the cheerful breakfast parlor filled with the aroma of bacon, eggs, and fresh tea, she discovered that Phoebe was not there to greet her.

"Where is the Lady Phoebe?"

"My lady does not tell me where she's bound each day. But now with the death of Lord Ramsay, I imagine some things will be changing here at Thistledown."

Victoria's curious mind set to work. "And your name?"

The maid curtsied. "Doris, my lady."

"How long have you been in the employ of this house, Doris?"

"Five years, my lady."

Victoria speared a piece of bacon from the sideboard. "And does Lady Phoebe have no female companion or chaperone?"

"No. She didn't like going out much, and when she did, Lord Ramsay would accompany her."

Victoria didn't want to be indelicate and therefore merely said, "I think it will be very hard for her to be alone here while in mourning."

"She'll find a way to keep herself busy. Always has. Never been one to stay inside longer than she must."

"What does she do?" Victoria pushed for more details. "I thought she preferred her books and the indoors?"

"My lady loves the outdoors too. I 'spect she rides her horse. She's always had a soft spot for animals. Like you and that big dog Lady Phoebe talks about. You love the animals too."

"Yes, I do. And that reminds me that I must check on my driver and chaperone and see how the horse and my dog fare this morning. I will go to the stables as soon as I finish this delightful meal."

The maid nodded. "Will you be needin' anything else?"

"I'm fine and will not be asking more of you. You've been most kind."

The young maid left her to eat her breakfast, and afterward Victoria walked outside to find the stables.

The morning sun kissed her skin. The day promised to be unseasonably warm, and she longed to ride Sir Henry and feel the wind on her face. But that would have to wait.

She heard Simon issuing orders to someone about the horse and not being pleasant about his request. When she entered the stables, Simon stood on an upside-down bucket, arms crossed, watching over the grooming of the horses that would carry them back to town.

"Good morning, Simon. Where is Nicholas?"

"Readying the harness and lines, Lady Victoria. Are you wantin' to leave soon?" He jumped off the bucket and bowed.

"We need to go as soon as possible. I'd hoped to see Lady Phoebe this morning, but it seems she's already gone somewhere. Have you seen her?"

"She went riding by herself. Said she didn't need a chaperone since her brother was dead. There was no one who would care. She seemed quite cheerful for a sister in mourning."

"Simon. It's not for you to judge. People in mourning are not always clearheaded. I do wonder at her wisdom of riding out alone, though. Regardless, we must return."

Victoria noted the busy stable lads and grooms. Several horses whinnied, and she wondered if Phoebe may not be returning. It seemed something had caught their attention. Lord Ramsay kept a full stable.

"I'm going outside for a walk about the area, Simon. "

"Not without me you aren't, my lady. I'm not so stupid as to leave you alone with no chaperone."

"It's not necessary, Simon. Really, it's not," she said as she exited the stable doors.

Simon caught up with her and suddenly grabbed her hand. "Look. That's what excited the horses."

She followed his outstretched hand. Raptors. A pair of them circled the stables. They glided through the area as if on patrol for intruders They were hunting. But who was flying the falcons, and what or who were they hunting?

❧

Twenty minutes from town two riders approached. It didn't take long for Victoria to recognize her brother and Lord Witt.

"We're in trouble now," Victoria whispered. She couldn't ignore the twisting ache in her belly.

"I do hope you're not going to implicate me in this wild scheme of yours," Simon said with his usual aplomb. "It would be unfortunate for them to think this was my idea."

"I don't think you have anything to fear, Simon."

"Simon Cox! Have you lost your bloody mind?" Devlin rode up next to the carriage. "Nicholas, hold that horse!"

Simon puffed out his chest. "If you think I didn't try to stop this sister of yours, then you don't know me very well. Someone had to go with her, or she would have dragged poor Nicholas into the dark with her and only Lazarus to protect them."

Devlin flushed an angry crimson. "If I weren't so relieved to see you, Victoria, I'd turn you over my knee. What were you thinking? What were any of you thinking? You could have been attacked by Talon or highwaymen and killed or worse."

"Devlin, please. Lord Witt, can't you make him see reason?"

Witt's jaw tensed. "I'm on your brother's side."

Victoria let out a sigh. "I need to speak to both of you about an urgent matter. Forgive me for sneaking out in the middle of the night. I only did what I thought must be done. Please don't scold me like a little child. And don't blame Simon or Nicholas."

"Snoop, this is not Yorkshire. And even in Yorkshire you would not be permitted such reckless abandon. I suggest we return home to discuss what has happened and what is so urgent."

Devlin and Witt rode their horses on either side of the buggy and escorted them back to the townhouse. "Victoria, I want you to report to the blue drawing room in fifteen minutes, and Lord Witt and I will talk to you about what has happened since you left this house last night. Simon and Nicholas, I will talk to you later."

When Victoria entered the house, Madeline stood there, holding out her arms, and Victoria welcomed the embrace. When Madeline pulled back, she said, "Devlin was terrified for you when he realized you were gone. I've never seen him so worried. I love you, Victoria, but you should not have left. I know you've craved adventure for a very long time, but this was beyond the pale."

"I had good reason, but I'm sorry I worried everyone."

"Your brother is quite angry, but I'll try to help you." Madeline took her hand, and they entered the Blue Room.

Devlin followed a few seconds after Madeline had seated herself. Victoria paced the room near a set of curtained windows.

Devlin stood near the fireplace, his hand behind his back. "Snoop, come here."

Victoria went to stand in front of him. "I'm sorry. I didn't think about how it would worry everyone. I just thought about how lonely and sad Lady Phoebe must be."

Devlin wrapped his arms around her and pulled her close. "Do you have any idea how frightened I was for your safety? I would be in Bedlam myself should anything have happened to you."

"Forgive me, Devlin. I am sorry. I hoped to help solve the mystery without anyone's help. I wanted to do something on my own, to prove that I am a capable woman and not in need of additional male assistance."

"And?"

"And...I should not have been so hasty. As it turns out, Nicholas, Simon, and Lazarus were quite enough for this detection opportunity." She couldn't help lifting her chin a notch. She smiled. "Yet I suppose if I'd thought it through, I should have considered the danger to them and not just to myself."

Devlin held her back at arm's length. "You are never to take such a risk again, Snoop. I think I've echoed those exact words to you several times since you arrived in London, and yet they appear to fall on deaf ears. If you consider more risks in the future, please consider my sanity." He gently wiped a tear from her cheek. "Now sit down, and I will invite Lord Witt to join us as soon as you've had a moment to compose yourself."

Madeline said, "I'll ring for tea." She hugged Victoria close and quickly kissed Devlin before ringing the bell. "I'll have a light meal brought as well."

Within moments the four of them were seated, and Madeline poured the tea. She looked up as she spoke. "It's been a harrowing morning. Devlin, where do you think we should start? You and I certainly came to a dead end at Bethlem."

Devlin nodded and sipped his tea and then settled the cup in its saucer. He looked at his sister. "Snoop, tell us why you made the decision to go to Thistledown Hall in the middle of the night. Had you learned of something?"

"It wasn't any one thing. I worried about Lady Phoebe because I knew she would have no one with her last night when she was informed of her brother's death. I couldn't sleep. I thought she'd be distressed and in need of a friend. And because of Lord Ramsay's death, I couldn't help but think there was something more we were missing.

"According to Lady Phoebe, she has a twin sister."

Madeline gasped. "Where is her twin? Why does no one speak of her?"

"She's one of your patients on your ward in Bethlem, Devlin. It's Chloe."

"Impossible! I would have been informed if she were the sister of a nobleman. She's permitted access to the grounds. I consider her one of the healthier patients."

Witt shook his head in disbelief. "What if she were somehow responsible for her brother's death, my attack, and the attacks on the others? It makes no sense, Lady Victoria."

"There's more. Forgive me, Lord Witt, for talking about such indelicate matters in front of you. Lady Phoebe states that she hated her brother. That he and her father were intimate with Phoebe and Chloe." Victoria blushed, her eyes glistened with tears. Madeline reached across the table and held Victoria's hand.

"Go on, Victoria. You're doing a fine job of explaining all this. You're very brave."

Victoria took in a deep breath. "Thank you. Now let me explain about Lord Stone's connection."

"Stone!" Both Ravensmoore and Witt said simultaneously.

"Listen," Madeline remonstrated. "Go on, Victoria."

The three listened to the story that Victoria had heard from Lady Phoebe's lips.

Lord Witt asked, "Do you believe she told the truth?" He gulped down the remainder of his tea.

"I do believe her. But she said that Chloe is timid and could never hurt a fly, let alone kill their brother. Although they both hurt tremendously from what they've had to endure, I discovered that neither seems the type that could carry out the events that have led to this day."

Devlin stood and walked to a window. "I'm not convinced," he said, staring outside. "It's the word *seems* that can sometimes trip us up when searching for the truth."

Devlin turned and looked directly at her. "Snoop, I'm going to send you on an adventure. I want you to take Lazarus into Bethlem with you for a private talk with Chloe. I want you to spend the day with her, get to know her as well as you can. Ask all the important questions. I will give you a letter to present at the entry desk, and you will be permitted access to the grounds. Chloe has privileges, so that will be of no serious concern.

"I want you to find out how Chloe's story matches up with that of Lady Phoebe's. But be aware that Chloe will not have been told that Lord Ramsay is dead. I don't want you to tell her what has happened. I don't know how she might react to the news, although from what you've shared, I don't think it would devastate her. Reactions to death are unpredictable, and I wouldn't want you in harm's way.

"However, to be absolutely certain that you are protected, I want you to take Lord Witt with you. Witt, are you up to the task? Are you strong enough?"

"I would lay my life down for Lady Victoria. You have no need to worry," he said, all the while looking at Victoria while he spoke to Devlin

"While the two of you attend to Lady Chloe, I will talk to Simon and Nicholas and find out what they experienced at Thistledown Hall. Then I will take my wife along to pay our respects to Lady Phoebe. She may need help planning the funeral for her brother."

⚜

Victoria arrived at the entry area of Bethlem, along with Witt and Lazarus, where all visitors had to report upon arrival if they wished to see anyone. She'd brought a large hamper of food with them, which Witt carried. "We wish to visit a patient in the west wing who is receiving treatment from my brother, Lord Ravensmoore." She handed the missive that Devlin had written to the surly-looking clerk, who scanned the request.

"All appears to be in order. However, I must insist that the dog not enter. It is against the rules."

"I believe my brother explained in his letter," Victoria pointed to the note, "that Lazarus would be permitted to attend this visit with us. It's very important for the patient's well-being."

"No dogs. I must insist."

"And I must insist," Witt stepped forward, and at the exact moment, as if directed, Lazarus stood and put his paws on the desk and stared into the clerk's astounded face, "that we follow orders from Lord Ravensmoore."

The flustered clerk reared back in his chair. "I will have one of the guards escort you to the area, and then you may proceed outside with this patient. If she acts up, there will be guards about the grounds who will assist you."

"Thank you." Victoria nodded her approval, reached into the hamper, and pulled out a ham sandwich wrapped tightly and tied with a bow for just such an occasion and handed the offering to the clerk, and then she turned to Witt with a smile of accomplishment. He offered her his arm as if they were being escorted into dinner as the guard led the way for them into the depths of Bedlam's corridors.

When they reached the room where they'd previously met with the Chloe and the other women, no one was there. "Where is everyone?" Victoria asked.

"Must be back in their cells," said the heavily whiskered guard.

"Their cells? But I thought—" She looked helplessly at Witt.

"I know the way." The guard continued down the corridor and led them through a maze that dead-ended into two huge barred areas.

Crying and singing mixed with voices that whispered to non-existent others kept some of the women company, in their minds at least. Others walked in tiny circles, and they seemed to concentrate on the ground as if searching for something lost. The smell of urine and feces mixed in straw made Lazarus whine and brought Victoria close to vomiting. She watched Witt swallow a lump in his throat and harden himself to the sights, sounds, and smells as they proceeded

Victoria chewed her lower lip while they walked past the dozens and dozens of women confined in the dank, dingy areas they called cells. "God, help them," she whispered. "What a horrible existence."

Witt put his arm around her and pulled her close to his side as they continued looking for Chloe. "It's a bloody shame to be housed like this. Doesn't anyone care about these people?" he asked the guard.

"They're no better than animals. That's why they are kept in cages. Today the woman Chloe will get to go outside because of you. Just like an animal being took outside to relieve itself."

Witt grabbed the guard by the neck and threw him up against the bars of the cell. Witt's gray eyes glinted like cold steel. "Don't ever let me hear you talk like that again. If you do, I will make certain you have no work in all of London. Do you understand? Now take us to the woman named Chloe and quit wasting our time."

Lazarus growled his own warning. The guard nodded his head, looking as though the fear of God had shot through his soul. Witt let go. The man nearly slumped to the ground, seeming surprised at the vehemence of Witt's attack. He straightened his shoulders and shrugged back into his stained and ill-fitting jacket. "Follow me."

At the very end of the barred area to their left, Victoria discovered Chloe hunched in the corner, where she rocked herself back and forth on the floor, her hands wrapped protectively about her knees, as if in attempt of holding herself together. She looked up when they approached. Her eyes widened, and her lips turned up at the corners when Lazarus trotted over to the bars and put his big head up against them.

"Lazarus. You've come to visit." Chloe crawled over to where Lazarus sat. She put her hands about either side of his face and rubbed. "You are a sweet, sweet dog."

Victoria felt tears sting her eyes. "We would like to visit with you too, Chloe." Victoria knew that Chloe hadn't been told about the death of her brother. "Would you like to come outside with us?"

She looked into Victoria's eyes as if pleading. "I would love that."

The three of them found a willow tree to sit under while they talked and ate. A slight breeze helped to quell the odor that clung to Chloe's clothes and skin. Victoria wished she could, this minute, help the woman get cleaned up and take a long, warm bath.

"I'm so glad you came to visit," Chloe said. "I thought I'd never get outside again. It's been at least a week."

Chloe daintily ate her sandwich that had been cut into four squares like any woman of breeding would do. She didn't gobble down the food like a starved animal but daintily ate as though she sat at the table with the regent himself.

After Witt finished a sandwich and drank from his flask, he rose and stretched. "It's such a beautiful day, I think I'll walk about the grounds so you two can have some time to chat about whatever it is that women chat about. I'll leave Lazarus with you, and I will be in sight should you need anything."

"That's very kind of you, sir," Victoria said. "We will be just fine, won't we, Chloe?"

"Indeed. Lazarus will be our protector."

Victoria watched Lord Witt walk away. She enjoyed the look of his broad shoulders and strong, muscular stature. He made her feel safe. And lately she had wondered if her dreams of love of adventure had been unrealistic. She was learning that each step of living such a dream was full of real risk. Not the risk that the penny dreadfuls touted, but real, life-threatening risk. Fear tried to steal joy and life. Fear was the devil's playmate, and she refused to be its toy.

"Chloe," Victoria reached out and took the woman's hand, "tell me how you came to be here in Bedlam. I want you to share your story with me."

"Will I get in trouble?" She stroked Lazarus' back. "I don't want to get in trouble."

"No, Chloe. You won't get in trouble. I promise."

"I promise. That's what he said. I promise that I won't you leave you. I'll come back. You'll see. Everything will be all right. I love you."

"Chloe, who made that promise to you?" Victoria watched a glazed-eyed expression shade her face. She was thinking of that time.

"William promised me. He was going to ask my brother if he could marry me. He was so handsome and sure of himself."

"What happened then, Chloe?"

Chloe looked away. "I don't want to talk anymore. I want to go for a walk with Lazarus. Can we walk with Lazarus?"

"Of course." Victoria put the food away and closed the hamper.

She moved it closer to the tree so she could retrieve it later. Then she looped her arm through Chloe's. "Come, Lazarus."

Lazarus looked back at the hamper of food and then at Victoria.

Victoria simply arched a brow. Lazarus's ears went up, and he decided to follow them.

"Smart dog." She smiled, and Chloe did too.

"Do you know how long you have been here in the hospital?"

"A long time. Too long. Someday I will go home, but not now. The time is not yet right."

"And when will the time be right?"

"When Talon comes to take me home."

"Talon?" The pounding of her heart nearly deafened her. "Chloe, do you mean to tell me you know Lord Talon? Who is he? Where is he? Chloe, this is very important. You must tell me how to find Lord Talon."

"I cannot do that. I wouldn't want Talon to get mad at me. He's very protective, and if he thought I'd betrayed him, he might not come to visit me anymore."

"Do you mean the person who calls himself Lord Talon comes to visit you here in Bethlem?"

"Yes. Lord Talon comes to visit me."

"Then you are not Lord Talon?"

Chloe stopped unexpectedly. "Lady Victoria, I may be in Bedlam, but I am not a lunatic."

"I'm sorry. I didn't mean to infer such a thing. It's just that so much depends on Lord Talon. It's urgent that my brother speak to Lord Talon."

"I do not think that would be wise." Chloe twisted a piece of auburn hair around her finger. "Lord Talon does not want to meet Lord Ravensmoore. Talon fears Ravensmoore."

"But why?"

"Because Talon must protect his beloved hawks. If your brother meets Talon, the hawks will have to be destroyed, and Talon has worked too hard to train the hawks for their special duties. Talon will not give up his hawks."

"Why would the hawks have to be destroyed if Talon meets my brother?"

"Because then the truth will be known and the truth will not set Talon free. The truth will kill Talon."

Victoria faced Chloe. "I want you to answer one question for me, Chloe, and it must be the truth."

# CHAPTER 22

*Fear is the pain arising from the anticipation of evil.*
—ARISTOTLE

WITT AND VICTORIA raced to Thistledown Hall on horseback. When they arrived, two footmen came to accept their horses.

"Have you seen the earl and countess of Ravensmoore? Are they here?" Witt asked.

"They've gone hunting with Lady Phoebe," said one of the footman. "She's using her brother's hawks, I believe."

"No!" Victoria said, looking toward the sky. "She mustn't release the hawks. Where would they have gone?"

"To the mews behind the stables."

Victoria and Witt galloped toward the stables and the mews beyond. They dismounted outside the mews. "I'd prefer you stay here," Witt said.

"Not a chance. That's my brother and sister-in-law at risk. I will not stay behind like a cowering woman awaiting bad news when there may be something I can do to help. Lady Phoebe is my friend, even if she is dangerous, and I might be able to help her see past what she imagines to be real to what actually is reality."

They entered the mews, and Witt demanded he take the lead and placed himself in front of Victoria. It was apparent almost immediately that only one hawk was missing from its cage. "Something is not right." Witt opened the cage and examined the other birds that remained behind. "These are not the same, based on feathers we've found and the size of the talons. I don't think these are the hawks that are carrying out the attacks. I thought that Talon may have been using red kites. That's what we saw during one of your riding lessons."

"Then where are they?" Victoria asked.

"When you were kidnapped by Talon," Witt said, "he took you to the mews we found on the west road. They were in the trees. I wonder if there may not be another mews in the trees near here. It would make the most sense, for the falconers knew nothing about the type of hawks we were looking for and did not train these hawks to be aggressive in the way that Talon's hawks fight. We must look elsewhere."

Devlin and Madeline cantered in and met them outside of the mews. "We saw you arrive." Madeline said, "But we were too far away to call out to you. Lady Phoebe slipped away from us while we rode. She didn't want to talk about herself, only Chloe. She insists that she has never met Talon, doesn't know who Talon could be, and refuses to believe that Chloe is a danger to anyone."

"I'm so glad you're all right," Victoria said. "You were in danger."

"We're fine, Snoop," Devlin said.

"We've been praying in earnest as we rode," Victoria said, nearly out of breath. "Chloe says that Phoebe knows Talon."

Devlin looked around the area and then back to each of them. "The twins may be protecting each other. It's hard to know if one or both of them are involved in these grizzly deeds. And it's possible they are protecting Talon. But I believe I understand what is happening, and Lady Phoebe is the key."

"I suggest we separate into teams," Witt said. "Ravensmoore, I suggest that you and the countess search the east side of the estate behind the stables. Lady Victoria and I will take the west. If any of us find the hawks or Lady Phoebe, fire a shot so we can locate each other."

Devlin nodded agreement. "And no matter what happens, do not confront her. Get her to talk about her sister. Tell her that you've just visited with Chloe. If Lady Phoebe mentions Talon, don't push her for information. Ask her what her hopes are for the future."

"And if we cannot find Phoebe, what then?" Madeline asked.

Devlin frowned. "Then we will meet back here in an hour and figure out what to do next."

They separated and began their searches. Victoria prayed that Phoebe would be found safe and that Talon would be captured. She worried that Lord Witt suffered silently from his wounds, but the seriousness of locating Talon and the hawks took precedence over everything. They rode for nearly an hour, searching the woods in silence, and still there was no sign of Lord Talon or Lady Phoebe.

"The hour must near be gone," Victoria said. "We should return."

The horses spooked. Victoria's heart hammered, but she tried to remain calm.

"I imagine you are looking for me."

A young man dressed in breeches, cravat, and waistcoat wore a hat pulled low over his brow and stood barely fifteen feet from them. He blended in so well with the forest that Victoria thought she could have ridden past him unawares.

"I am Lord Talon." He held an enormous hawk. "I believe we've met already, Lady Victoria."

"I think that was all your pleasure, Lord Talon. You kidnapped me and left me with your hawks. Not very hospitable."

"Victoria." Witt sent her a warning glance.

"I apologize, Lord Talon. I didn't mean to be rude."

Talon bowed, and in that moment the hat slipped from his head and long dark strands framed his face.

"Phoebe!" Victoria said, surprised at the vision of Phoebe, half herself and half Talon. She knew something was wrong, but she'd never thought anything like this was even possible, yet the shock of seeing her holding the hawk both terrified and mesmerized Victoria.

Witt pulled his gun and fired the warning shot.

Wings flapped. Talon released the hawk. It knocked the gun from Witt's hand and returned to its master.

Victoria's stomach tightened, and her horse quivered.

"You shouldn't have done that, Lord Witt. It's a dangerous game you play. You have alerted Lord and Lady Ravensmoore. Or have you?"

"What does that mean?" Victoria asked. "Have you done something to them?"

"Let's just say they will not be coming to your rescue." Talon's voice came from Phoebe's face, and it was an odd mix of personality and physical form.

"Are they all right?" Victoria asked.

"Both are well. I have no desire to hurt them. I merely had Wellington here scare their horses off when I tricked them into searching for Lady Phoebe on foot. Poor judgment on the doctor's part. I thought Ravensmoore would have known better. I understand that he is an excellent physician."

"I heard no warning shot," Witt said.

"No, you wouldn't have. All I had to do was tell him to drop his pistol or I would unleash my hawk on his wife. If he tried to shoot the hawk, I told him that you both would die. He had no way to know if I was telling the truth or not, so he made the wise decision to surrender his weapon." Talon pulled Devlin's pistol from his waistband. Now the pistol was in Talon's right hand and the hawk remained fisted in his left.

Victoria recognized the pistol and remembered what her brother had said. "We've just come from visiting Lady Chloe at Bethlem."

"Ah, Lady Chloe. How is she? Well, I hope. I try very hard to protect her. It's not easy when she's locked up in that horrid place."

"Lord Talon. Tell me about your hawks. How many do you have? How do you train them?"

Victoria read anger in Witt's eyes, and her fear grew for him.

"I've trained five. Wellington here is the strongest and bravest of them all, fearsome and bold, just like the real Duke of Wellington."

"You must be very proud." Victoria took a step forward.

Talon motioned her back. "Careful," he whispered. "Be very careful."

"Tell me when you fell in love with hawks, Talon. I don't know much about them," Victoria whispered. "May I come closer to Wellington, or will that alarm him?"

"You may proceed. Wellington won't bite unless I tell him to, and I'm sure you will give me no reason to do so. Phoebe told me you were a good friend and that you could be trusted. You must forgive me, though. I am not of like mind."

Victoria slowly walked toward Talon and had no idea what she would do. She just thought it necessary to connect with Talon so no one would get hurt. He'd kidnapped her and didn't hurt her. Perhaps some part of Phoebe was still present. "Is it difficult to teach them to fly?"

"It's very difficult, but even more so to get them to return. My hawks are not like your dog. They won't go fetch a stick and bring it back unless carefully trained to do so, and even then a treat must await them or they will not remain very loyal. Hawks are pernickety. Like people. Very pernickety."

"So how do you get them to return to you?" Victoria now stood within six feet. Wellington's massive talons forced her to reevaluate her ill-thought-out plan. This creature's power and skill frightened her, but she couldn't let her anxiety show. Hawks might be similar to horses and other animals regarding their ability to sense fear.

"He's almost hypnotic, isn't he, Lady Victoria?"

She'd been staring at the raptor's eyes and then at his thick talons. Suddenly his wings flapped and spread wide, which terrified and mesmerized her at the same time. Victoria jumped back. "Lord Talon. Don't."

"It's all right. He's just restless. He wants to fly." Talon stroked the head of the bird that fisted his protective leather glove. The tether hung from the glove, swinging to and fro as if in anticipation of the hawk's release. "He needs to hunt."

"And what is Wellington going to hunt, now that Lord Ramsay is dead, Talon?" Victoria grew bold. "What are you needed for now?"

Talon tilted his head and looked at her and blinked much like the hawk. "I don't know what you mean. I will continue to take care of the hawks, of course."

"But Lady Phoebe no longer needs the hawks. Do you, Phoebe?"

"Lady Victoria, you risk too much," Witt warned. "Step away."

"It does not matter what Lady Phoebe needs." Talon ignored Witt's remark. "I make the decisions. She was too weak to do what needed done. Now all that remains is to rescue Lady Chloe from her imprisonment, and then all will be well. All will be as it should be."

"Would you fly Wellington for me?" Victoria asked.

"I like you, Lady Victoria, but I am not a fool. If I fly Wellington, Lord Witt is certain to try for the pistol I procured from your brother and shoot me, and I cannot let that happen. If you will step back, Lady Victoria, I will fly the hawk."

Witt stepped closer. "No. It's too dangerous. That hawk nearly killed me. I won't allow you to loosen it on Lady Victoria. She's unprotected."

"I suggest you not take another step, Lord Witt. I may be forced to shoot you. And if you hadn't noticed, I am the only one capable of protecting Lady Victoria."

She turned her back on Talon. "Lord Witt, I want to see the hawk fly. Please don't interfere."

Talon released the hawk and aimed the pistol at Witt.

Victoria threw herself at Talon, knocking him to the ground. The pistol fired. The ball found its way into Wellington's breast, and Talon screamed as he watched his beloved hawk fall from the air.

Witt was next to Victoria and Talon in an instant.

"Victoria! Are you all right?"

"I'm fine." She rolled off of Talon, bringing the pistol with her.

Talon rolled over and hit the ground with his fist over and over again, crying, "No! Not Wellington! Noooooo!" He finally gathered himself. Tears streaked down his shocked and devastated face. "I must go to him. Please." He looked at Witt.

"Let Talon go to his beloved bird, Lord Witt," Ravensmoore said as he rode toward them.

Witt nodded and helped Victoria to her feet. "I thought for a moment you'd been shot. Don't ever do that again." He hugged her close.

"Talon is cunning, but he risked too much," Devlin said.

"You're all right! Where's Maddie?" Victoria asked. She couldn't quite take in what had just happened. "I thought you and Madeline were on the other side of the estate without horses."

"We were. But it didn't take us long to get the horses back. We did hear the warning shot, and I sent Madeline back to the house for help. It seems you've saved the day, little Snoop. I'll have to talk to you later about how carelessly you take care of yourself after all I've done to get you well."

"I had to do it, Devlin. I was afraid he was going to kill Lord Witt, and I couldn't let that happen."

Devlin said, "I thought you were guarding my sister, Lord Witt. It seems you were fortunate she was guarding you."

"I believe God watched over these events, my brother. I wish to go to Talon. I feel sorry for him."

She turned to see Talon stroking the dead hawk.

"We'll all go," Witt said and picked her up in his arms as they walked to where Talon crooned to the bird.

"I will have to come up with a new remedy," Talon said as he stroked the dead hawk he'd named Wellington. "I will reassure the others that I will take care of them now that Talon is gone. I have my bees and my laboratory, but I will find a way to care for you too. Perhaps I can bring you back. Perhaps the Lady Chloe will help when she comes home. Talon did hope to free her himself. I will miss him."

Victoria looked from her brother to Lord Witt and then at a new personality of Phoebe's. "Hello. What is your name?"

"I'm Celeste. Who are you?"

"Don't you know? You don't remember me?"

"I know I've never met you. Can you help me with this hawk? I'm afraid his master is gone, and I don't know if I can bring either of them back."

Victoria's heart broke for this poor lost soul. Phoebe was lost within Celeste, just as she'd been lost within Talon. Victoria wondered where Phoebe was in this mix of personalities and if she could ever be sorted from the others. The physical and psychological damage committed against her had been too great to bear, so she hid in plain sight, like a chameleon, among the other personalities in her psyche.

"I will help you, Lady Celeste. We cannot bring them back. But God is merciful."

# CHAPTER 23

With him is strength and wisdom: the deceived and
the deceiver are his.

—JOB 12:16

THE EVENING OF June the third, Lady Victoria joined
Lord Witt, Devlin, and Madeline around the dining
hall table. Of course, Lazarus had opted for the fireplace, as the evening had turned cool.

"Devlin, what is going to happen to Lady Phoebe and Lady
Chloe?" Victoria sat close to Lord Witt, and their fingers inter-
twined under the table. The heat from his hand warmed hers, and
she thanked God for her blessings. "Have Parliament and the courts
made a decision?"

"There was great debate, as you can imagine. In the end it was
decided that Lady Phoebe would be committed to the new wing of
Bethlem for those who have killed and been deemed insane. The
details of the twins' abuse from an early age at the hands of both
her father and brother was the deciding factor in allowing Lady
Phoebe to live. But her mind is so confused and the personalities of
Lord Talon and Lady Celeste such an integral part of who she has
become that she may never go well."

"Before you say no, brother, hear me out. I want to go see Lady
Phoebe."

"I don't think that would be a good idea, Snoop. She is very ill."

"That's all the more reason that I should visit her. I'll take Lazarus. She'll like that, and I can read to her from Jane Austen's books."

"You cannot be left alone with her, Snoop. She is too dangerous, and one personality may outride the decisions of another. You could get hurt, and I won't allow that to happen."

"Good. We'll all go."

"That may be for the best," Madeline said. "And what of her sister Lady Chloe? Will she be allowed to live in the same wing with her sister?"

Devlin looked at each of them. "I'm releasing Lady Chloe. She's well enough to go home. The sad thing is that now she has no sister to live with her. But she will be permitted to visit Lady Phoebe. And Chloe will have the assistance of a companion who will need to be with her for a long time until she makes the difficult transition back into society."

"That's so sad," Victoria said. "I mean, it's a good thing that she'll be released, but to not be able to have the company of each other outside of Bethlem is horribly sad." Tears sprang to her eyes, and Witt handed her his handkerchief.

The next day they entered the area where Lady Phoebe would live out the rest of her days. Lazarus stayed close to his mistress. Victoria shuddered when she saw her friend confined within a straitjacket. She sat in the corner of a cell in a chair that Victoria recognized. It was the chair from Phoebe's library. The one that she kept the Jane Austen novels hidden under to prevent her brother from finding them.

Victoria asked, "Would it be all right if I spoke to her by myself with all of you a bit further off? There is nothing she can do to me."

Devlin nodded. "Go ahead. But she may not say anything at all."

"She'll know I'm here."

Victoria sat in a chair that Witt moved close to Phoebe's cell and squeezed Victoria's shoulder as he left her. She hoped that she could reach a place in Phoebe's mind to give her hope. Lazarus sat by her and suddenly barked as if Phoebe were foreign to him.

"It's all right, my Lazarus. You know our friend, Lady Phoebe.

"Hello, Phoebe. It's me. Victoria. Do you recognize me?"

Phoebe stared through the bars of her cell window. Sadly, Victoria realized that her deluded friend stared outside at the birds flying and talking to each other.

"You miss your hawks, don't you? I'm sorry about Wellington. I know he was your favorite."

At the mention of Wellington's name, she turned her head and looked at Victoria with eyes that appeared black and fathomlessly sad. Then her face appeared to shift, and a smile came upon her lips. "Do not feel sorry for me, Lady Victoria. I am stronger than the others. I will survive this place, and I will escape. You'll see. You will all see."

Victoria's heart beat fast. "You're not Lady Phoebe or Talon or Celeste, are you?"

"I hate to disappoint you. But no. My name is Archer. You may know me as the father of lies."

Victoria swallowed hard and steeled herself with a prayer. "Phoebe, do not believe the lie."

# CHAPTER 24

Let him kiss me with the kisses of his mouth: for thy
love is better than wine.

—SONG OF SOLOMON 1:2

VICTORIA WALKED ARM in arm with Lord Witt on a brilliant sunny day in mid-June in the gardens of St. James
Park behind Carlton House. The gardens bloomed with so many
tulips she imagined they might be in Holland if she didn't know
better.

"I can't believe it's been almost three months, Lord Witt. It seems
several lifetimes since I arrived in London seeking adventure and
met you right here in St. James Park, where our adventure together
began."

'I think perhaps you found more adventure than you hoped for
that morning when you and Lazarus ran into the mist." He stopped
and turned to her with a mischievous smile on his face. "I'd like to
take you on another adventure, Lady Victoria."

"Another adventure?" Her eyes brightened with curiosity, and
she arched a slim blonde brow. "Do explain what you mean."

"Remember when your brother was forced to stay at the palace
when Lord Stone was attacked? He tried to convince the regent that
it was unnecessary that he care for Lord Stone, as the regent had his
own physician. His majesty promised that he would make it up to
him at a later time, because Devlin very much wished to take you

about London on your first night in town. He was not happy to allow me the enjoyable task."

"Enjoyable task? Hmm. I like the enjoyable part but quite resent the task aspect."

"I've learned since that *task* is not the word, but at the time I wasn't so sure." He smiled.

"Heavens. Spare me your compliments, Lord Witt. Perhaps I should find a beau who appreciates the unique qualities I possess. What do you have to say about that?"

"I don't think another beau will be necessary. In fact, it tends to create quite a scandal among the ton when a married woman takes a beau."

Victoria stopped so fast she lost her footing on the third step leading up to another section of the gardens filled with blood-red, white, and yellow roses, all perfectly beautiful and smelling of the fragrance of heaven. Witt helped her regain her balance and prevented catastrophe again.

"Did you say 'married woman'?" Her breath caught. "Do you mean? Are you asking—"

"Allow me to explain." He got down on one knee, which brought all the couples and persons walking near them in the park to come to a halt. Whispering, staring, and even pointing fingers surrounded them.

"My dear Lady Snoop." He smiled. "I love calling you Lady Snoop. I'm asking you to be my bride, my wife, and my best friend. I consider you the only woman who could ever put up with me. I hope you will not consider the prospect of living a majority of our time together in the country tedious. I will endure the journey to London or wherever you wish for adventures of your liking. But for now, I pray you will join me for a great adventure of the heart."

Victoria wondered what she'd ever done to deserve such an astonishing fate. God did indeed have a plan for her life. "Lord

Witt, I think this might be the best time to tell you that, as hard as it might be to understand, I need to reveal that I may be *difficult* to live with because, as you already know, I tend to have a very curious nature, which is not always understood or welcomed by some and utterly annoying to others."

'Lady Victoria." He looked about at the others in the park who were intently focused on them. "I imagine that our audience is expecting that I am about to be rejected due to your careful consideration of my question. I pray you will not make too spectacular a scene if that is to be the case, because I must tell you that I will not take no for your answer. It's simply unacceptable and would be far too unbearable a prospect to my future to imagine it without you."

"My dearest Witt." She stood before him, pulled off her glove, and placed her bare palm on his warm cheek. "*Yes* seems such an infinitesimal word for a heart so overflowing with joy. I would find myself miserable without you too. So, yes. Yes! Yes, indeed I will marry you."

Witt stood and gathered her into his arms and very publicly bestowed her with a kiss that endured for so long that the crowd could not resist applause. When the kiss ended, she whispered to him, "Kiss me again, Jonathon. I love the sound of your Christian name on my lips. Jonathon. I do want to make an impression."

"Oh, but you have made an impression. That's why I'm going to enjoy kissing you again and again," he said, merely an inch from her lips.

"I mean," she said, "I want to impress every couple walking here today in these beautiful, lush gardens. I want them all to know and remember that even the most unlikely of couples can find love and adventure if they refuse to hide their true selves and revel in the knowledge that each of us are wonderfully made by the One who created us for this grand adventure."

"Well, then. Let us not disappoint. The crowd is growing larger." He covered her mouth with his own and so thoroughly enjoyed the kiss that he forgot the onlookers were even there.

# A NOTE FROM THE AUTHOR

Dear Reader,

First of all, I must thank Jo Ann Ferguson of RWA's Beau Monde for sharing her pictures and experiences about hawks with me. And to Emma Ford who wrote an engrossing book titled *Falconry: Art and Practice.* Any mistakes in this novel are mine alone regarding the training and actions of birds of prey. My imagination took many an interesting twist while creating this work.

I am grateful that you chose this book, *Chameleon,* to read from all the other books calling to you from brick-and-mortar bookstore shelves and those in digital cyberspace. I appreciate that you spent your time escaping into the past with me to explore the world of Regency England and the characters I populated it with who struggle with their own flaws and challenges, much as we do today. I also loved portraying Lazarus as an early version of a pet therapy dog, although I don't think they considered this treatment modality at the time.

There is still much that is not understood about Dissociative Identity Disorder (DID), which used to be referred to as Multiple Personality Disorder. You can learn more about this mental health issue on the NAMI (National Association on Mental Illness) website.

I hope that I was able to convey what this disorder may have looked like during England's Regency period.

The history of mental illness and its treatment is a long and complicated battle for sanity often filled with misunderstanding. Even with today's modern treatments and therapies many patients still face difficulty and stigma both within and outside of the church. Families and loved ones pray for relief of those affected by depression, anxiety disorders, and the many other mental health disorders that prevent quality living and a life passionately filled with purpose.

It is my greatest hope that someday the secrets of the brain and mind that harbor illness will be unlocked so that true peace of mind can be experienced by everyone. I pray that you enjoyed this story and that in some small way it brings you encouragement for your future. I hope you look forward to my next book, *Mysteries of the Heart*, which will make its appearance in 2013.

Remember the words of Isaiah: "The Spirit of the Lord God is upon me; because the Lord hath anointed me to preach good tidings unto the meek; he hath sent me to bind up the brokenhearted, to proclaim liberty to the captives, and the opening of the prison to them that are bound" (Isa. 61:1).

—Gratefully,
Jillian Kent

# COMING IN 2013 FROM
# JILLIAN KENT...

## MYSTERIES OF THE HEART

# CHAPTER 1

ERCY WHITTINGTON GULPED for air as another wave battered her, pulled her under, and scraped her along the coast floor. She suddenly surfaced and prayed, "God, help me. I have nothing left."

Sand squished through her fingers, then she tumbled with another wave away from it. Again and again she reached for the sand.

Sand meant a shoreline. "God, help me," she prayed again, choking as her mouth and throat filled with salt water.

Sand. Again. Precious sand. She reached for it, felt its rough wonder in her hand.

She'd made it! "Thank You, Jesus." Tears stung her eyes as she vomited sea water. Coughing and sputtering, she dragged herself onto the beach.

Too weary to care that she wore trousers instead of skirts, she closed her eyes and vomited again. Vaguely it occurred to her that the trousers—her surgeon's attire—had saved her life...along with the prayers God had seen fit to answer. Lying limp, she only had the energy to kiss the wet sand before falling into an exhausted sleep.

An annoying brush of twigs drummed against her cheek.

Mercy opened her eyes to stare through several spindly branches.

She bolted upright when the crab pinched her cheek, then scuttled backward on the sand. The sound of her heart pounding in her ears, Mercy watched the creature dance diagonally across the hard, wet sand. She drew in a ragged breath and focused on the now calm ocean that last night, as it raged, nearly took her life.

"Interesting little devils, aren't they?"

Mercy twisted around, the crab forgotten at the sound of a deep masculine voice tinted with humor.

"Wh–who are you?" Her voice trembled, much to her annoyance. Her arms supported her from behind, and her hands and fingers splayed across the sand for support.

A man's shadow fell across her, causing her to squint as she tilted her face upward. His nearness caused her to push further away from him.

"I'm not going to hurt you, if that's what you're thinking. You're safe enough, for now."

"Where am I?" She took her eyes off him only long enough to glance around, her gaze shifted beyond him to the desolate sea. "Where did you come from? I see no ship. Are you a pirate?"

He grinned. "Do I look like a pirate?" At that moment, a breeze lifted off the ocean, whipping a strand of dark hair across his tanned face. He had at least two days' worth of stubble and indeed had the look of a pirate, no matter what he said.

"All you need is an eye patch."

His grin widened. The next moment he shifted, and she drew back, wondering what he was going to do. His broad shoulders loomed over her. But all he did was sit down next to her. "I hate to disappoint, but I'm not a pirate. And the ship I'm on is in a nearby cove in hopes of evading the devils.

"I'm Lord Eden at your service. And I have the pleasure of—?" He left the question hang in the air between them.

"You have the pleasure of nothing. Am I in Scotland or England?"

He blinked. "England, of course."

He leaned near and picked a piece of seaweed from her hair, and as his thumb brushed her cheek, a jolt of fear passed through her. "Don't."

Thoughts of danger raced through her mind. His shirt blew open nearly to his waist. Grateful for the heat of the sun that scorched the beach, she hoped he hadn't seen her blush. She'd thought that kind of reaction well in control now after her work of the last six months.

His gaze traveled the length of her, and she remembered her male garments. She could almost read what must be going through his mind. Finally his look came back to hers. "Do you mind me asking how an English beauty ended up on this beach with no one to defend her? And wearing pants, boots, and a waistcoat?"

She thought about the events of the last two days.

"I have no intention of telling you anything." She placed both palms on her forehead and leaned her elbows on her knees. "Did you tell me where we are?" she asked.

"Not far from Brighton. Maybe a day's sailing."

She stood and brushed the sand from her pants. "May I go with you?"

"I'm thinking the men won't take kindly to your boarding the ship, especially the captain, who believes in voodoo and is more likely to sacrifice you than provide you transportation."

"What's voodoo?"

"A woman in pants.

"I was hoping for a swim, but I guess that will have to wait for now." He got up and walked in the direction of where he'd said the ship waited in the cove.

"Wait. You will take me with you... won't you?"

"I guess we'll find out." He nodded toward the cove and kept walking.

Seagulls walked the beach, and in the distance a puffin dove into the ocean and returned to the sky with its catch.

She watched Lord Eden in front of her, black breeches, Hessians, and a white linen shirt hanging loose.

She took a deep breath and ran to catch up with him. "Wait." He didn't stop. "How do I know you can be trusted?" She trotted along the sand. "Please, wait."

He stopped and turned to look at her, quirking a brow. "You don't know if you can trust me or not, but I guarantee you that you can't trust them." He pointed down into a cove.

She sucked in a breath, her heart hammering in her chest at the sight of several swarthy-hued men performing some kind of pagan dance with masks and movements that looked uncivilized indeed. Several small boats decorated the shore, and further out she saw the ship.

"Is there no other way?"

"Where is it you want to go?"

"Yorkshire."

"You can walk until you find a village. Perhaps someone will take pity on you and offer you transport."

"But—"

"I'm going to London." He pointed out to the sea. "So is this ship. So make your decision now, for soon they will see you and then there will be no turning back."

"Surely you wouldn't leave me here with no escort?"

"I am not in a position to take you anywhere. But if you want to come with me now, I will do my best to keep you out of harm's way."

"That is not very honorable for an Englishman. Are you quite certain you are English?"

He bent and pulled a knife from his boot.

She took several steps back. "What do you intend?"

"Are you coming with me or not? I'm offering you transportation to London, and only to London. The accommodations will be rough, and you will need to remain in my cabin at all times. Is that understood?"

"That depends on what you plan to do with that knife." She took several more steps away from him. She'd never get far if he really wanted to do harm.

"I'm going to disguise you as a lad. Are you willing? I have to cut your hair."

"My hair!" Her hands immediately felt for the long strands of hair that had come loose in the water. "No. You will not cut my hair."

"Then how do you propose to look like a lad? Did you not get a good look at the men I travel with?"

"There must be another way. Perhaps I could tie it up." But even as she said it, she knew it wouldn't work. Not in these circumstances.

She squeezed her eyes shut. *Lord, I do not think this wise, but running off on my own could be just as risky.* She opened her eyes. "All right. Cut it!"

"This might just work." He drew near and grabbed a handful of her dark hair. "This may hurt, for although the knife is sharp, it's sure to pull at your scalp. It will have to be very short. Are you ready?"

"Do it."

"Stand very still." He sawed away at her hair.

When she thought of all she'd endured in the past months, she considered crying over the loss of her hair absurd, but she still had to fight back insistent tears.

She bit her lip to keep from crying out. Finally he stopped. The yellow sand was covered with what had once been her crowning glory. Gingerly she put a hand to her head. Her cropped hair felt shorter than his lordship's, which fell unfashionably below his ears and yet was not long enough to be pulled back in a queue.

Before she could say anything, he stuck the knife back in his boot. "There now. Pull your shirt out of your pants and cover your backside."

"Why?"

"Because it's obviously female, and if you are going to be my new," he cleared his throat, "*valet*, you must look the part."

Her eyes grew round. "Your what?"

"Well, it's not like I'm asking you to be my mistress. I'm trying to help you without knowing the details of your family or your position. Do you want to tell me who you are now?"

She lifted her chin. "I don't believe so."

He looked at her and frowned. "Be clear that when we get to the ship that you do not open your mouth to speak. Your lips are too feminine, even without saying a word, and—" He picked up a glob of mud and smeared it on her cheeks and chin.

She spit mud out of her mouth. "What are you doing?"

"I'm making you presentable to a shipload of men who would not hesitate to take advantage of a woman. You have the ability to appear as either. I suggest you follow my lead and my orders once we enter the cove and again on board."

He started down the rocky trail.

Gritting her teeth, she followed him.

As they grew closer to the black sailors, she saw they were naked from the waist up. The dancing and celebrating, if that's what it was, stopped the moment they saw her behind Eden.

A tall, lean black man with a necklace of ivory around his neck came up to them. "Who this?"

"I found him, Fox."

"Share him." The man rubbed a hand through her newly cropped hair, grabbed a handful, and pulled her head back to study her face.

Eden smacked the man's hand away. "Not bloody likely. I'm taking him to the ship."

"Get in that boat, boy," Eden directed her. "Now!"

She scrambled into the small boat, and when she looked out over the ocean, she saw the masts quivering in the wind. Mercy swallowed hard. She'd just been thrown overboard last evening from a ship, and now she was about to board another. When she looked back, Eden was pushing the small boat into the water, and the men on shore ran to get in the other boats.

"Are you all right?"

She nodded.

"You take one set of oars, and I'll take the other. Make it look good as we near the ship so you don't look as inexperienced as you are. The others will follow."

Mercy didn't dare cause trouble. She'd never heard of Lord Eden or voodoo, but she desperately wanted to get home, not to London for a number of reasons she didn't care to think about yet, but to York. But as they approached the ship, Mercy wondered if she shouldn't have just refused Lord Eden's hospitality, if one could call having her hair chopped off hospitality.

"Don't say a word." Lord Eden pushed her ahead of him.

When she reached the top and peered over the edge, her blood seemingly chilled in her veins but her feet kept moving. She slid over a rail and fell to her knees on the deck, looking up into the eyes of a half-naked man squinting hard at her through bloodshot eyes.

"What'd ya catch, Lord Eden? Look me in the eye."

Mercy raised her mud-caked lashes to his gaze and nearly choked with fear. She thought he must have seen through her disguise, but she prayed God would show him only courage reflected in her eyes.

She gulped and waited for what would happen next.

Lord Eden grabbed her by the back of the shirt. "He'll clean my cabin. It's been a long journey."

"I imagine your cabin needs cleaning, Lord Eden." He laughed, and the deck hands roared with laughter when he repeated his statement in a language she'd never heard.

Eden kept his hand firmly on her neck and guided her into the depths of the ship to where his cabin awaited them. He opened the door into a room that held a bed for a single person, a table, a chair, and two trunks.

"This will be very close quarters. I'll leave you alone as much as possible."

Mercy looked at the tangled bed sheets. "Where will you sleep?" She looked up at him and his eyes danced.

"With you, of course. I can't have Skinner thinking you have time on your hands. He can think whatever he wants, but I guarantee you his thoughts are from the devil."

She shivered.

"You're cold." He grabbed the dark wool blanket from his bunk and draped it around her shoulders. "I suggest you get out of your wet clothes."

She gaped at him. Could he really be that dim-witted? "And what would I wear?"

"Your clothing, after it dries." He grinned. "Lock the door behind me." He left and pulled it shut.

"But—" Mercy let out a long, low sigh of irritation, locked the door, put her back against it, and sank to the floor of the cabin. The effects of her near-drowning and all that had led to her being aboard the other ship and then tossed overboard crowded in on her. Lord Eden, Captain Skinner, and his ship of unusual sailors had opened a floodgate of panic and despair. She wanted her family. Needed them more than ever.

She pulled the blanket tight and realized if she didn't get out of her clothes, she soon wouldn't have a dry blanket. Exhaustion taunted her, and she closed her eyes, wanting everything that had happened to go away. Common sense and the need for comfort drove her to her feet to shed her wet clothing. The odor of the sea and...she breathed in the scent of the blanket. Cinnamon, musk, and the natural scent of him. This combination pleased and surprised her.

She eyed the two trunks, looked toward the door, and wondered when Lord Eden might return. Guilt flashed through her. Need won out.

The scent of clove and sandalwood lifted with the lid of the first trunk. She gently searched through the first layer to find something to wear while she slept. Perhaps a shirt of Lord Eden's would do. She picked up several sets of trousers, all too big for her to consider. A black silk shirt caught her eye. She pulled it from the trunk, and an oak box fell to the floor making so much noise that she glanced to the door fully expecting Lord Eden to fill the doorway, a dark frown upon his face.

Mercy held her breath in fear of being caught stealing. When nothing happened, she let out a pent-up breath. She was only looking for something to cover her under these extraordinary circumstances. Mercy picked up the oak box. It was heavier than it appeared. And then she reprimanded herself, thinking this was something her sister Victoria, whom the family affectionately referred to as Snoop, would do, but not her. Mercy respected others' privacy, and she expected others to respect her privacy. Perhaps she'd spent too much time in London last year with her sister. That a brought a smile to her face.

Her hand followed the smooth grain of the box until her finger found a rough edge. *A lock of some sort?* She felt along the edges, but nothing. She pushed on the area with her thumb and gasped when the heavy head of what looked to be an ancient spear slid from the box and landed on the cabin floor with a thud.

WALLA WALLA
RURAL LIBRARY DISTRICT